THE
RUBBER
FENCE

ALSO BY DIANA STEVAN

A Cry From The Deep
The Blue Nightgown

*For Dana,
Thanks for coming to my book launch!
Diana Stevan*

THE RUBBER FENCE

A NOVEL

Diana Stevan

Island House Publishing

THE RUBBER FENCE
Copyright © 2016 by Diana Stevan
All rights reserved.

This is a work of fiction. Names, characters, businesses, organizations, places, events, and incidents either are the product of the author's imagination or are used fictitiously. Any resemblance to actual persons, living or dead, events or locales is entirely coincidental.

No part of this publication may be reproduced or transmitted in any form or by any electronic or mechanical means, including storage and retrieval systems, without permission in writing from the author or publisher, except by a reviewer, who may quote brief passages in a review.

Library and Archives Canada Cataloguing in Publication

Island House Publishing

ISBN-10: 0994040199
ISBN-13: 978-0994040190

Cover design by Ares Jun
Cover Photograph: Ann-Christine Höglund
Formatting and layout provided by: Quantum Formatting Service

Printed in the United States of America

For Rob,
my love.

Time's glory is to calm contending kings,
To unmask falsehood, and bring truth to light.

~William Shakespeare, *The Rape of Lucrece.*

1972

The year that:

Apollo astronauts explored the moon's surface;
The TV series, *All in the Family*, was breaking new ground;
Gloria Steinem launched her feminist magazine, *MS*;
The Equal Rights Amendment was finally passed in the USA;
The Vietnam War was still on;
Family Therapy was in vogue;
And Joanna Bereza started her internship on a psychiatric ward.

ONE

THE MORNING HAD barely started, but Joanna Bereza felt like she'd already run a marathon. She parked her old Toyota in the Manitou General Hospital lot, checked her hair in the rear-view mirror, and grabbed her satchel from the backseat before hurrying past other cars jockeying for spots. She glanced at her watch hoping the hands on the dial would tell her something different. She wished she had a good excuse for being late, but she didn't. As usual, she'd lost track of time. She'd been unable to decide on what to wear for her first day. *Trivial,* she said to herself. Now she was running like a fool.

And for what? The sprawling grey stone complex in front of her looked more like a prison than a place of healing. Taking her residency in psychiatry at this stage in her life was beginning to look like a crazy idea. With so many unknowns, it was also scary. No wonder her heart was racing. Well, there was no turning back now, not after she and Michael had sold their home and moved into an apartment so she could further her studies.

She hesitated at the steps leading to the double glass doors and let a couple pass. Her pantyhose had twisted around her hips as if it too was unsure of where it was going. After a few adjustments, she took a deep breath and climbed the steps.

The bustle in the hospital corridor of staff and patients in search of a cure did little to calm her mind. She was headed for 2B, the infamous psychiatric ward. The hospital had worked hard to erase the stigma it had acquired after the ward had been shut down in shame forty years before. Back then, the mentally ill had been hospitalized against their will and were given hydrotherapy or lobotomies or electric shock treatments, which broke their bones and destroyed their souls.

On the second floor, she headed toward the doors labeled 2B. Her pulse quickened. She was about to enter a field where the guideposts were still being built. Since the mind was the most unexplored territory of human beings, how could any shrink know the answers to what troubled a patient? And yet, this is what she had signed up for.

She sighed. *This is for you, Grandma.* She swung the right door open.

Her nostrils were immediately assaulted by the strong odour of Pine-Sol. Though 2B wasn't a locked ward, the unpleasant smell underlined her feeling that something dirty was still going on. It didn't help that the walls were overdue for a fresh coat of paint, and the chairs—in one waiting area that she passed—looked like Salvation Army cast-offs.

She walked by one silent room after another, some with patients lying or sitting on their beds, others empty. The only sound was the clicking of her heels on the linoleum tiles. She tried to shake her apprehension, but she knew that once something bad had gone on in a place, a stain remained that was hard to remove. Same as it was for people. One wrong move, and you could be marked for life.

She passed a few patients standing near their doorways staring at the floor or at something unseen. She considered briefly what she might do if one of them turned violent and attacked her. She'd heard of incidents where staff had been bitten or kicked, and help had arrived too late to restrain or sedate the patient. But, she reminded herself, the staff of today had better control of the aggressive ones, thanks to the new psychotropic drugs.

Just ahead, an elderly man wobbled out of his room. His face was contorted, and his hands and legs shook as he struggled across the passageway to join another patient. His erratic movements were textbook—an unfortunate side effect of drugs used to treat psychosis. It was bad enough to see it in a filmed lecture, but to view it firsthand made her frown, so she looked away.

She continued down the corridor and passed an emaciated woman in a faded blue chenille robe pacing and mumbling to herself, her attention riveted on the well-worn floor. As she shuffled along in her tattered terry cloth slippers, she counted the grey and white squares. "Ten, eleven, twelve,—fourteen, fifteen."

The old woman's skipping number thirteen reminded Joanna of her own superstitious tendencies. Even though she knew it was foolish, she was careful not to step on any sidewalk cracks—*break my mother's back*—or walk under a ladder. *Something else to work on.*

By the nurses' station, she spotted Roberta Underwood, a statuesque redhead. She appeared to be scolding a nurse's aide, who held a stack of clean bedding in her arms. Joanna had met the head nurse the week before at a mental health conference.

The aide left the station with tears in her eyes. It didn't seem to bother Roberta. When she saw Joanna, she said without missing a beat, "Welcome to 2B, Dr. Bereza. The temporary home of adolescents, drunks, and the barely living. To be or not to be."

Joanna couldn't help but smile. "I'm sorry I'm late. Thank

THE RUBBER FENCE

you for taking the time to show me around."

"It's my job." Roberta didn't return the smile. She looked at her watch. "I won't be able to show you the whole unit now, but we'll cover what we cover." It was obvious from her tone that she was put out.

Joanna scolded herself again for being late. This was not a staff member to cross. Roberta had previously worked at Selkirk, the province's long-stay loony bin, where she'd run the program with an iron hand.

The tour began in the nurses' station, the hub for patient records and storage of patients' medications. Across from it was the lounge, where the mentally ill could take breaks from their dismal rooms and stare at one another instead of their bare walls. Joanna then followed Roberta down another corridor, past more patient rooms, until they stopped near a door marked ECT. She caught her breath at the sight. Since 2B was now being touted as being leading edge in mental health, a room for electro-convulsive therapy was the last thing she'd expected to see.

Peering through the open door, Joanna saw a janitor dip his grey stringy mop into a bucket of soapy water and wring it out. He washed the floor around the machine, carefully lifting the attached cords, as if they were snakes that might bite.

Joanna's palms began to sweat as her grandmother's face, pale and drawn, filled her mind. She said to Roberta, "I thought after *One Flew Over the Cuckoo's Nest*, ECT had gone the way of the dodo bird."

Before Roberta could reply, a deep voice from behind declared, "Is this our star student?"

Joanna turned to see a tall, middle-aged, balding man in a fine navy wool suit. She might have considered him pleasant looking, if not for the way he carried himself. He had an air of superiority and a glint in his eye suggesting he was doing them a favour merely by showing up.

"Dr. Eisenstadt," said Roberta. "Our new resident—"

"Joanna Bereza," Myron interrupted. He took Joanna's hand in a firm grip and appraised her in more than a professional manner. Uncomfortable under his scrutiny, she let go of his hand and shifted her gaze to Roberta.

"You can call me Myron," he said.

"All right. Myron." Though it was unusual to address a superior by first name, Joanna wasn't surprised he'd asked her to. With society loosening up in general, first names amongst health professionals were becoming universally accepted, even with patients.

Myron's eyebrows rose as he said, "I read your research project in the *National Psychiatric Review*. It's not every intern that's published before they've even seen a patient."

Joanna's cheeks flushed. Was he complimenting her, or had she detected mockery in his voice?

"What kind of research?" asked Roberta.

"I reviewed the traditional responses to depression."

"She did more than that," said Myron. "She questioned the validity of prescribing ECT, stating that the data available was too unreliable."

Flustered, Joanna rushed her words. "I guess that's why I'm surprised to see it on 2B. I thought the machines had been phased out everywhere, except in long-stay mental institutions."

"Where they throw away the key?" He grinned. "You see, Dr. Bereza, we're still in the dark ages. Patients here run kicking and screaming as we chase them with electrical cords."

Though Joanna knew he was goading her, her stomach turned. Swallowing her discomfort, she smiled. "I'm looking forward to working here. I read your recent paper on major depressive disorders. My university professor told me you're the leading expert in the country."

"Who was that?"

"Dr. Peterson."

"Smart man." Again, Joanna couldn't tell from his smug look whether he was joking or bragging.

"Don't flatter him," said Roberta. "We're having enough trouble keeping him down to size."

"I thought you liked my size," he said with a smirk.

Roberta blushed, and Joanna caught a moment between them that was hard to interpret. She glanced at Myron's left hand and saw a wedding ring; Roberta's hands were ring-free.

"You'll see that shock therapy—" Before he had a chance to finish, a patient made a beeline toward him. Joanna recognized her as the woman who'd skipped the number thirteen.

"Dr. Eisenstayed," said the patient, mispronouncing his name with a frozen smile. "Something's wrong. I'm feeling better. I'm not supposed to have a treatment today." She tugged at his sleeve as if to make sure he'd heard her.

Myron took in Rose's nicotine stained fingers. "There's nothing wrong," he said, removing her fingers from his jacket. "You just go over there and relax."

Rose's agitation grew, but she didn't move.

"You heard Dr. Eisenstadt," said Roberta in a stern voice. "Be a good girl and wait over there."

Rose shuffled to the lounge. "Goofy shrinks! Somebody should stick electric wires up their assholes and see how they like it."

Joanna stifled a laugh and said to Myron, "You have to admire her feistiness. Involuntary admission?"

Myron nodded as a thin, wiry man trooped past them bellowing like a TV evangelist addressing a large congregation. "Sinners, beware. The Almighty is watching, and he doesn't like what he's seeing. Get down on your knees and pray if you want to beat the devil!"

"We suspect the preacher is palming his meds again," said Roberta.

"Is he really a minister?" Joanna asked.

"No," said Myron, "but we call him that, for obvious reasons."

The preacher continued sermonizing as he passed Rose in the lounge. "And I say to you again, Lucifer preys on the weak. Hang on to the sleeve of God, and the devil won't touch you."

"Cocksucker!" Rose said to his back.

The preacher sent Rose a blistering look, which missed its mark since she didn't give him a second glance.

Upon seeing the exchange, a middle-aged brunette in the lounge crossed herself and rubbed the beads on her prayer rope, one bead at a time, saying, "Lord Jesus Christ, son of God, be merciful on me, a sinner."

Joanna watched the woman, then said to Myron, "What's her diagnosis?"

"Depression. Maria's father wrote her from Greece. Don't know what he wrote, but whatever it was, it hit her hard."

"It's all Greek to me," said Roberta, laughing at her own joke. She then added in a sober tone, "She wouldn't get out of bed after that, so her husband brought her in."

Joanna shook her head. "The power of family connections. Even by Canada Post. Was the letter translated for her chart?"

"We considered it," said Myron, "but we couldn't find anyone on staff that could read Greek."

THE RUBBER FENCE

"I gather her husband couldn't?"

"No," said Myron, shaking his head. "Anyway, her antidepressants are working, and she's about to be discharged."

Joanna nodded, but she couldn't see how this tidying up of the patient's problem was anything but temporary. Psychotropic medication was just a bandage covering up a mental sore. Though tempted to say something, Joanna knew it was too early in her residency to question his treatment plan.

Myron looked at his watch. "Time to see what the night brought on the ward."

TWO

IT WAS ONLY eight in the morning, but already the observation room was a beehive of activity. Joanna stood in the doorway and scanned the three rows of metal folding chairs, filled with staff and students trading stories. They were ignoring for now the one-way mirror showing the interview room, which was simply furnished with a brown couch, two naugahyde arm chairs, and a laminate coffee table with the requisite box of tissue. Tucked in the corner was the video camera used to record interviews for instructional purposes.

Squeezing past the staff at the back, Roberta sat down with Myron in the front row and opened her red binder. Joanna found a spot behind them beside a towering man with dark skin and a buzz cut who turned out to be an intern like herself.

"Jerome Sousa," he said, extending a hand in her direction.

His hands were warm. "Joanna Bereza. I haven't seen you at the college."

"I graduated four years ago. I've been working in Jamaica since. I'm planning to go back once I finish my residency."

She smiled, thinking how nice it would be to go to Jamaica. It had been awhile since she and Michael had gone on vacation. They were overdue for one, but now with her studies, his work schedule, and their reduced income, they'd be lucky to go anywhere in the next four years.

"Let's get started," said Myron to Roberta. "How many do

THE RUBBER FENCE

we have?"

"Three," she said, staring at a form in her red binder. "A rape victim, a slasher, and a paranoid schiz. It must've been fun in emerg. last night."

"Love that full moon," said someone with a husky voice from the back of the room. The staff chuckled.

"She's all yours, Sam," said Myron. "Maybe she'll howl for you."

Joanna turned to see a ruggedly handsome man of about thirty, leaning against the doorframe. He was dressed in a T-shirt and jeans, and with his long brown hair in a pony-tail, he looked more like a hip musician than an aspiring shrink. She'd seen him before—just this past week across a sea of tables in the campus cafeteria. One of her class-mates had mentioned he was quite the brain.

Myron said to Joanna, "Sam is our senior resident. If you need to know anything about ward procedure, he's the one to ask."

As Sam left the room, their eyes met. He nodded, and Joanna smiled back.

"How did the rape victim end up on our ward?" asked Myron.

Roberta scanned the patient's admission sheet. "Emergency determined she was suicidal."

Jerome whispered to Joanna, "A few months back, a woman hanged herself on 3C. I'll bet emerg. didn't want to put this one on a medical ward and risk another mishap."

Through the mirror, Joanna watched a female nurse escort a young woman with a bad blond dye job into the interview room.

"That's Sylvia Jackman," said Roberta. "She's anxious to get out of here."

Wearing a tight blue sweater, jeans, and sunglasses, the blond patient looked around warily before sitting down on the sofa. Sam, close behind, shut the door and took a seat opposite her.

Myron said to Joanna, "Sam has elected to do another rotation on this ward, so it can't be that bad. Pay attention. In a couple of weeks, you'll get a crack at this." He smiled wryly before turning back.

Roberta leaned forward and turned the volume knob on the wall that separated the two rooms. Sam's voice came through. "Can you tell us what happened?"

"You know what happened," Sylvia said with irritation in her voice.

"Look, I know it's hard—"

"You know it's hard? What do you know?" She scowled. "They didn't line up to take turns with you."

Joanna wished Sylvia would take off her glasses. She wanted to see if her expression matched the edge in her speech.

Sam bent forward. "You're right, but we need to know a little more so we can help you."

The patient sat motionless for a few seconds, taking her time to answer. Maybe it was the word "help" that encouraged Sylvia to let her guard down and remove her sunglasses—revealing eyes that appeared navy from a distance. She surveyed the mirror and the ceiling, as if she were planning her escape. *Was she looking for hidden mikes or what?* Joanna knew Sylvia couldn't see through the mirror, but it was unnerving to have someone stare back. Maybe patients could see an outline or a slight movement—just enough to make them wonder about the size of the crowd behind the glass. Joanna made a mental note to check the mirror from the other side as soon as she could. She was sure

THE RUBBER FENCE

it did nothing to ally patients' fears when they walked into that room.

Sam stretched his denim-clad legs and folded his hands in his lap.

Sylvia stared at him intently for a few seconds and then said, "I freaked out. They kept coming at me." She sighed. "I dunno— I dunno how many there were. Everything was a blur. After,...after..." She stumbled and looked down, unable to continue.

Sam waited. Joanna liked that he didn't jump in to fill the void.

"I'm sorry," said Sylvia, visibly choking back tears.

"It's all right," said Sam. "Take your time."

Sylvia glanced at the mirror again before continuing. "They dumped me on the street. I lay there for a while, I dunno how long. I was very sore. I couldn't move, but I knew I had to in case they came back." She glanced occasionally at the nurse, whose face remained enigmatic.

"That must've been terrifying for you," said Sam in a soft voice.

She nodded. "I pulled myself up and walked to a grocery store a block away. I used the phone there to call my friend Cheryl. She picked me up and brought me to the hospital. I didn't want to come. I had to leave my kids with my mother. They dunno what happened, but I could tell they were scared. I guess I looked a mess." She raised her hand to her eye, as if she had a bruise there that was bothering her.

Joanna's eyes misted over, and she hoped no one could see. It could be embarrassing if anyone noticed how easily she fell apart.

With the session ending, Myron turned down the sound and

said, "I'm sure her clothes acted as a red light."

"As in a red light district," said Roberta.

Joanna found Myron and Roberta's comments troubling. Did they truly believe that Sylvia had asked for it? She had little time to consider the implications because Sam returned to the observation room.

"Good job," said Myron to Sam, who was now standing at the back.

Sam shrugged. "It was like pulling teeth at first."

"Let's ask our female resident," said Myron. "Joanna, what do you think this young woman needs?"

"Besides a new hairdresser," said somebody in the back, eliciting titters from a few nurses.

Though annoyed by the black humour, Joanna couldn't blame the staff. It was either laugh about the misfortunes of others, or cry yourself to sleep every night.

"What, no ideas?" said Myron, raising his eyebrows.

"I expect," she said, swallowing hard, "after this trauma, she's going to need some help to get her rage out, and...and hopefully to see justice done."

Sam jumped in. "See, Myron, they *are* teaching students something at the university."

"Well, Joanna," said Myron. "You have an ally."

She hoped Myron was right. The way things were going, she'd need one.

Roberta whispered to Myron, who then announced, "That's it for the morning. The other two patients aren't available for intake right now."

Joanna followed Jerome to the door, where Sam was waiting. He said to Jerome, "Wanna shoot a few hoops after lunch?"

"Sure."

Sam smiled at Joanna over Jerome's shoulder, as if she were the one who'd agreed to play. His eyes sparkled like a cool, inviting lake on a hot summer day. He then grinned in a way that made her wonder if he'd been reading her thoughts.

She felt her cheeks redden. "What?"

"Nothing. I was just thinking it's good to have a female resident for a change. We get a lot of patients who prefer to talk to women."

"Is that right?" she said, smiling. "So, what's next on the agenda?"

Sam said, "Use the rest of the morning to get settled. The residents' room is down the corridor on your left. Pick an empty desk. There should be a procedures manual in one of the drawers. If not, you can find one in the nurses' station. After that, you can review the patient records—get a feel of who we have on the ward."

Was he kidding? Did he expect her to do all that in one morning? He must have noticed her bewildered expression, as he added, "You have to hit the deck running. It's the only way you'll survive."

"Ha. Should I start shaking now or wait until after I've had my morning coffee?"

Sam laughed and started singing, "New York, New York", as if the hospital was the city, and if she made it there, she could make it anywhere.

Jerome joined in and did a few tap steps.

She was heartened by their kidding. Maybe if she hung around them, she'd loosen up. Michael was always telling her she was too uptight.

Just then, a mild and unassuming young doctor with granny

glasses—a man who could blend into the woodwork if you let him—came up to them and said, "Does one have to tap dance to get into this circle?" He was in some of her classes, but she hadn't yet spoken to him.

Sam stretched out his hand. "Sam Berman."

"Dennis Williams."

"Good to have you on board."

"Thanks. Is he as tough as they say?"

"Myron?"

"Is there anyone else I should be concerned about?"

Sam snorted. "No, Myron's the one. Just be ready to take a little heat."

"I hate to say this to you," said Dennis, "but when I first saw you, I thought you were a patient."

Jerome chuckled. "When we get through our stint on 2B, we're all going to look like this honky." The others joined in the laughter.

After more introductions, Joanna considered what a curious mix they were: a hippie, a tall Jamaican, a married woman, and a young man who seemed too delicate for a profession that was still finding its feet. They were all different, but they were all working toward the same goal—an exciting but frightening one. In their quest to be the best, they were all taking a risk. She had heard of doctors who had cracked themselves or lost sight of their families, or even worse, misdiagnosed patients who then committed homicide or suicide under their watch. To be a psychiatrist was a goal worth pursuing, even if the path to it was fraught with peril.

THREE

ONE FLOOR ABOVE 2B, a new life was about to be extracted from the loins of a chunky young woman. Layered in sweat, Theresa Boychuk breathed deeply with each contraction.

It seemed like only moments before she had come to the realization her future was doomed. She and Eugene had been living for the last ten months—the entire length of their marriage—in his parents' basement suite. Her relationship with her mother-in-law was prickly at the best of times, but had reached an all-time low in the past twenty-four hours.

Theresa had gone upstairs to the living room the day before to get a book she'd left on the couch. She shouldn't have left it there, as Dr. Benjamin Spock's *Baby and Child Care* was a book her mother-in-law criticized.

When Theresa had walked into the room that day, her mother-in-law was smoothing out the wrinkles on the plastic-covered wing chairs. "Did you see my book?"

"I don't know why you need it. Mothers have been using common sense to raise children for centuries."

When Theresa didn't reply, Mrs. Boychuk said with a bite, "I couldn't stand the mess and put it in the magazine rack."

Before Theresa had a chance to get it, her water broke on the newly finished hardwood floors and threatened to seep down the uneven floor boards into the neighbouring hallway.

"Look what you've done!" shrieked Mrs. Boychuk. She ran

to the kitchen and was back with a sponge before Theresa could shake the paralysis that had set in when she saw the liquid flowing from between her legs.

"Eugene!" Mrs. Boychuk hollered.

Eugene rushed in like a soldier commanded by his sergeant. His face flushed red as he took in the scene.

"I told you she wouldn't be ready. By the time you pack, she'll have it here. I don't know why no one listens to me."

With fear mounting, Eugene stared helplessly at his wife.

His mother softened. "My poor Eugene. You have your hands full."

"I don't want to have it here!" Theresa whimpered.

"You won't," Eugene said without conviction. He took his wife by the hand, like a parent with a disobedient child, and led her from the pristine living room to their crowded quarters downstairs. Theresa sat immobile on their bed while Eugene grabbed nightgowns, panties, and socks from the chest of drawers and threw them into a tan overnight bag he'd taken out of their closet moments before.

Less than ten minutes later, Theresa's eyes widened when she heard the thumping footsteps of the woman she'd grown to hate coming down the stairs.

Her mother-in-law appeared in the doorway, her face that of a prison guard ready to snap. She stood there scowling for several moments and then flipped her expression like a coin in a toss. In a saccharine tone, she said, "I'll get the car."

"It's all right, Mom," said Eugene. "We'll manage."

"Are you joking? I wouldn't think of you going alone." Ignoring Theresa, she patted Eugene on the shoulder and left as abruptly as she had arrived.

Theresa hissed, "What's she talking about? You're not

THE RUBBER FENCE

going alone. You're going with me. Me, dammit!"

"Mom's just a little excited."

"She's always excited."

Eugene frowned, his forehead lined like ruts on a Manitoba highway after a bruising winter. He put all his attention into closing the small suitcase as if the act was critical to the outcome of his wife's labour.

All the way to the car—now parked in front of the house—Theresa muttered about her mother-in-law's intrusion, but Eugene walked on without saying anything, like he was in a fog and needed all his senses to stay clear of any obstacles.

Mrs. Boychuk was no sooner seated in the back seat when she said, "I don't know what's so hard about packing a few things. Why does she need so much? My husband never had to pack for me. I was ready months in advance."

Theresa sat quietly in the front seat, tears staining her cheeks, while Mrs. Boychuk carried on like she wasn't there.

When the three reached the emergency entrance, Eugene leapt out of the car and got the overnight bag out of the trunk. Then, after helping Theresa move her great girth off the front seat, he said, "I have to park the car. You'll have to go in with Mom."

Alarmed, Theresa gave Eugene a desperate look—one that he ignored. Couldn't he understand how vulnerable she felt? She would rather have walked the extra distance than be alone with her mother-in-law. Mrs. Boychuk had been the main source of tension even before they were married. She had done everything she could to prevent Eugene from tying the knot. The fact that he hadn't listened had been one point in his favour, but the little backbone he'd shown then had disintegrated over time.

Theresa had thought their stay at the Boychuks was going to

be temporary. But two weeks had stretched into a month, a month into ten, and now it seemed they were destined to live there a few more years so Eugene could get his engineering degree. The thread that had held Theresa together was his promise that after he graduated, they'd find their own place. Until then, she'd have to put up with Mrs. Boychuk's constant barbs, and given their current struggles, Theresa was no longer sure she could last that long.

Still, preparation for the birth had gone well. Eugene had attended prenatal classes with her, despite his mother poohpoohing the whole notion. Now, all Theresa had to remember was to breathe deeply with each contraction. She tried to force her mother-in-law's criticisms out of her mind and focus on the hard labour ahead. Mercifully, Mrs. Boychuk hadn't followed Eugene into the labour room. She was sitting in a hospital lounge somewhere waiting for the baby to arrive.

Theresa had been shaved and cleaned for the upcoming battle. She wasn't afraid of the birth, or even of having a baby and taking care of it. She was more afraid of the woman Eugene called mother. Since Mrs. Boychuk had little good to say about her daughter-in-law, what would she be like when the baby came home?

Another sharp pain erupted in her lower abdomen, and she cried out. Even with her banshee yells bouncing off the walls, Eugene hovered nearby, whispering reassurances. He may have been apprehensive, but he was proving to be surprisingly supportive. The agony of labour seemed lessened with him by her side, especially with the final push fast approaching.

"Are you sure you don't want anything for the pain?" asked Dr. Gebbard.

"I'll never...oh, oh, OW!" She shook her head, but her

THE RUBBER FENCE

screams told a different story.

"She wants to do it natural," Eugene stated offhandedly as if he'd said it a hundred times before. He'd made his thoughts known that he didn't agree, but he *did* agree that there was no point in arguing with a woman. The nurse smiled, nodding her approval. She was a petite young woman of Filipino extraction, looking no more than fifteen.

It was then that a second nurse came into the room, approached him, and said in a hushed tone, "Your mother would like to see you."

"Eugene," Theresa gasped.

"She collapsed in the hallway," the second nurse said. "We're just checking her out now."

Eugene's eyes bulged with dread. "Oh, God! I have to go." He tried to extract his hand, but Theresa held on, insisting that he stay. The doctor and nurse did not take sides, but a tug of war ensued, and they were about to separate the two when Eugene wrenched his hand away. "I'll be right back," he said as he quit her bedside.

He stopped by the door looking like he was leaving one war zone to go to another. His face pleaded with her to understand, but all Theresa could manage was another scream.

As he disappeared from view, Theresa couldn't help but smile a sad, odd smile. She whispered to her unborn baby, "It's okay, honey. Mommy's here, and I will always be here for you no matter what—no matter what."

Within seconds of Eugene's departure, Theresa gave a whoop, signalling that the baby was ready to begin its journey down the long canal.

She strained and pushed. Beads of perspiration gathered in a line on her brow. The nurse wiped them away gently as if she were cleaning an open wound on a child.

"Just a little more," said the doctor. "You're almost there."

Theresa bore down with all the strength she could muster. When the baby squirmed through, bloody but intact, her body shook with relief. "Oh, hallelujah." Tears filled her eyes.

The doctor caught the infant, tapped her lightly to elicit her first cry, and then handed her to the waiting nurse, who cleaned the baby with warm towels before placing her on her mother's chest. Theresa trembled, partly from the cold that swept over her, but mostly from the joy that coursed through her like a wave crashing triumphantly on the shore.

"You did a great job," said the doctor. "You were very brave."

Theresa looked at her infant, snuggled on her right breast. Marvelling at the miracle before her, she said a prayer of thanks and touched her baby's rosy fingers.

It was only after the umbilical cord was cut and the placenta delivered that Eugene rushed back into the room. "Oh, honey," he said, with wonder at the loving sight before him.

"You have a beautiful baby girl," said the doctor, patting Eugene's back. "Congratulations."

Theresa turned away, shielding her baby from Eugene. She didn't see his crushed look, nor did she know he was wishing he'd never left her side.

FOUR

JOANNA OPENED THE apartment door and breathed in the aroma of spaghetti sauce—tomatoes, garlic, basil, and oregano.

"Joanna?" Michael's voice boomed out.

"I'll be right there." She hung up her jacket and then caught a glimpse of her strained face in the hallway mirror. She frowned. *You knew it would be hard. This is what you wanted.* Sighing, she ran her fingers through her hair and entered the dining room.

One of Michael's philosophy books lay open on the table, a sign that he had interrupted his work in order to make dinner. He was at the stove stirring the sauce, the steam of boiling noodles swirling around his face.

She hugged him from behind. His body softened in her embrace, and he turned to kiss her, the remnants of spaghetti sauce transferring from his mouth to hers. She licked her lips and his. "Mmm. Tastes good." She caressed his back and let her hands wander down, appreciating how toned he was.

"You're getting me all excited."

"That's the plan," she said, smiling.

He gave her another kiss, this time more deeply, causing her limbs to tremble. He could always turn her to pudding.

Stirring the sauce, he said, "You're going to love this."

"I already do. Just proves again that you're the better cook."

"If you think you're going to succeed in getting out of your turn tomorrow…"

Joanna laughed. That had been her ploy exactly. Ever since she had decided to further her studies, Michael had begun to help more. His help hadn't come without some argument; he'd grown up with a doting mother. She poured herself a glass of wine. "Want one?"

"No thanks. I'm having a beer." He took a swig from the bottle by the stove before sprinkling garlic powder on the sauce. "How did it go today?"

"It was rough. A rape victim ended up on the ward. You should've heard the innuendos."

"Was she a floozy?"

"Michael, why would you say something like that?"

"Right." His expression immediately turned sour. She wished she hadn't reacted with such an edge in her voice. He was just kidding…or maybe not? He could be a woman's champion, but occasionally, chauvinism surfaced. It was a familiar argument. She looked at him again. He was still pouting. She hoped he'd let it go. The last thing she wanted was a fight. She stared at his back while he ladled the sauce onto each plate of hot noodles. After a few moments, she cleared the table and set it for two. The air was thick with the unspoken, but nothing more was said until they sat down.

Joanna twirled her noodles. "So…did you have a good day?"

"Yeah, until you got home."

"Oh c'mon, Michael. I didn't mean to bark at you. Let's not spoil the lovely dinner you made."

He looked at her briefly, as if he were contemplating another retort, but then he said with a softened tone, "It was the usual. One hundred students listened attentively to my lecture on

THE RUBBER FENCE

original thought. I spent the first half arguing that there was such a thing, and the second half rejecting the idea."

"Well, that must've gone over well."

He smiled. "Got to keep them on their toes, you know."

She took a mouthful of spaghetti and savoured the flavour. "Are you sure you don't want to do this every night?"

"Ha."

She sipped some wine. "Remind me again of why I went into psychiatry."

"It was something about an old lady dear to your heart."

"Yeah," she said, shaking her head. "You know, nothing much has changed. They still have one of those damn ECT machines on the ward. I thought for sure they'd be gone by now. You'd think with better meds…" Her voice trailed off. "I feel like I'm reliving a nightmare."

"It didn't happen to you."

Joanna swallowed a few more mouthfuls before saying, "I'm hardly thirty, and already I'm getting wrinkles."

"I was going to talk to you about that."

She waved her fork at him. "Don't…"

"You look beautiful."

Half-smiling, she said, "I just need a good night's sleep." She took another sip of wine. "I was thinking, did I go back because I didn't want to face the truth?"

"Joanna, we've gone over this."

She played with the napkin on her lap. "Maybe if we could've had a child, I wouldn't be looking for another challenge."

Michael's face hardened. "We can have a good life without kids."

"I just…I just wish my mother and father weren't so

disappointed."

"Yeah. They look at us as if someone had died."

Joanna grimaced. "Someone did. I miscarried twice."

"I can't go through the rest of my life talking about this. Can't we give it a rest?"

She nodded. Michael was right. They went in circles. Every time, she brought up their past failures to have a child, they ended up at an impasse. She didn't do it to massage the hurt. All she wanted was to raise the possibility of adoption again. The meal ended the way it had started—in silence.

That evening, Joanna lay on the bed staring at the ceiling. It was an old, rental apartment with peeling paint in the corner, like the edges of her marriage. Michael was in the dining room working on the next day's lecture. She figured he was taking longer than usual because their talk, or lack of it, had put a damper on the rest of the evening. Maybe he hadn't grieved like she had, or maybe he didn't care as much, she couldn't tell. The fact that she couldn't carry full term had settled on her like a sore that wouldn't heal. To cover it up, she worked harder. Which was pretty crazy given that her hard work might've been the reason she'd lost her fetus. She had beaten herself up for that. She was sure her mother and Michael's mother still blamed her. Their generation of women had stayed home and taken care of the children.

She tried to stay awake, hoping he'd come to bed soon, but she drifted off. Their plan of lovemaking had fizzled like a wet firecracker.

FIVE

FIVE DAYS AFTER giving birth, Theresa left the hospital feeling sore, weary, and apprehensive about what lay ahead. She and Eugene had fixed up a spare room for their baby across from their bedroom, painting three walls yellow and wallpapering the fourth with illustrated nursery rhymes. It was better than crowding her into their room where there was barely enough space for a bed and dresser let alone a bassinet.

Right from the time she came home, Marlene tossed and turned in her sleep. Theresa hadn't expected a cranky baby. It was one more thing on top of the competition that arose between Theresa and her mother-in-law as to who was the better mother. *At least I can breastfeed my baby.* That had to count for something.

One evening—while the family was finishing up a meal of pork chops, mashed potatoes, and gravy—matters between the two women came to a head.

"Thanks, Mom. This is my favourite supper," said Eugene, smacking his lips to underline his compliment.

"I know," said Mrs. Boychuk. "That's why I made it for you."

"It was good, Sophie," said Mr. Boychuk, wiping his mouth with his napkin.

Theresa's stomach churned at all the fawning and praising. Fuming, she kept her head down, swallowing the potatoes but not the compliments thrown around the table.

"I've always done what you like, Eugene," said Mrs. Boychuk in her sweetest tone. "Even when you were tiny, like Marlene." She gestured with her fork at him. "You know, you were a different baby; you were bottle fed. None of this dirty breastfeeding for you." She said it in such a warm way that Theresa was startled and wondered for a moment if she'd heard it right.

Mrs. Boychuk went on. "I sterilized those bottles every night. Do you remember, Walter?"

"I remember."

Scrunching her face in disgust, Mrs. Boychuk said to Theresa, "I don't know why you insist on breastfeeding."

Theresa's eyes darted from Eugene to her father-in-law in an appeal for support but both men avoided her glances. Walter rose to get sugar for his tea, and Eugene bent under the table on the pretext of picking up something that had fallen. Theresa hoped it was courage he was looking for and would find some before he sat up again.

Theresa steeled herself and said, "Breastfeeding is the most natural thing in the world. It has everything a child needs."

"You don't know what you're talking about," said Mrs. Boychuk, her voice rising. "You don't know how much she's getting. You feed her and two hours later, she's hungry again. You can't tell me she's getting enough."

"You can't tell me she's not," Theresa muttered too softly for her mother-in-law to hear. And with that, she stood up abruptly and carried her dirty dishes to the sink, clattering them as she put them down.

Walter avoided his wife's looks and brushed imaginary crumbs off the table with his hand. Eugene had come up for air

THE RUBBER FENCE

and was now looking from one woman to the other as if he hoped they had accomplished a truce in his absence.

Theresa caught her husband's eye and motioned with her head suggesting he'd better leave the kitchen with her or he'd be sorry.

Instead of rising to join her, Eugene lowered his head and played with his crumpled napkin.

Theresa said bitterly, "I'm going to see *my* baby."

Chastened and with his shoulders hunched, Eugene got up and followed his wife out the door.

As the young couple made their way downstairs, they could hear Mrs. Boychuk's shrill voice hammering her husband. "Did you see that? All I do for her and this is the way she treats me. Is this the way to treat the grandmother of her baby? She's got no manners, that girl. I don't deserve this; I don't deserve this at all."

With her mother-in-law's diatribe ringing in her ears, Theresa resolved to stick to her instincts. She figured that Mrs. Boychuk's love of bottles had to be at the root of Eugene's insecurity. With that in mind, the young mother vowed that nothing and no one would stop her from nursing Marlene.

After that evening, matters only became worse between her and Eugene. His lack of support tore whatever fabric was holding their marriage together. Feeling alienated, Theresa no longer confided in her husband when he came home from the university. She even kept quiet about the time she and her mother-in-law almost came to blows.

The incident that led to an irreversible falling-out happened on the day that Theresa had woken up to find she'd slept in. The clock on her nightstand read eight a.m. For a moment, she'd thought she was dreaming, but the next, she marvelled that

Marlene had made it through the night without waking.

Theresa hurried to the nursery and found her baby in the crib, sucking on the rubber nipple of a bottle of formula propped up by a stuffed teddy bear. Theresa went ballistic and rushed to the kitchen where she found Mrs. Boychuk making cinnamon buns. The aroma would've been sweet if not for the acrimony that lay between the two women.

Theresa yelled, "How dare you give her a bottle!"

"Before you get on your high horse, missy, I was just trying to give you a good night's rest. You should thank me instead of coming in here and bawling me out. Didn't your mother teach you anything?"

"Leave my mother out of this."

Mr. Boychuk came into the kitchen carrying a newspaper. "What's going on here?"

"I can't please Theresa."

"Don't you *dare* give *my* baby a bottle again!" Her face red with rage, Theresa stormed out as quickly as she'd come in. She would have to talk to Eugene about moving out. They would have to find some way to make it work.

Mrs. Boychuk poured a cup of tea for herself and her husband at the kitchen counter. "That's gratitude for you. I try to help out, and what do I get? I'm spit on, that's a fine t'do. What Eugene saw in her, God only knows. Lazy, good for nothing, she-devil..." She leaned on the counter and started to cry.

Misery etched on his face, Walter shifted in his seat at the lace cloth covered table. "Sophie, no point in getting upset over this. She's just young. She doesn't know any better." He paused

THE RUBBER FENCE

as Sophie wiped her tears with her apron and brought two cups of tea to the table.

"You're right," said Sophie, sitting down. "She doesn't know anything, especially how to treat a mother. If I had treated my mother that way, she would've shown me the back of her hand."

He looked at her for a moment. "Maybe you should leave well enough alone."

"What? You, too? You think I was wrong?" The fire in her eyes warned Walter that he'd soon find out the definition of hell if he wasn't prudent. "You expect me to just take it and not say anything. What kind of a man are you?"

"No, it's not—" Walter's voice wavered, "—it's not that you said anything wrong. It's just that—"

"Just what? What are you *just*ing about?"

"Nothing. You know what's best."

"If I know so much, how come nobody listens?" She gave him a long hard look.

He avoided her scrutiny by picking up the *Winnipeg Free Press* and burying his head in the "Sports" section. He let out a big sigh when Sophie went back to making her cinnamon buns.

When Eugene had come home that evening, Theresa was still worked up over what had happened. She told him about the bottle. "I can't do it, Eugene. She's driving me around the bend."

"Theresa, I just got in the door. It's been a hard day. Can't we talk about it in the morning?"

She glared at him as if he was the devil incarnate. "It's always tomorrow. It's always, 'We'll talk about it tomorrow'.

You know damn well that's not going to happen."

When he stood there with his arms by his side, not saying anything, she said, "Go. Run to Mama." She slammed the bedroom door in his face.

When he tried to open it, he couldn't. For all he knew, she had blocked it with a piece of furniture. He didn't want to force it, make a commotion, not with his parents upstairs. Frustrated, he went upstairs to the living room where his father was sleeping in his chair, and his mother was glued to the TV.

Upon noticing Eugene, Mrs. Boychuk said, "Turn down the volume."

After turning the knob, Eugene sat down beside his mother on the sofa and stared at her until she said, "What is it?"

"Mom ... you know how sensitive Theresa is about nursing Marlene." He could feel the strain in his throat as he spoke. "Why did you put a bottle in the baby's mouth?"

"I won't do it again, believe me. If I thought she'd go crazy, do you think I would have said anything? Not on your life." She waved her finger at Eugene and said, "But I tell you one thing: I'm not going to let some pipsqueak shit all over me."

Eugene gnashed his teeth. "She ... she didn't do that."

"How do you know? You weren't home." Mrs. Boychuk softened her stance. "What did I do that was so bad? Theresa hasn't been sleeping. Look how tired she's been. Her nerves are on edge. That poor girl needs her rest. I thought I was helping her." She blew a raspberry. "That's gratitude for you. Next time, I'll mind my own business."

Eugene felt defeated but he knew that if he kept pushing, it could lead to an outcome he didn't want. His mother could turn a cold shoulder faster than any woman he knew, not that he knew many.

THE RUBBER FENCE

He remembered a time when he was six—he had dropped one of her china plates by accident. She had screamed, "What's the matter with you? That was a wedding gift!" Scared of her loud voice and piercing eyes, he apologized at least five times. It wasn't enough. She continued to moan about her china dish. When she had exhausted her complaining, she had the nerve to say, "You can say anything you want to me. You know that. You can tell Mommy anything."

So he did. He told her how terrified he'd been when she'd yelled. That only made her angrier. When he'd asked her to stop yelling, she denied that she'd been yelling. She then screamed that he must have made it up. She went on and on and on until his head hurt, and his stomach ached. After that, he knew he'd best keep his opinions to himself and only say what he thought his mother wanted to hear. Why couldn't he walk away like his sister had done? She and his mother no longer talked. He guessed that was why he wasn't prepared to take that gamble.

To make peace, he said, "Mom, you know I think you're great." He winced as he said it, but he kept going. "We both appreciate your help, but I ..., I think you know that Theresa, well, she needs to do this her way."

Mrs. Boychuk said nothing but looked at him as if he were a stranger.

"Mom...?"

"If that's what you want." There it was again—bitterness poisoning the words he wanted to hear. "But you'll see; she won't be able to manage. She's going to crack up if she keeps this up."

Eugene left the room feeling as if he were caught in some kind of vortex with no way out.

SIX

THE WEEK AFTER her orientation, Joanna was scheduled to meet Myron for a session in his office, but since a few of his overhead lights had burned out, they instead met in one of the interview rooms—a narrow space with a small desk and two visitor chairs. There were no distractions such as windows or posters or any other form of art for relief if matters between them became tense.

The room may have been austere, but there was nothing simple about Myron's presentation. Everything about him was polished—his crisp white shirt, fine herringbone suit, diamond patterned socks, and polished brown brogues. They sat across from one another like opponents in a chess game, each eyeing the other for any body language that could be used in their battle of wits. She wasn't sure what to expect, but she knew from her initial observations that he planned to keep her guessing.

Hoping to develop some rapport, she said, "I heard you're an American. A liberal one."

Her opening seemed to disarm him. "Yes, I am. Do you follow our politics?"

"It's hard not to, with the war on TV every night."

They began to chat about recent news—the Kent State University students who'd been shot to death while demonstrating against the war in Vietnam and the current uproar over the break-in at the Democrat Party headquarters in

Washington. But after exhausting the topic of the government down south, there was a brief lull during which the strain between them surged once more.

Breaking the uncomfortable silence, just as she was about to make some inane comment about the heavy rain that day, he said, "Is it what you expected?"

"What do you mean?" She wasn't sure if they were still on the topic of American politics.

"The ward." He smiled, as if he'd just scored a point.

"Oh." Joanna leaned back. She wished the chair was more comfortable. "Yes and no. I didn't expect such a wide range—confused old folks on the same ward as schizophrenics and alcoholics. Even a few adolescents." Her brow furrowed with the thought.

"It's not ideal, I agree." He folded his hands in his lap. "Anyone having a psychotic break, whether it's from intoxication or some kind of family drama, ends up here." He shifted in his chair as if she had blamed him for the problem. "Anything else?"

"Well, there's not much to report yet..." She hesitated.

"Something's troubling you."

Unsure of how to share what she was thinking, she looked instead at a black mark on the wall behind him. Maybe a patient had thrown something out of frustration.

Joanna regarded Myron again and decided to take a chance on his sincerity. She cleared her throat. "I was bothered by the woman Sam interviewed last week at intake. Sylvia Jackman?" She said the patient's name in the form of a question, one that implied he might not remember the young woman he'd seen only a week ago.

"Our self-defeating personality."

He did remember, but why wouldn't he? Gang rape wasn't a

common occurrence. And he'd also encouraged some mocking remarks about her appearance. "What makes you say that?"

"Her behaviour suggests that."

Joanna frowned, knowing Myron was referring to a diagnosis in the psychiatric bible, a small coil-bound book with a gold cover called the *DSM-II—Diagnostic and Statistical Manual for Mental Disorders*. It provided shrinks with a wide range of labels they could apply to someone behaving outside the norm. It was supposed to be a guide, but some psychiatrists treated it as gospel.

"Yes," Joanna said, "that's true, but she's a product of her environment."

"So?"

His gaze was unnerving. She sighed. "This is a woman who grew up poor, was molested when she was eight, had two abortions, and was recently raped by a biker gang." Joanna shook her head at the thought of all Sylvia had been through. "And she's still living with her mother and trying to raise a child with no support from the father. He was, or maybe still is, a drug addict. With a history like that, who wouldn't feel defeated?"

"Joanna," said Myron in a condescending tone. "You're going to find that most of the patients who end up here have been brutalized or terrorized in some way."

"I'm not arguing about that." Her heartbeat accelerated as she pressed her point. "It seems too simple and unfair to fit everything that happens to anyone into a neat little category, like self-defeating personality. I find it hard to accept this kind of labelling for Sylvia. It ignores all the environmental factors that played a role in her hospitalization."

"It's the best we've got." He studied her for a moment, then said, "Look at the evidence. She's a young mother. What the hell was she doing going to a party dressed like a whore?" Myron's voice rose like that of an evangelist working his congregation. "What did she think was going to happen? She wasn't dressed for a Tupperware party."

Joanna frowned. "Maybe she was naïve and lonely. Maybe she just wanted some love, some attention. Maybe she thought that was one way to get a guy interested in her."

"Oh, they'd be interested all right."

"Maybe for a few hours she wanted to forget she had responsibilities." Joanna paused when she realized she was getting too emotional. She added softly, "Is that so wrong?"

Myron brushed his right leg, as if there was some lint on his wool pants. "No, but she has responsibilities."

"True enough, but I can't imagine how she must feel trying to raise a child with no one to help her. Women in her position have so few options."

Myron arched his eyebrows. Surely, he agreed with her? But the way he looked at her with such a penetrating gaze, she could only guess at what he was thinking. Like patients, residents were also under the microscope.

Joanna pulled out of the hospital lot. There wasn't much traffic on the drive home, giving her a chance to reflect on the group meeting Myron had held with the residents that afternoon. He was in fine form.

She could still hear his words. *'In order to be boarded, you have to pass your written and oral exams. We, at the hospital, are responsible for preparing you for the orals where you will have one hour to interview an unknown patient...'*

That'd be the time when everything would have to come together. But until that test interview, there would be a lot of ground to cover—a lot of course work as well as a fistful of patients to assess and analyze in depth.

As far as Joanna could see, the hospital was one big obstacle course. As a doctor, you were assigned patients who expected to get better, even if you had little idea about how to help them. She would need to find a way through the labyrinth of psychiatric musings and be humble enough to admit she didn't know what to do when she didn't. She hoped she would be up to the challenge.

SEVEN

BECAUSE OF THE ongoing bickering with her mother-in-law, Theresa's nerves were frayed. And although she had always prided herself on her good health, she was now suffering with headaches, stomach upsets, and sleepless nights. It didn't help that her baby's cries had intensified. Her screams were like an auditory report card on how well the women in the house were doing, and at the moment, they were both failing miserably.

One morning, Theresa woke up to Marlene howling. The young mother's heart pounded as she raced to the nursery and found her baby tangled in a thin receiving blanket; her legs and arms flailing and the blanket swirling over her head.

Theresa pushed the blanket away and picked up Marlene. In an effort to calm herself and her baby, Theresa sang, "Daisy, Daisy, give me your answer true. I'm half crazy all for the love of you. It won't be a stylish marriage; I can't afford a carriage..."

Soothed by her mother's voice, Marlene's cries subsided to a whimper, and she laid her head on her mother's shoulder.

Theresa moved her hand down Marlene's back and felt her wet nightgown. "Aw, sweetykins. No wonder you were crying so loudly."

Taking a diaper from a side table, Theresa sang some more while she held Marlene. "But we'll look sweet, upon the seat, of a bicycle built for two..."

Theresa arched herself, hoping to relieve the sudden sharp

pain in her lower back. She wished she had a changing table, as the crib was too low, and she had to bend over to reach Marlene. The whole idea of dealing with large safety pins made Theresa anxious, especially when she couldn't count on Marlene to lie still. She took a deep breath and lowered her infant onto the crib mattress.

In the kitchen upstairs, Eugene tried to block out his baby's sobs by burying his head in the newspaper. Theresa's singing and Marlene's cries competed with the percolating coffee and the sizzling of the French toast that Mrs. Boychuk was preparing.

Eugene kept glancing at the doorway as if at any moment his wife might barge in asking him to take over. It had been a rough few weeks. The baby's demands for a feeding every two hours made it impossible to have a good night's sleep. Maybe he could grab a nap in the car at lunchtime. He was glad he could at least escape the house. He didn't feel guilty, either. Why should he, when he was working hard at his studies and even bringing home some money from his weekend work at the government liquor store? Of course he knew that his being out meant Theresa was left with his mother for long stretches of time. But what could he do about that? They were both stubborn women. With the cries intruding on his thoughts, he got up from the kitchen table and walked over to the counter to get the sugar bowl.

"I could have got that for you," said Mrs. Boychuk as she flipped the egg-soaked bread. "You poor thing; I don't know how you slept. I could hear that baby crying all night. Maybe Theresa's milk isn't coming in like she thinks."

"I'll be fine. It's Theresa who's—"

THE RUBBER FENCE

"She can sleep during the day, for heaven sakes. But you—you have to study. It's a good thing I can help. Thank God, I still have my health. For how long, I don't know ... touch wood." And with that, she touched the breadboard. "Heaven knows, I don't need any more scares like I had at the hospital."

"The doctor said it was nothing serious."

"You talked to the doctor?"

"Yes, Mom. You were there."

"I don't remember him saying that. Maybe you talked to him when I wasn't there."

Eugene shrugged. "He said that you hadn't had any liquids for a while, and you were suffering from dehydration."

"What the hell does he know? I drink. You see me drink. My fridge is full of juice."

Eugene immediately regretted saying anything. He could see the tension in his mother's face as she transferred two slices of French toast onto a melamine dinner plate. He knew she hated anyone challenging her, yet there was his wife to think of. He couldn't win. Eugene's choosing his mother at the time of Marlene's birth had driven a wedge between him and Theresa. But what could he have done differently? He hadn't known his mother's fainting wasn't serious.

With a grim expression, Mrs. Boychuk brought his plate of French toast and a bottle of pancake syrup to the table. "I don't know how taking care of one baby is so hard. What's hard about it? I raised you and took care of my sick mother at the same time." Her eyes were wide and reproachful, as if he had something to do with his grandmother's illness. "I thought I'd never finish the washing. All those sheets! She wet the bed, poor soul. It wasn't easy. It was hard work. I know about sleepless nights. You don't think I know? I know. Ha! What's one baby?"

Eugene had heard this all before. Marlene screamed again in the background. He took a sip of coffee and, hoping for a break, started toward the kitchen door. "I'm going to see if Theresa needs any help."

Mrs. Boychuk stopped him with her hand. "No, I'll go. You eat. What's it for me? I don't do anything all day anyway." She took off her apron and flung it on a chair as she swept out of the room.

He exhaled sharply and went to the fridge to hunt for jam. Passing the sink, he caught a glimpse of himself in the mirror above it. His headache had deepened the furrows on his brow. He knew he should've gone to help Theresa, but he just couldn't take it. He had never been good at fighting, and now, with two women pushing at him from either side, his head was spinning. For a moment, he thought he might be coming down with the flu, but he quickly ruled that out as he had none of the other symptoms. Still, he felt dizzy, like he was about to fall from a high tower into a bottomless unknown.

Theresa tried to keep Marlene warm with a receiving blanket as she placed a diaper under her. She had to work quickly as the rails dug into her chest and the bending was hard on her back. With her baby's renewed thrashing, Theresa found it almost impossible to get her changed. Somehow, with one kick of her tiny left foot, Marlene had managed to cover her face with the blanket.

"Poor little sweetie pie. Mommy's hurrying."

Marlene wailed harder.

"Theresa!" yelled Mrs. Boychuk, from the doorway. Before

THE RUBBER FENCE

Theresa had the chance to reply, her mother-in-law rushed to the crib and said something sharp to her in Ukrainian.

Theresa hadn't understood all of what her mother-in-law had shouted, but she knew one word, *the devil.* Mrs. Boychuk skillfully picked up the baby and proceeded to arrange the diaper under her bare bottom.

Stunned, Theresa said, "What are you doing?"

Mrs. Boychuk rocked Marlene in her arms as if Theresa wasn't in the room. Marlene continued to sob like a needle stuck on a record, playing the same notes over and over, each one more piercing than the last.

"How dare you!"

"I saw what you were doing." Mrs. Boychuk fired the words at Theresa. "You could have choked her!"

"What are you talking about? Give me back my baby!" Theresa pulled at Marlene, but her mother-in-law held on. "Let go, you witch!"

"Eugene!" Mrs. Boychuk screamed, and Marlene echoed with a holler that matched her grandmother's volume.

In a matter of moments, Eugene entered the room. "What's going on?"

"Ask your wife!"

Theresa blanched. She hated when her mother-in-law referred to her in that way. "My name is Theresa," she said, her voice barely audible.

Eugene looked confused and stood glued to his spot. "Theresa? Are you going to tell me?"

It wasn't his words that were so upsetting, it was the tone he used. She felt all her energy drain away and her body shrink like Alice's had after she'd taken that drink in Wonderland. She saw Eugene turn to his mother, who was busy consoling Marlene.

Hadn't he noticed how distressed his wife was feeling? Didn't he see the fierce looks his mother threw in her direction? Did he care? Theresa decided no, he didn't. Nothing had changed from the time he'd left her bed in the delivery room. Mrs. Boychuk was the winner, once and for all. She was the one he wanted.

Eugene came over to her and touched her shoulder. "Theresa, it's okay." Tears trickled down her cheeks as he hugged her against his narrow torso. Her body stiffened, as if none of her limbs could bend.

Mrs. Boychuk made clucking sounds to the baby, who was still crying.

With Eugene holding her, Theresa felt a glimmer of hope take hold. She raised her head from Eugene's chest and was about to say something when her mother-in-law shrieked, "Tell him! Go ahead, tell him!"

Eugene pulled away from his wife and looked from one woman to the other.

Theresa began to shake. With her head down, she said to Eugene, "She…she…she came in here and took the baby. I…I was just changing her—"

"Liar!" yelled Mrs. Boychuk. "I came in, and the baby was choking! She was standing by the baby and the blanket was over Marlene's face. Thank God I came in when I did. My God—my God, she couldn't breathe."

"No, that's not true…I was…"

Ignoring Theresa, Mrs. Boychuk said to Eugene, "Son, I told you something like this was going to happen. Don't say I didn't warn you."

"Theresa, did you…?" Eugene said, challenging her this time with more than words. His face was that of an accuser. She took his doubt in and let it seep through her entire being. It filled her pores and her veins until she felt she was going to burst like a balloon, leaving no trace of Marlene's mother.

"Damn it all, Theresa. Did you or didn't you?"

This was not the Eugene she knew. It was as if her world had turned inside out and upside down. Theresa opened her mouth, but nothing came out. She glanced at her mother-in-law, who'd managed to get Marlene under control. *How did she do that?* They presented a calm picture—one that she'd been cut out of. Theresa stared at them as if they were blurred and she was trying to get them into focus. Although the distance between them was only a few yards, there may as well have been a canyon between her and her child.

And still, Eugene waited for her to say something in her defence. "Theresa, if you don't say something pretty quick …"

His tone was the same. He didn't understand. Theresa folded like an accordion after its owner has decided there was nothing worth playing. She crumpled into a heap on the floor and began to rock, back and forth, back and forth.

"Theresa, don't." Eugene stood there, bewilderment on his face. He made no move to comfort her.

"I guess *you'll* have to deal with her," Mrs. Boychuk said in a huff. "Like my mother always said, you make your bed, you lie in it." And then, without waiting for an answer, she left the room with Marlene, but not before casting her daughter-in-law one last disparaging look.

Theresa lay at Eugene's feet in a fetal position making a strange grinding noise.

EIGHT

JOANNA FOUND HER university courses bland compared to the ongoing drama in 2B, where human struggles played out like some bizarre symphony with a lot of wrong notes and clanging chords. About to experience her second round of intake patient interviews, she wondered what peculiar behaviours would be on display this morning. Knowing that the observation room filled up quickly, Joanna arrived early and found a seat near the front between Sam and Dennis.

There were a few new faces. One of them—she learned through Sam—was Dr. Bernie Stein, a short man with a pencil-thin moustache. His brown wool serge suit, crisply ironed shirt, and polished loafers portrayed another shrink who liked to be in control. Although she was critical of that kind of obsessiveness, she wished she had more of that quality herself. Perhaps then, she wouldn't feel so scattered.

Bernie had just returned from a family holiday and was regaling Myron with tales of topless beaches on the Riviera. His kibitzing manner suggested he had less to prove than Myron and might be a valuable ally should Joanna need one.

The other doctor, sitting with Bernie and Myron, was a physically imposing man in his early sixties. Despite the new rules of dress, he wore a white lab coat over his shirt and a red plaid bow tie that underscored his ruddy complexion. "Welcome," he said to her in a husky voice with a hint of a

THE RUBBER FENCE

Scottish accent. "It's nice to see more female doctors coming through."

"Joanna," said Sam, "meet Dr. Bryce Morley, our chief of psychiatry."

"Dr. Morley, I've been looking forward to working under your guidance," she said, shaking Bryce's hand. It was large and warm, like a giant teddy bear's.

"Bryce will do, my dear."

Joanna was taken aback by the head doctor's *my dear* remark, but accepted it as an eccentricity commensurate with his age and position.

"Like your tie," said Myron to Bryce. "Is it Robbie Burns' birthday today?"

"You're a funny guy. At least you're aware of our Scottish bard."

While the two senior shrinks traded comments, Sam whispered to Joanna, "Myron may run the ward, but he reports to Bryce. He wouldn't be too upset if Bryce dropped dead from a heart attack. He'd love to take over."

"Nice," said Joanna sarcastically. She wondered how a man with that kind of killer drive had ended up in psychiatry.

She switched her attention to the interview room, where Jerome's session had been aborted before it started. His elderly patient had to use the bathroom. They'd heard the man speak with a distinctive British accent, and in his Harris tweed jacket, he looked more like a gentleman out for a walk in the English countryside than a mental patient in a city hospital.

As she and the others watched Jerome follow the nurse and patient out of the interview room, Myron said to Roberta, "He seems more eccentric than disturbed. How did he get in here?"

"He exposed himself to some woman in a grocery store. She

called the police. The cops came right away, and when he told them the Queen would hear about it, they brought him in here."

"Could be brain damage from a stroke or just some attention-getting. Get the social worker on this right away. We have enough seniors plugging up the ward. Now, what do we have next?"

Roberta read from the cardex. "Theresa Boychuk. Nineteen. Postpartum psychosis. Her husband and family stated that Theresa began acting strangely a day ago. Her mother-in-law claims Theresa tried to kill her baby. She is contemplating pressing charges. The admitting nurse tried to talk to Theresa, but according to her family, she stopped talking just after the alleged incident took place. I think that's about it."

Myron said, "Joanna, do you have the chart?"

Joanna held up a file. She could feel the thumping of her heart as she left the observation room.

When Joanna introduced herself to Theresa, she saw a young and seemingly shy woman, not the kind capable of violence against a child. But then again, as her mother always said, *still waters run deep.* You couldn't always tell by looking at someone what was going on in their mind or heart.

Carmen, a nurse who looked as though she could have been Lena Horne's younger sister, sat down and waited for Theresa to do the same. The young mother hesitated, looking like she was ready to bolt. In the next instant, she fixated on the one-way mirror as if she were trying to determine its meaning.

Joanna pointed to the empty chair. "Theresa, you can sit there if you like." Theresa's eyes darted around the room before

THE RUBBER FENCE

she sat down. Joanna positioned herself on the sofa with her back to the mirror.

"I understand that you're a new mother. You have a little girl?"

Theresa nodded.

"I also understand that your husband and mother-in-law brought you in last night. Did a nurse explain to you that people who are involved in your care are on the other side of that mirror?"

Theresa stared at the unseen people behind the glass but said nothing. Carmen gave Joanna a look that was hard to interpret.

Joanna continued. "They're watching our interview. It's a one-way glass." Not knowing if the young mother was truly violent, Joanna lowered her voice to calm her. "It's not easy being here. You just gave birth a few weeks ago. You've had a lot to deal with."

Theresa met Joanna's gaze briefly before looking down.

"What's surprising is how tiny babies are," said Joanna, "and yet they can be very frustrating. Most women find taking care of a baby one of the biggest challenges of their lives. Some women get depressed almost immediately after giving birth." Joanna knew she was beginning to ramble, but for the few seconds their eyes had met, she thought she had penetrated Theresa's wall.

Theresa then stared at her fingers, giving no indication she was listening.

Joanna struggled with what to say next. She'd said everything she could think of to break the young mother's barrier of silence. She had run out of ideas.

◇◇◇

In the observation room, Myron grew restless. "Why in the hell did Joanna sit there? We can't see her with her back to us."

"Perhaps she doesn't want to be seen," said Roberta. There was a chuckle from somewhere in the back.

Joanna's voice came through again. "There's no manual that comes with your baby—nothing to tell you how to raise it."

Myron fumed. "What in the hell is she doing now?"

Bryce mused, "I think, Myron, it's called establishing rapport."

"All this feely stuff should be left to social workers."

"What?" said Bryce.

"Nothing." Myron whispered to Bernie, "I wish to hell he'd get a hearing aid."

A half-hour passed with little progress. Outside of a quick glance, Theresa hadn't given any ground. Joanna talked in measured tones, but nothing she said engaged the young mother. When Carmen raised her eyebrows and crossed her legs a fourth time, Joanna began to show some anxiety. She kept glancing at the mirror.

"I can't help you if you won't talk to me," she said, dropping her voice even lower.

Roberta shook her head. "Ain't that the truth?"

"Quiet! I can't hear what she's saying," Bryce barked.

"We know that," muttered Myron.

Theresa looked everywhere but at Joanna.

Joanna lowered her shoulders in defeat and nodded, a sign that the interview was over.

◇◇◇

THE RUBBER FENCE

The four interns sat at old wooden desks in a converted hospital room with a bank of windows on one side and reviewed their morning. Intake had gone well except for the patient that Joanna had interviewed. She was the only one they were stuck on.

Sam stretched his long, jean-covered legs and said, "Hey, you did good. There was no way she was letting you in."

Jerome said, "Honey, you'd have to talk to The Man Upstairs to get through to that one."

"Thanks," said Joanna. "I would get a mute patient for my first interview. You have to admit, if Myron was trying to put me in my place, he succeeded. Thinking back, I never should've questioned him about his research."

Sam shook his head. "He's got thicker skin than that."

"If you say so." She wasn't convinced.

"You were gentle," said Dennis. "I liked what you were doing."

"Maybe too gentle," said Joanna. "She probably has a lot of repressed anger."

Sam's brow furrowed. "Not so repressed. Judging from the admission report, she tried to suffocate her child."

Yes, there was that, and that was troubling. Joanna opened up Theresa's file and reviewed the emergency nurse's report. When she had asked the Boychuks if the baby had been examined by a doctor, Mrs. Boychuk had replied, "I got there in time, thank God. The baby's fine, but if I had come in a few minutes later, it might have been too late."

The admitting nurse had also noted the husband's meek behaviour in the presence of his mother. Although that did give a clue about the family dynamics in the home, it didn't explain Theresa's loss of voice or the attempted infanticide.

As if Sam had been reading her mind, he said, "What could

be going on in a woman's life to make her want to hurt her own child?"

Joanna twisted her lips. "Maybe what's happened to her is nothing more than raging hormones post delivery. The literature is full of cases where women have gone bananas after giving birth."

"She's a tough one," said Sam, "which means I'll probably get her, but what will I do with her? I've never had a baby. Especially one that's very tiny and very frustrating. And I don't even have a manual."

Joanna laughed and threw a pencil at him. Sam ducked, but the look they exchanged unsettled her. She couldn't afford any complications.

NINE

THERESA DID BECOME one of Sam's patients, and even though Joanna could understand the assignment given his previous rotation on the ward she was disappointed. Sure, she'd been upset with her initial interview, but she wasn't one to run away from a challenge. She was intrigued by the young mother and had hoped she'd get an opportunity to try again. Nevertheless, as a fellow resident, she would be privy to any success or failure on Sam's part. So far, Sam hadn't gotten anywhere.

Two weeks had passed since Joanna had started her residency, and of the three new interns, only Jerome had succeeded in getting off to a quick start. He continued to work with John Barnwell—the eccentric old gentleman who'd been caught with his pants down. He was still on the ward because the social worker was having a hard time finding a suitable placement.

Sam must've sensed Joanna's disappointment in not getting a patient of her own, as he invited her to join him in his follow-up session with Sylvia, the rape victim. He told Joanna he wanted a female present to offset any seductive transference between patient and doctor. Although Sylvia had been discharged the week before, Sam was playing it safe.

Sam and Joanna met with Sylvia in the interview room, only this time there weren't any observers on the other side of the glass, at least none that they knew of. On occasion, staff did pop into the observation room just to see if anything was going on. Manitou General was a teaching hospital, and patients were informed of that upon admission.

Sylvia was dressed as provocatively as she had been at intake. Her thin T-shirt was cut so low that Joanna wondered how Sam could focus on the task at hand.

Biting her candy-pink lower lip several times, Sylvia described her experience seeing her attackers in court the week before. "Those goddamned bastards. They all sat there in black leather, jeering me and cursing me. I felt stupid for even showing up."

"They jeered you in the courtroom?" asked Sam.

"No. In the hallway. I had to walk past them to get to court."

"What did they say?"

"They said, 'You asked for it, bitch'. They called me a cunt. Yeah, right. Like I asked for it. Fucking assholes."

Sam clasped his hands over his thighs and said, "When does your case go to trial?"

"Next month, if I'm lucky."

Joanna said, "It'll be good to have it over with."

Sylvia made a face. "I dunno if I can take much more. They have my number. My mother says someone's been calling, telling me to keep my mouth shut. It's gotta be them."

"Have you told the police?" asked Joanna.

"Yeah, I called. Big help they were. Where were they when I had to walk down the hall past those fuckers?"

Sam sighed. "I'm sorry you have to go through this. They don't make it easy."

"No." Her voice stuck as if she had swallowed a large pill the wrong way.

THE RUBBER FENCE

"If there's anything further I can do, just let me know."

"Sure. If you have any pull with the law, call me."

Sam smiled. "How was your appointment with the social worker?"

"All right." Sylvia didn't sound impressed.

Sam said, "With what you've been through, I think it would be a good idea to keep seeing her. You don't need a psychiatrist. The way you reacted was very normal."

She nodded.

Sam got up. "I hope things work out for you."

"Thanks." Sylvia stood up—she was a few inches shorter than Sam—and gave him a hug. He looked uncomfortable but didn't pull away.

Joanna got up as well and shook Sylvia's hand, surprised at how cold and clammy the young woman's fingers felt. "I hope you can get beyond all this soon."

"All I want is for those bastards to get what they deserve. Fat chance that'll happen, huh?" Sylvia looked at Sam as if he had some role to play in the justice system.

"Good luck with everything," said Sam.

"Thanks."

After the young woman had gone and was well out of earshot, Joanna said, "Affectionate, huh?"

"You'll get that. More than most areas of medicine, psychiatry strikes a chord that's deep. It's hard for the patient not to feel close to you after they've spilled their guts."

Joanna thought of how the reverse was also true. She already felt something for Theresa, and she wasn't even Joanna's patient. Even though intimate matters were exchanged in a psychiatric interview, a doctor couldn't become friends with a patient. It wasn't therapeutic for either person involved. It was difficult to stay objective if the psychiatrist cared too much. Patients were only a part of their doctor's life for the length of time it took to cure them.

When Joanna left the room, she tried to dismiss her feelings about Sam. She told herself it wasn't surprising given her problems at home.

Just that morning, she had caught Michael admiring himself in the mirror while applying his aftershave lotion. He'd always been good at grooming, but this time, it was different. He was taking more time, as if he were preparing for a big date. Though she told herself there was probably nothing to worry about, it was his self-absorption that troubled her. He didn't seem aware that she was even nearby. At the time, she wondered if there was some student on his mind—someone he'd been flirting with, much like he had done with Joanna in their better days. When she said, 'Smelling good', he seemed startled. He thanked her and continued to stare at his image.

Okay, so she wasn't sure about Michael, but what proof did she have about anything? Just because he seemed distant these days didn't mean he was fooling around. They were probably going through a phase—not unusual for most couples. And yet, knowing how easily he flirted—a bone of contention in mixed gatherings—she couldn't help but feel insecure. Still, she told herself to be cautious and not give in to any urges. She had no excuse to be foolish. Not with someone she worked with.

TEN

JOANNA SQUIRMED DURING Myron's lecture on ECT. It wasn't the subject that bothered her as much as his manner. He delivered his talk in the residents' room with such zeal, he could easily have been a salesman for the machines. She looked at the others—Jerome, Dennis, and Sam. They all seemed engrossed in what Myron was saying. ECT had been discovered by an Italian neurologist in the 1930s to induce seizures. What bothered her was the fact that psychiatrists still didn't know how it worked. Though it provided temporary relief from the agonies of the mind, it also erased memories. Therefore, it was a toss-up as to what was worse—living with the troubles that got you admitted or losing pieces of your life, never to be retrieved again.

Her mind drifted to the walls where she'd hung posters to brighten the place—*Today Is The First Day of the Rest of Your Life* and another with a quote from Henry David Thoreau: *If a man does not keep pace with his companions, perhaps it is because he hears a different drummer. Let him step to the music which he hears, however measured or far away.* Thoreau's way of looking at the world made sense. Unfortunately, those who stepped to a different beat were often unwelcome in a world that had little tolerance for different drummers. It was easier to put them out of sight, like on 2B or in the provincial asylum.

When Myron had first seen the posters, he'd smirked and

said, "Too hippy dippy for me." It was a comment about the posters, but Joanna thought it was also a veiled comment about her.

Now, his brusque but confident voice broke through her reverie. "I'm going to show you some old footage, so you can appreciate how this treatment has improved." He played the videotape. At first there was static, but then a black and white film showed a rabbit undergoing primitive electro-convulsive therapy. Its legs shook violently as the electric shock was discharged into its body.

Over the film footage, Myron said, "ECT induces a grand mal-like seizure."

The sequence showed the rabbit shaking for less than a minute, but it was unbearable to watch. The animal lay helpless, its body secured by wide leather straps to a table. Joanna flinched and averted her eyes when the next subject, a mature cat, was similarly treated and writhed as a result. She now understood why animal advocates were trying to put a stop to psychiatric experiments on these helpless creatures. Myron pressed pause, and the image froze with the cat's legs up in the air—a grotesque sight, as if the animal had been stuffed in that awkward position.

"When it was first introduced," Myron said, "there were arm and leg fractures; patients bit their tongues."

"No kidding," mumbled Joanna. She remembered reading Ken Kesey's *One Flew Over The Cuckoo's Nest* in a psychology course and wondering afterward if she should reconsider her choice of profession. What propelled her forward was her hope that psychiatry was moving out of its infancy stage. For too long, patients had been viewed as subjects to be experimented upon. Glancing at her fellow residents, she could see that the tide was changing. They were like her—compassionate and willing to

THE RUBBER FENCE

consider the new behavioural therapies. Perhaps she was too hard on the doctors of the past who could only act on what research had shown them.

Myron hit play again and the next shot was of a man thrashing. The narrator was saying, "The current is passed across the head so the heart is not affected." The closing shot was of an old asylum—a two-story structure with a stone façade that was anything but welcoming.

Myron turned off the video player. "Today, we give them sodium Brietal and Anectine to control the shakes and sedate them. As you'll soon see, we've come a long way."

Joanna recognized the patient in the ECT room as Rose Andalucci—the one who had tried to convince Myron she didn't need any more shocks. Now, she was lying semi-sedated on a gurney while the staff—Myron, Roberta, Carmen, an anesthesiologist, and all four residents—stood around her, waiting for the treatment to begin.

After Carmen had swabbed the inside of Rose's arm, the anesthesiologist inserted a needle. Although only half-conscious, Rose was aware enough to cringe at the sight of it. Next, Carmen attached the blood pressure, oxygen, and heart monitors.

Myron said to Rose, "I want you to start counting backwards from one hundred."

Rose's eyes glazed over as the anesthesiologist changed syringes. "One hundred, ninety-nine, ninety-eight, ninety-seven ... ninety-six ... ninety ... five ... ninety ... nine ... fie..."

The electrodes with the sponge tips were positioned on each side of Rose's greased temples. Joanna's palms grew moist, and she yawned a few times--something she did when she was overly anxious. Rose was near the age her grandmother had been when she died.

Joanna glanced at the others. Dennis, who was right beside her, was the only one who showed any sign of discomfort. His hands clenched and unclenched in time with Rose's breathing.

The anesthesiologist placed a black, rubber mouthpiece over Rose's teeth.

Myron said to the residents, "The mouth guard keeps her from biting the inside of her mouth."

"How reassuring," whispered Joanna to Dennis.

The anesthesiologist placed an Ambu bag over Rose's mouth and compressed the bulb a few times to give her oxygen.

Myron timed the machine at two-hundredths of a second and motioned everyone to stand back. "Juice!"

Sam depressed the button on the appliance. The meter registered one hundred and forty volts. Rose's body contracted almost imperceptibly. First her head and heels went up slightly, then her fingers turned in on themselves. Her eyelids blinked, and her mouth quivered. The heart monitor registered jagged spikes.

When Rose laboured in her breathing, Myron signalled for the Ambu bag again. The bulb was squeezed, and Joanna looked at the monitor recording Rose's heartbeat and pulse.

It had only been a minute or so, but it seemed much longer. Nausea gripped Joanna as if she were on the gurney, and her underarms became wet, promising stains on the shirt she was wearing. Finally, Rose inhaled deeply and the staff relaxed. Joanna's knees buckled with the strain, and she grabbed Dennis's arm.

"You okay?" asked Dennis, giving her a concerned look.

Myron glanced over as well. "Missed your breakfast,

THE RUBBER FENCE

Joanna?"

Embarrassed, Joanna said nothing.

"You'll toughen up," said Myron, in an offhand manner. Rose continued to tremble. Myron said to Roberta, "Better consult the cardiologist. This shouldn't have happened."

"Her physical was fine."

"I still want his opinion."

As they were exiting, Sam said to Joanna. "It's always rough the first time."

Though she appreciated his support, she was still woozy and in no shape to reply. She excused herself and ran to the ladies' restroom where she splashed cold water on her face. Is this what her grandmother went through? Joanna remembered her grandmother's ashen face after treatment. *No wonder she disappeared on me.*

ELEVEN

JOANNA SPENT THE rest of the morning in the nurses' station reviewing the conflict procedures manual. It was hard to concentrate because the ward clerk, Annette Monsetti—a woman in her fifties with a squat figure and dyed black hair—was on the phone giving hell to someone in maintenance over the light bulbs not being bright enough. It also didn't help that her mind kept racing back to Rose in the ECT room. She was anxious to review Rose's file, but it was on the desk in Roberta's office, which was directly behind Annette.

Joanna looked through the office's glass windows and saw Roberta, Sam, and Myron in conference. She didn't have long to consider what they were discussing, as an outburst from across the way in the patient lounge commanded her attention.

John, Jerome's elderly patient, was reading out loud from a newspaper and commenting in his British accent. "Bloody Rights! Nixon's aide said there was no whitewash in the White House."

Theresa, who sat a few chairs over from John, peered at him like he was a lunatic and then went back to staring at a black and white abstract painting that bore a strong resemblance to a Rorschach inkblot. Joanna surmised the artwork was some hospital administrator's idea of a joke.

John folded his paper with a flourish and announced, "Of course, his speech was whitewash. It was all eye-wash. And hogwash. And it WON'T WASH!" He then stood up and stomped out of the lounge.

During the last bit of John's harangue, Roberta exited her office and said to Annette, "Mr. Barnwell thinks he's in Hyde Park. If he keeps that up, I'm gonna write the queen myself and tell her that one of her royal subjects is loose and to come and get him."

Joanna chuckled just as Myron came up to her with Sam at his side. "Looks like you're about to get your first patient. Sam is adamant about Theresa getting a female therapist."

"She's all yours," said Sam, handing her a file.

"You're kidding."

"Just a senior helping out a junior."

"All right," said Joanna with a grin.

Myron nudged Sam. "Although with those locks of yours, it could have worked. Theresa may not have noticed you were male."

"Ha, ha," said Sam, rolling his eyes.

Myron tapped the file folder in Joanna's hand. "We'll have to continue to watch this one closely. If she tried to kill her baby once, she could try again."

Although Joanna was elated at getting a second chance with Theresa, she began to feel anxious. Their first meeting had gone so poorly.

After Sam and Myron had gone off, Joanna studied Sam's case notes, which raised more questions about the young mother's diagnosis. Theresa's behaviour and the complaints from her in-laws suggested post-partum psychosis—a mind out of control—but was she really out of control? Someone who refused to talk could also be labelled controlling. It wasn't as if her vocal cords had been cut leaving her no choice. Since there were no clear answers as to what had taken place in the home, Joanna reminded herself that no one on the psychiatric team was any wiser.

Joanna found Theresa propped up in her bed getting help with breast milk expressing equipment from a nurse's aide. Small glass jars of milk sat on the night table along with a worn Harlequin novel. She waited by the door for Theresa to finish expressing her milk. The young woman seemed so compliant—almost robotic in her actions. What was she thinking? Had she given up on breastfeeding her baby? Knowing the young mother was separated from her baby brought a wave of sadness that enveloped Joanna like an unexpected downpour on a sunny day. She felt an ache in her chest and attributed that to her own loss. Would she ever have a baby of her own or was that experience forever lost to her?

The nurse's aide spotted Joanna in the doorway and said, "Theresa has enough milk here to feed two babies."

"Lucky baby," said Joanna as she walked into the room and sat down on the visitor chair beside Theresa's bed. The young mother tucked her breasts back into her nursing bra and stared at the jars of milk beside her, as if she was surprised at the quantity.

Joanna said to Theresa, "From what I read in your file, your husband comes by and picks up your milk every day."

Theresa's long brown hair half covered her eyes, and what gaze was visible seemed fastened on her chest.

"Remember me? Dr. Bereza? I interviewed you after you arrived on the ward. In the room with the one-way mirror." Joanna hoped she hadn't insulted the young mother. Just because she didn't talk, it didn't mean she had no memory. "I'm going to be working with you."

Theresa stared at Joanna for a moment and then hid behind her hair again.

"I promise you won't have to do anything you don't want to do."

Theresa's face remained buried under her hair.

Joanna frowned. She felt her insides turn, much like they had when she'd first interviewed the young mother. She was beginning to think that Sam referred Theresa not because she would benefit from a female therapist, but because she was an unreachable patient—one that would tax even the most seasoned psychiatrist. Joanna studied Theresa's body language—slouched torso, crossed legs and arms. What chance did Joanna have of breaking through that silent exterior? Sure, case records were full of patients who didn't talk in therapy sessions, but it was unusual to have one who hadn't said one word to anyone since admission. To say Joanna was apprehensive would be an understatement. Given this shaky beginning, Joanna couldn't help but be pessimistic.

Joanna smiled weakly at Theresa and said, "I'll see you again tomorrow."

TWELVE

THE HOSPITAL CAFETERIA was a zoo at lunchtime, but the atmosphere—with its chatter and smells of minestrone soup and beef stew—was a welcome refuge from the sad stories on 2B. Joanna carried her tray to the round table in the far corner where Bernie, Sam, and Dennis sat eating their lunch.

She was hardly seated when Dennis stood up. "If you'll excuse me, I just have enough time to call my aunt to see how my mother is doing."

"Good luck," said Bernie.

After Dennis had picked up his tray and left, Joanna said, "Is his mother sick?"

With his mouth full, Bernie nodded.

Sam said, "She went over to see her sister in Frankfurt and came down with something. She's in the hospital over there. Apparently, the doctors are trying to figure out what's wrong with her."

"That's too bad," said Joanna, taking a serviette from the metal container on the table. She unwrapped her salad and began picking at it, though eating wasn't foremost on her mind. She wanted to find out more about Rose. She waited until Bernie had squirted a little ketchup on his plate, then said, "I saw my first ECT this morning."

His warm brown eyes met hers. "How did it go?"

"Not so good. There were some tense moments."

"Rose had trouble," said Sam. "We don't know if the tranquilizer she received compromised her breathing."

"ECT can be tricky," said Bernie, dipping his fry in ketchup.

Joanna sighed. "It wasn't what I expected. I'd only seen it before in movies."

"Yeah, horror movies," said Sam.

Joanna exchanged glances with Sam. He seemed in tune with her. *Was Michael ever like that?* If he was, she couldn't remember.

"What did you expect?" asked Bernie.

"A calmer treatment. I didn't expect her body to writhe like that, as if she was fighting a bad nightmare. I thought the drugs would have eased the shaking. She's so frail." Joanna sighed. "It seemed more like a punishment. I know she's depressed, but…isn't it natural for someone her age to be depressed? Her friends are probably dying, or maybe they're all dead. Her body's falling apart. Who wouldn't be depressed?"

Both Sam and Bernie seemed amused by her speech.

"Pass the salt," said Bernie. Joanna passed it and waited for an answer.

After wiping his mouth with his napkin, Bernie said, in a matter-of-fact tone, "There are some paranoid features to Rose's personality. And with depression, if all else fails, ECT is still the treatment of choice."

Joanna's brow furrowed. "Interesting choice, considering that scientists still don't know how it really works."

"That's true, but it works."

"And we're here to use anything that works," said Sam sarcastically. "No matter how it works."

Bernie shot Sam a look. To Joanna, he said, "Don't take everything Sam says as gospel. He still has his training wheels on."

"And may they never come off," said Sam. "You see, even though I've reached the exalted position of senior resident, I get no respect."

"When you start dressing like a shrink," said Bernie, "you'll get all the respect you want."

"Is that all it takes? Tomorrow, I'm coming in a three-piece suit."

Joanna laughed. She had to admit, these were two doctors she enjoyed talking to. She ate a forkful of salad and then said, "I just don't get it. There's so much about the treatment that's unpredictable. I mean, look at Hemingway. He shot himself soon after he was shocked. I read somewhere, maybe it was in the *Atlantic Monthly*, that he told his agent, 'How can they expect me to write when they take away my memories?'"

"Joanna," said Bernie softly, as if he were humouring a small child, "Hemingway was known to be despondent at the time and a very heavy drinker. Prime ingredients for suicide. You can't blame that on ECT."

"Blame what on ECT?" asked Myron as he arrived with a beef dish and a glass of water on his tray.

Joanna said, "We were talking about Rose's treatments. How many will she be getting?"

"As many as it'll take," he said, sitting down.

That wasn't the answer she'd been hoping for, but then again, why was she expecting anything different from a psychiatrist who was the expert in electric shock therapy?

After a few bites of his entree, Myron waved his knife at Joanna. "The problem is not ECT. The main problem is that the patients go back to their families, their whole network—therein lies the root of it. All the stuff that troubled them gets stirred up

THE RUBBER FENCE

again. That's why we have problems convincing some that it's a good treatment. It does work. What doesn't work are the families they go back to."

Sam said, "If we could only bubble-wrap the patients and send them to a new environment, ECT would get better press."

Joanna stared at Sam. She hadn't expected anything positive about ECT from him. Maybe she was truly alone in her opinions.

Using his napkin, Myron took some fatty beef out of his mouth and put it on the edge of his plate. "I wish to hell this cafeteria would get a better cook." He reached for the salt-shaker and shook it over his plate as if he were trying to dispel bad spirits. He took another bite of stew and grimaced. "Nothing I do makes this taste any better." He pushed his plate aside and gulped down some water.

Joanna swallowed hard. "Myron, has anyone interviewed Rose's family?"

Myron leaned back and said to Sam, "I have a feeling she's not going to stop until she gets the case."

"Could be." Sam smiled, confusing Joanna further.

That wasn't what she wanted and Myron hadn't answered her question. She was arguing against ECT, but what could she offer the old woman instead? Would drugs and psychotherapy really improve the old woman's condition? She'd been in the system so long, was she even malleable? Joanna felt doubt creep in; she was getting in over her head. She began to fidget with her napkin as she felt Myron studying her. She couldn't give up suggesting an alternative form of treatment. ECT was barbaric, that's all there was to it. Joanna reminded herself that Rose's record showed few attempts at getting to the root of her illness.

"You know," Myron said with a look of glee, "it might not be a bad thing for you to have a close look at Rose yourself.

Frankly, this is her fourth admission, and we're all getting a little worn down."

"Fourth? It's worse than I thought."

"Fourth or fifth. More than enough. You seem to have a special interest in this old woman. Perhaps you can offer her a fresh approach—one we hadn't considered in our wildest dreams."

"I wasn't asking to take her on, I—"

"Your passion for the elderly is refreshing," Myron interrupted. "Take her. Please. After all, this is a teaching hospital. We can all learn from one another's mistakes." He then grinned at Sam as if they'd shared some private joke.

Joanna felt her cheeks burning. Sensing she had walked into a trap, she couldn't think of anything to say.

"What?" said Myron. "Don't tell me you don't want her. You made such a vehement argument; I'm stunned that you're not more enthused about getting her as a patient. Rose is a perfect complement to Theresa. One old, one young. One fresh to the system, the other burned out."

"No, no, that's fine." It wasn't, but what could she say to reverse his decision? Myron had raised the bar, and she had no choice but to accept and leap as high as she could. It was one thing to criticize ECT, but now she'd have to come up with something to lift Rose's paranoia fed by years of shock treatment. What hope did she have in finding effective non-invasive therapy after all the damage that had been done? Why couldn't she get a first admission like Sylvia, the rape victim, or an elderly eccentric like John Barnwell?

While Myron went to get another cup of coffee, Sam and Joanna slid their dirty trays onto the rack by the kitchen. As if he could read her mind, Sam said, "She's going to be difficult, all

THE RUBBER FENCE

right. He's just trying to put you in your place—you know that."

Although Sam sounded supportive, Joanna didn't know him well enough to share her doubts. "I know," was all she said.

As the three of them walked down the corridor to the elevator, Sam eased the tension by changing the subject. "Myron, I hear you got a new Porsche."

"A red one. Hums like a charm. You be a good boy, and you'll get one too."

"What did you do with the wagon?"

"The wife took it."

When they reached the elevator, Joanna was still reeling from the realization that Rose was now hers. "Myron, regarding Rose. I won't be able to evaluate her properly if she keeps getting shock treatment."

"For God's sake, Joanna," he said, his voice rising. "This isn't research, it's real life. Her course of ECT is non-debatable."

"I can't see—"

"Exactly. You're an intern." Myron paused, which served to underline his message. "However, if in the course of your work with Rose, you find something more remarkable than ECT to lift her delusions, let me know. I'll take note. Maybe you and I can patent it and both become rich."

His retort hit her like a blast of cold wind. And though she half-smiled to hide her annoyance, she could feel herself retreating. She wished she wasn't so easy to bully, a trait she'd acquired growing up. Her older sister had always taunted her, especially in her teen years. Though they were close in some ways, Eileen couldn't stand the fact that her younger sister had done better in school. Their parents, being the non-interfering type, had left Joanna to fend off the verbal attacks herself. Perhaps that was the other reason she had chosen to study the mind; her sister's was difficult to understand. She used to explode over the slightest thing. And because of that, Joanna had learned to tread cautiously whenever she sensed emotions rising.

This was something she'd have to explore in therapy, a requirement of her residency to be scheduled later on in her term. The thinking was that in order to treat a patient, you had to be aware of your own unresolved issues. It was essential not to mix your garbage, so to speak, with the patient's. It made total sense, but the idea of it made her uneasy. What if she wasn't up to the task? What if, in the end, she was too flawed herself to help anybody?

THIRTEEN

WITH DIANE OFF at some charity meeting and the kids away at a friend's place, Myron welcomed the solitude at home. After the crazy day he'd had, the last thing he wanted was to listen to Diane chirping about her fund-raising ideas and whether they should have this couple or that one over for dinner. All he craved at the moment was a shot of scotch and a chance to look at the paper before bed.

Myron took off his shirt and analyzed his body in the bathroom mirror. His chest was flabby, his hairline was receding, and the circles under his eyes showed a man who wasn't getting enough sleep. Perhaps that was why his ulcers were acting up. Bending closer to the mirror, he stared at his face. He was only forty-three, but his forehead was already permanently lined. He grimaced and made a half-hearted promise to exercise more, telling himself that he'd sleep better and look more his age if he did. He still liked to play squash, but time for a game seemed impossible to schedule.

Something had to change, but what? He liked running the ward, but he still had to answer to Bryce, who got the glory when 2B ran well. With the old Scotsman at the controls and a new, tight-fisted board, Myron found the stress hard to manage. But he also knew that if he wanted to inherit the throne, he'd best act like a chief-in-waiting. He was the one who was supposed to solve the ongoing problem of patients who didn't belong there and who sent the ward's statistics skyward. Alcoholics, drug addicts, the elderly waiting for a home, acting-out teens—the list of patients occupying much needed beds unnecessarily was endless. These were social problems, not psychiatric ones. But what could he do? At least, he was making headway with the depressed and psychotic ones. ECT had snapped so many out of dark corners. And yet, he was meeting with resistance—from a new resident, no less. Not that Joanna had any power, but she seemed to be on some kind of mission. If she wanted to be an advocate for the downtrodden, she should've gone into social work.

Myron groaned as he threw his shirt into the hamper. He could see a time of argument coming, a questioning of his approach to madness. Five years back, he could have easily put her in her place, but now it would take finesse. Joanna was exceptionally bright and passionate about her work—traits hard to overcome in a fight. As if that weren't enough, there was the whole women's movement lurking in the shadows, ready to pounce on any man who treated one of its sisters unfairly, even in the halls of medicine.

He couldn't afford to blow it. Not if he wanted to become the head of the largest urban psychiatric ward in the country.

So why was he letting an upstart rattle him? When Joanna had pumped him about Rose during lunch, he'd heard the cynicism in his retort. He was smart enough to know it didn't serve him, but his scorn tumbled out before he could restrain himself.

He'd learned through analysis that he was still fighting his brother through other people. Curious in one way, but not so curious when he thought of his mother.

"My sons, the doctors," his mother had bragged to her

friends at a dinner to celebrate Myron's convocation. "I told them both from the time they were five, 'you make us proud. Be a doctor or a lawyer, that's a position. That's something to be proud of.' And they both made it. Can you believe it? We have two doctors in the family. Two! Herschel and I don't have to worry anymore."

Made it! What did that really mean? In his estimation, he hadn't. Not like his brother. Sidney was the one celebrities sought out for help untangling the knots that kept threatening to mess up their lives. Much to Myron's consternation, his brother had recently been on the cover of both *Time* and *Atlantic Monthly*. Inside the magazines there were interviews with Dr. Sidney Eisenstadt touting the relevancy of psychoanalysis. Myron found that surprising, given that the entire field of psychiatry was moving away from navel gazing. It was odd how his brother had managed to get the public's attention despite choosing a therapy the majority of psychiatrists were now rejecting. Of course he was jealous. Who wouldn't be?

If he had stayed in New York, he could have achieved more, he was sure of it. But he fell in love with Diane, a Canadian, and she wanted to live close to her parents.

Yes, he had made it all right. He had ulcers, a spoiled wife, two rebellious teenagers, and a jealousy of Sidney that knew no bounds. If that was making it, he wished he had failed.

He sat down on the bed and took off his shoes and socks. Diane would lose all respect for him if she knew what he really thought. As it was, she begrudgingly put up with his long hours and irritability that leaked out at the most inopportune times. He suspected she only did this because she loved the security his money bought.

She had free run with her Holt Renfrew account and didn't

hesitate to redecorate their architect-designed home in Tuxedo every five years. Besides the paid trips from pharmaceutical companies, she enjoyed family vacations in Miami Beach every winter, and their children attended St. John's Ravenscourt—the best private school in the city—even though it wasn't a Jewish one. What he couldn't understand was why she continued to hold him at arm's length. He paid the bills, yet he was the one who seemed to be begging her for what was his right as a husband. Their lovemaking wasn't what it once was, but she was still capable of seducing him when she wanted something.

Like the other night in their bedroom. She'd been in her temptress mood and had surprised him with a new negligee she'd bought at Eaton's. It was rose coloured; he would have preferred black, but he wasn't about to complain. It was still sexy; he could see the outline of her breasts—surprisingly perky after twenty years of marriage. When she walked slowly to their bed with the lights turned low, he was prepared for anything. It wasn't his fault that the phone rang—there was a crisis on 2B. She had asked him not to answer the call, but he was too nervous to let it go in case an emergency threatened to unravel all that he'd been striving for.

When he got off the phone and told her a patient had punched an orderly in the eye—this after the hospital employees' union had been complaining of improper safety procedures—she wasn't impressed. Even though he said he would take care of the ward problem in the morning, the mood had been broken. She'd turned without saying a word, put on her satin robe, and flounced out of the bedroom. She didn't slam the door, but she may as well have. It left him with a fierce headache. He hadn't experienced such pain since his brother beat him at tennis when he was fourteen.

THE RUBBER FENCE

He wanted to chase after her, grab her, and shake her, but he was afraid he wouldn't be able to contain the violence he felt. Instead, he got into his Porsche and headed for the perimeter highway where he let the speedometer climb to 130 mph. After driving at that speed for half an hour, he turned around and came home to find her asleep. In the morning, Diane didn't ask him where he'd been, and he didn't tell her.

If only he was a man content to go to his job, put in his time, and come home to a family with a TV blaring. *If only*.

FOURTEEN

ON SUNDAY, MICHAEL suggested a jog in Assiniboine Park and lunch afterward at the Beefeater's restaurant in Osborne Village. The morning turned out to be perfect—cool with no wind. They ran on the dirt path along the Assiniboine River under a leafy canopy of maple, elm, and willow tree branches. The sun's rays danced amongst the leaves, spilling light onto their shoulders. It was as if nature's majesty had commanded them to take a break from the intensity of their lives.

They jogged past an older couple walking their dog. The couple smiled, looking as if they'd been together forever. Joanna wondered if she and Michael would still be together, let alone smiling, years down the road.

As they ran, they caught glimpses between the tree trunks of the fast flowing river. A couple of sparrows flew across their path and then arched upward, disappearing into the trees. The ground felt hard under her feet but Joanna welcomed the pounding. It helped her get her thoughts together.

She glanced at Michael and then returned her gaze to the winding path in front of them. She said without changing her pace, "Do you ever think that maybe nobody has any control over anything, and it's just happenstance what happens to anyone? That life is all an illusion? That none of this matters—none of it at all?"

He smiled. "I thought I was the one who questioned the

universe, and you were the pragmatic one."

"Not always." Joanna wiped away a bug that had flown in her face. "Yesterday, I saw an old woman get shock treatment. It was all I could do to keep myself from pulling the plug."

"That would've made an impression."

"Yeah." She laughed. "Well, joke's on me. I've now got her as a patient."

"There's a vote of confidence."

"You think so?"

"Absolutely. How old is she?"

"Sixty-seven, though she looks a lot older."

"What are you going to do with her?"

"Don't know. She's been in and out of institutions since she was a young mother. Some sort of panic, like claustrophobia, hit her in her twenties, and she couldn't go out or do anything. So they shocked her over and over again. The strange thing is, there's no mention in her file about any psychotherapy. Nothing at all. No attempts to determine what could've precipitated her fears." She glanced at him again. "How can a woman go through the system and not be given the opportunity to tell her story? I find it appalling."

"Maybe she was hostile."

"I don't think so. If she had refused, it would have been in her file."

"So now you've got her. You can talk to her."

"Right. She was virtually written off for the last forty years. I haven't got a clue where to start."

"Start at the beginning."

"Not so simple. Given what she's been through, I doubt she could remember with any accuracy. Thanks to ECT." Joanna's legs were getting tired, and her right shoe rubbed on her instep.

She thought of stopping to adjust the tongue but they were nearing the end of the trail. "What if she won't talk to me?"

"You've just been shaken by that mute patient."

"Maybe you're right. I just wish I had some idea of what to do."

They ran without speaking for a few minutes. Joanna admired how effortlessly Michael ran. Perhaps he wasn't weighed down by expectations the way she was. She exhaled deeply. "I feel so stuck. On one hand, I'm pleased I got her. Maybe I can do something different—at least stop those electrical charges that only confuse her."

"There you go."

"I need to come up with something better, or else Myron won't support me."

"Joanna, do yourself a favour. Give it a rest. All this worry is beginning to show on your face. You're going to be old before your time."

"What's that supposed to mean?" She wondered if he was comparing her to his young students.

"Can't we just run? Isn't it enough that you're immersed in it every day of the week?"

Joanna frowned. "It's a difficult case."

"Look," he said, turning to her briefly. "I don't mind talking about your work some of the time, but it's constant with you." He stared ahead; a grim expression settling over his face.

"I know," she said, her running now laboured.

"I don't want the pressure of—"

"I wasn't asking."

"Weren't you?"

"Forget about it, okay?"

Michael said, "I can't do this day in and day out."

THE RUBBER FENCE

"Nobody's asking you to."

"Talk to one of the shrinks. Not me."

Joanna knew that Michael had a point, but she felt uneasy. If she couldn't talk to him about her fears and frustrations, who could she talk to? She couldn't admit to her fellow psychiatrists that she was scared. That was akin to committing professional suicide. Her mother wouldn't understand, nor would her sister, who had enough problems of her own, struggling with a second marriage. As for her girlfriends, they'd fallen by the wayside after Joanna had gotten married.

It was the end of the trail. Joanna and Michael had slowed down to a walk, their breathing shallow. Joanna stretched her calves while Michael drank some water.

She eyed his bottle. "Are you going to drink all of it?"

"Did you forget your water again?"

She sheepishly nodded. Annoyed, Michael handed her the bottle. She took a long drink before giving it back. When he raised the bottle to see what was left, he scowled and then swallowed the few remaining drops. Joanna walked ahead, pushing a tree branch out of her way. It snapped back fiercely, as if it too hadn't had its share.

After a quick shower at home, they lunched at the neighbourhood restaurant. Joanna had hoped for a light banter even though she realized she had put a damper on their outing with her rumination about her patients. With the subject of work off limits, they lapsed into a silence they couldn't recover from, leaving Joanna to wonder how she could feel so lonely in the company of the man she loved.

FIFTEEN

STYMIED BY THERESA'S refusal to talk, Joanna arranged for the young mother to spend some time in the occupational therapy room where there was no pressure on the patients to converse. Here, they could be cajoled into knitting, painting, or some other craft. By using their hands, they could quieten their minds and relieve some of their emotional pain that kept them stuck on the ward. At least, that was the theory.

Joanna walked into the O.T. room about halfway through Theresa's allotted time. The occupational therapist, a slender woman with a blonde ponytail and granny glasses, pointed out the young mother who stood with her back to the door at an easel in the far corner of the room.

"How's she been doing?" asked Joanna.

"She's been quiet, keeping to herself."

Joanna nodded, and the occupational therapist went back to helping an older woman glue pieces of a photograph that had been ripped in four pieces.

To get to Theresa, Joanna had to walk past five other patients sitting at tables working on crafts, and a heavy-set young man in a striped T-shirt and jeans sprawled in the middle of the floor. He was alternately spanking and hugging a teddy bear. Joanna suspected he was re-enacting what had happened to him as a child.

As Joanna moved closer to Theresa, she noticed how

THE RUBBER FENCE

tentatively the young mother was applying paint to the canvas. She had painted a contorted tree with black snake-like branches stretching across a white background. Its wide trunk was blood red and had a large black hole in the middle. In the bottom right-hand corner of the painting, Theresa had squeezed in a rendering of a tiny girl. In contrast to the tree, the figure had been drawn solely in black and appeared to be cowering.

For a few moments, Joanna stood unnoticed behind Theresa. When the young mother turned, Joanna said, "She's very small, your little girl."

Theresa ignored her therapist's remark and added more black to her painting.

Undeterred, Joanna said, "She doesn't seem to have much power with that big tree looming over her."

Theresa's lips quivered as she embellished her painting with more black branches; this time with thicker strokes. She worked with greater urgency, covering more of the canvas in the nightmare colour. Sensing her anguish, Joanna waited, reminding herself to keep the interaction calm so that her patient would feel safe enough to let out whatever she needed to let out.

Theresa obsessed about the trunk as she painted one layer over another. Finally, she put her brush down and stared at her creation.

Joanna said, "A lot of feeling there. What can you tell me about it?"

There was no response. Instead, Theresa took off her smock and laid it on a nearby chair. She then returned to her painting and stared at it.

"Lots of hurt there," said Joanna. "A lot to handle." She may as well have been talking to someone on the other side of the room for all the acknowledgement she received. But rather than be discouraged, Joanna framed what had happened as progress. Theresa had expressed herself through art. These were baby steps toward learning how to deal with her pain constructively.

Joanna still didn't have the foggiest idea of whether Theresa had committed the crime of attempted infanticide. Since no charges had been laid, Joanna presumed the young mother was innocent. But was she? There were too many documented cases of women refusing to press charges even though their husbands or boyfriends had battered them. What if this was a similar situation? Perhaps Eugene and his mother wanted to keep the record clean so that it wouldn't follow baby Marlene. It was one thing for families to tell medical personnel their fears or make wild accusations, but if there was criminal intent, the police needed to be informed. So for now, the question of Theresa's guilt remained in the emergency record, but for her sake and her baby's safety, the complaints needed to be investigated. To do that, the young mother would have to tell her side of the story.

SIXTEEN

IN THE NURSES' station, Joanna reviewed Rose's file. Up to her late teens, the patient hadn't reported anything unusual in her history, but somewhere around the age of twenty-two she had mentioned unending crying jags, hearing voices, and seeing faces staring at her everywhere she went. What had propelled her over the edge? Was there some trauma revisited, or was her behaviour attributed to genetics—some inherited predisposition to mental illness?

Sam's voice penetrated Joanna's train of thought. "You're setting a bad example for the rest of us. It's the end of the week; time to put it to rest."

She looked up to see Sam with Jerome, who grinned in the way that only he could.

"Should we tell her the escape route?" said Jerome, winking. His dark eyes sparkled, and the laugh lines around his mouth were deep with practice.

"What escape route?" asked Joanna.

Sam said, "Harry's."

"Isn't that a singles bar?"

"If it'll ease your mind," said Sam, "I'd only be too happy to chaperone."

"Oh, that'll make her feel really comfortable," said Jerome with a touch of sarcasm.

Sam ignored him. "It'll take your mind off these bent

creatures for an hour or so. All work and no play..."

She checked the time. "I don't know. I forgot to check whether Michael was home for dinner."

"Phone him," said Jerome. "Tell your husband you'll be a little late."

"She's got a husband? Damn!" said Sam with a glint in his eye.

Joanna couldn't help but laugh.

"I'm sure he gets out once in a while," said Jerome.

She waffled. She knew that Michael wouldn't hesitate to have a good time if the opportunity came up. He'd called from a pub or a bar many times to tell her he'd gone out with a fellow prof or a student for a drink. She, on the other hand, had been boringly responsible. After she'd gotten married, she had avoided that kind of social activity, but not because she didn't enjoy it. Rather, she found it hard to connect with those who were unattached. They were still looking—playing the field.

She looked at Sam and Jerome again; their smiling faces irresistible. Hanging out with them could pay off if any problems on the ward arose in the future. It was always good to have teammates for support if the waters turned rough. Convinced that it wouldn't hurt to go for an hour or two, she said, "Okay," and closed the file.

The official hospital hangout was just a few blocks away. It was a cozy retro bar with an orange neon sign that flashed *Harry's*. Inside, the darkened windows did nothing to dampen the spirits of the jubilant crowd jammed into every booth and onto every bar-stool.

THE RUBBER FENCE

Sam and Jerome ordered beer and found a table by the wall. Rather than join them right away, Joanna took her glass of wine and walked over to Carmen, who was standing with a few nurses by the long oak bar. Sidling up to her, Joanna said, "I'm so glad to see you. I was afraid I'd be the only married one here."

"What do you mean married?"

"Your ring..."

"Oh, that," said Carmen. "Force of habit. It keeps the wolves away. No, I'm not married anymore. The asshole left some time ago. Oops." She chuckled. "I swore I'd stop calling him that. Must be the booze."

Joanna looked around at the rising gaiety. She was glad she had come. She sipped her wine and wondered how many people there were looking for a relationship. She then noticed Jerome coming their way. The way he moved his hips when he walked made her think that the stereotype of black men being loose-limbed was pretty accurate.

Jerome winked at Joanna and said to Carmen, "Hey, how you beautiful women doing?"

Carmen smiled. "Doing better now that you're here." Jerome burst into an even bigger grin, if that were possible.

Jerome said, "Sam and I were talking about *Cabaret*. Have either of you seen it?"

"I saw it," said Joanna. "Loved the music."

At that moment, Sam walked up to them holding a mug of beer. Jerome said, "Joanna has seen *Cabaret*, too."

Sam nodded. "Those dance scenes at the Kit Kat club were worth the price of admission."

"You liked that, did you?" asked Carmen.

Sam laughed. "What's not to like?"

Joanna said, "What did you think about Michael York's

character?"

"I thought it was great," Sam said. "About time they showed homos on the screen."

Joanna cocked her head. "Really. He was one all right and yet he had sex with Sally Bowles."

Sam sipped his beer. "Some men swing that way. Can't make up their mind who they are."

Jerome grinned again. "I've got no trouble in that department. Do you, Sam?"

"No," said Sam, looking at Joanna intently.

Carmen laughed. "You're just little boys in short pants."

"Now, how did you know about my short pants?" teased Jerome. "You want to see them?"

Carmen giggled. "Now, why would I want to do something like that? You know you got the reputation of the devil."

"Where'd you hear that?" Then Jerome said to Joanna. "Is she coming on to me?"

Sam bumped his hip against Joanna's. "Didn't I tell you this place would relax you?"

She had to admit she was feeling less tense, though she wasn't as sure about Sam's familiarity. She peered over at Jerome and Carmen, envying their ease and ability to joke. It was obvious they found delight in one another. She and Michael had had that once, but somewhere along the way they had lost it. It was when she had miscarried, she was sure of that. She couldn't help but feel he had blamed her for both miscarriages. He'd said as much. She could still hear him say, *If you weren't so hell bent on taking care of your patients, you would've taken better care of yourself.*

And she had yelled back, *Go to hell!* She had stormed off with those words hanging between them like empty clothes pegs

THE RUBBER FENCE

on a line.

Now she smiled at Sam. "I'm glad you guys dragged me here." She raised her glass of wine. "To a good year."

"And may we all stay on the sane side of the rubber fence," he said as he clinked her glass with his mug.

"What do you mean, 'rubber fence'?" said Carmen.

Joanna said, "It's a term Lyman Wynne, a family therapist, came up with to describe the boundaries around a family. He said the boundary stretches like rubber when any member tries to escape the family script."

Carmen tsked. "He got that right."

Simon and Garfunkle's "59th Street Bridge Song" came on the jukebox and a crowd near them started singing along. Soon, Joanna, Carmen, Sam, and Jerome joined in. The Jamaican doctor's baritone voice stood out, and Joanna fell into harmonizing with him before the song ended. Afterwards, she had another glass of wine and found herself trading looks with Sam that trampled on her ideas of fidelity.

When Joanna finally left Carmen and the guys at Harry's, she was feeling high from the wine she had imbibed and high from her time with Sam. He had touched her fingers when he took her empty wine glass, and again a desire had swept through her. She sensed that he could see it in her eyes. It was dangerous, she knew that, but she had experienced an attraction she hadn't felt in years. It was unnerving. She was a married woman, for God's sake. Then she reminded herself she wasn't dead. It was only a feeling, nothing she would act on.

◇◇◇

When she got home from Harry's, Michael was still out. In the morning, he reminded her that he had told her about the meeting. Had he told her and she'd forgotten? She dismissed it, not because she wanted to avoid another argument, but because she didn't want to believe there was someone else he had his eye on. While she was brushing her teeth, she vowed to write any of his future meetings down on the calendar.

SEVENTEEN

WITH EACH SUCCESSIVE day, Joanna became more troubled by the definition of mental illness. She'd see a couple of older male patients playing cards in the lounge and conclude—after observing their calmness and occasional laughter—that they were no more insane than the staff that passed by. But she also knew that the traits of insanity could emerge unexpectedly, and too many of these incidents could bring a sufferer to the emergency room door. Who didn't have crazy reactions on occasion—those moments in time when all reason was lost? It was a fine line that humans walked, as if on a tightrope. One misstep, and over you went.

Rose was a case in point. After every discharge, she had reported good days to her family doctor, but then something would set her off, and back she'd come to the ward, delivered by her well-meaning sister and brother. What were those triggers? Joanna was determined to find out.

It felt serendipitous that soon after Rose had been assigned to Joanna, her sister phoned and asked to speak to the psychiatrist in charge. Before taking the phone, Joanna reminded herself of the danger of talking to relatives or friends when the patient wasn't present. She hadn't established trust with the old woman yet, so she would have to be careful not to divulge confidential information that could come back to haunt her.

Joanna took the phone from Annette and said, "Hello. This

is Dr. Bereza."

"I'm Mrs. Marks, Rose's sister. I was thinking you might want to talk to me." The woman sounded like Rose, only less edgy.

"Yes, I do," said Joanna.

"What are you doing to help her?"

"Rose has just come under my care. Dr. Eisenstadt has been giving her ECT, and we need to finish it. We're hoping it will lift her depression."

There was a pause and then, "She's had it before you know."

"Yes, I'm aware of that."

"What about her paranoia? It gets worse every time she gets these treatments."

"I understand. Do you have any idea of how it started and when?"

"Well, you know she's always been weak. She likes her men, you know. That's her downfall. Always the men. My brother and I have tried to talk to her about this, but she won't listen. Just goes off and does what she wants. Now, she thinks we're all against her."

"That must be hard." Glancing at the patient lounge across from the nurses' hub, Joanna thought the three patients sitting there might think the same thing about the people in their lives. The mentally ill, as far as she knew, all felt alone. "I'd like to meet with you and Rose. Would you and your brother be available to come in next week? We can discuss this further then."

After arranging a time, Joanna ended the call. Though the phone call was brief, it had opened a door she hadn't expected.

Following her exchange with Mrs. Marks, Joanna went to

THE RUBBER FENCE

Rose's room. The bathroom door was ajar, and a horrific retching sound came from inside. By Rose's bed, there were a few crumpled tissues, but no reading material, flowers, or toiletries of any kind. The other bed in the room was empty and unmade, save for a rubber sheet. It would be filled soon by another confused soul. After a few minutes, Joanna heard the toilet flushing and then the tap running before Rose came out, looking more pale and drawn than usual.

"You okay?" said Joanna. Rose had had another bout of ECT that morning.

"I always throw up when they electrocute me. Lot of damn good it does!" Her unsure steps back to her bed underlined the point.

"It's probably the sedative that disturbed your stomach." Joanna wanted to believe that rather than think it was a side effect of the electrical charges that had been discharged in Rose's brain.

"My head's like a bloody freight train. Chugga, chugga, chugga." Rose's voice withered as she spoke. "Nothing they give me stops the pounding." She held her head gingerly then patted the blanket flat before she sat down, as if any wrinkle would add to the noise in her head.

Joanna felt caught in some limbo she couldn't define. The fact that she had felt nauseous too just from watching the treatment made her feel she and Rose were sisters in a battle against some unseen force. She wanted to tell Rose she had doubts about ECT too, but how could she? Instead she said, "The nausea and headaches should pass. But if they don't, tell one of the nurses, all right?"

Rose nodded but turned her head to the wall, apparently indicating she wanted her visitor to leave. There was nothing there to look at except the silver chain to pull if a nurse was needed.

Joanna moved a chair to the side of the bed by the wall so she could face Rose. Sitting down, she said, "Your sister called. She wants you to come live with her."

"Why didn't she ask me herself?" she said, glaring at Joanna.

"She said you won't talk to her."

"Which sister is that?"

"How many do you have?"

"Three. I have three sisters."

"It was Mrs. Marks."

"Oh, that one," she said, making a face. "The busybody. I thought she died a few years ago. Ha, ha." She opened her night table drawer and rummaged through some papers, as if there was something important she needed to find.

"I gather you and your sister don't get along."

In a sing-song fashion, Rose said, "Ding dong, the witch is dead, cover your head, the witch is dead. Ding dong, the wicked witch is dead." She knocked her head a couple of times. "Nobody home. Ha, ha."

"Rose..." Joanna reached out to touch her hand.

"I want to go home," Rose said, ignoring Joanna's gesture. She then pushed her papers down and closed the drawer.

"You will. Soon. We just need to help you feel better first."

The light from the window cast a shadow on Rose's face, making it hard for Joanna to see the old woman's expression. "Here come more blanks."

"What?"

"Blanks. The treatment gives me blanks. I know something; I think I do. I don't know where it goes, but it goes. Phew." She slid one palm against the other, raising the top one as if it were a bird taking off in flight.

Joanna leaned forward in her chair. "Rose, I want to help you. I don't have all the answers—I wish I did, but maybe if we talk and you tell me more about the troubles that got you here, well maybe then we can stop the treatments. I can't promise, but I'll do my best."

Rose opened her mouth like she was about to reveal something, but then a curtain dropped and her eyes became dull. She had changed her mind or gone blank.

Joanna could see that the treatments had beaten Rose into submission. Electroconvulsive therapy was known to make aggressive patients more compliant—easier to manage. She wondered what kind of a young woman Rose had been. What dreams had she harboured? She still had some feistiness left, and as long as there was still some fight left in the old woman, Joanna would keep trying.

When Rose looked at her again, Joanna said softly, "I don't know how much you've talked to doctors, but most people find it helpful to talk about what's bothering them. It helps to get the junk out, so to speak—the stuff that's weighing us down. Like cleaning house."

Rose gazed out the window as if she were trying to measure how far she could fly if she tried. "One shrink I saw. We were supposed to talk, but he always fell asleep."

Joanna smiled. "That wasn't helpful."

"Of course it wasn't," snapped Rose.

"There was a note in your chart. Was that Dr. MacDiarmid?"

"The shit!" Joanna was surprised the old woman remembered his name. Perhaps Rose wasn't as far gone as

Joanna had thought.

Just then, a commotion outside the room distracted Rose. A young female voice yelled, "Fuck off!"

Rose brightened and yelled back, "You tell 'em, honey!" She stood up and shuffled to the door to check what was going on in the corridor.

Joanna followed. "We'll talk more another time."

Though Rose didn't reply, Joanna hoped she'd heard what she'd said. She stood beside Rose and looked down the corridor toward the nurses' station. There, a skinny teenage girl with bandages around her wrists was struggling to escape from the hold that Roberta and two male staff members had on her. Annette and a few patients stood a little distance away, taking it all in. From behind them, Myron came running. The girl gave Roberta a sharp jab in the ribs with her right elbow, forcing the head nurse to let go.

"Ow, you little…!" Roberta massaged her side while a burly orderly rushed in to help contain the teen.

With the girl finally restrained, Myron said to Roberta, "Best keep her in a room by herself until we get a chance to review her case."

Joanna left Rose, who was still grinning at the teen. She went to Myron and said, "She's so young. For someone so tiny, she put up a hell of a fight."

"Yes, she did. She's only fourteen." Myron kept his eyes on the teenager. She had lost this round, but she was spoiling for more by bucking the staff that had corralled her. Her arms and legs were being held, but she wasn't making it easy.

"Fucking weasels!" the teen yelled.

"A girl after my own heart," said Rose loudly before she hobbled back into her room.

THE RUBBER FENCE

Joanna shook her head and said to Myron, "That young girl shouldn't even be here."

"She won't be here long. Only until they can free up a bed in the adolescent unit. How's Rose? Making any progress?"

"Her sister called. Rose wasn't happy about it."

The young girl, escorted by two aides, walked by them and stuck out her tongue.

"Now there's a comment on our profession," said Joanna.

Myron shrugged. "You can't please them all." He sighed as they watched the young girl disappear into her room. "And how's Theresa doing? Getting anywhere?"

"I spent some time with her in O.T. Her anger spilled out on a canvas, so I'm hoping it won't be long before she starts talking. I'm letting her go home for a few hours this evening. I want to give her a chance to feed her baby and keep her milk up."

Myron's eyes widened. "Do you think that's wise? What if her mother-in-law is right?"

"If Theresa tried to harm her baby, why weren't the police contacted?"

"Domestic disputes are often covered up. We probably wouldn't have seen this one, except she withdrew into her own world. I'm guessing the family couldn't handle it and brought her in."

"Still, her husband didn't seem concerned when I broached the subject of her going home for a few hours. He said he'd supervise."

Myron looked at her as if there was more he wanted to say but then changed his mind. "Make sure he signs a release form."

EIGHTEEN

THAT EVENING, JOANNA waited in the nurses' station for Eugene. In the adjacent patient lounge, Dennis was playing checkers with his patient, Marty Feldman, an overweight young man dressed in pyjamas and a too small powder blue flannel robe with his name monogrammed on the chest pocket in red. While Marty waited for Dennis to make a move, he rubbed a stubborn black mark on his sleeve. He was still rubbing the uncooperative stain when Eugene showed up ten minutes later.

"What does this mean?" Eugene asked Joanna, referring to the form in front of him. "If something happens to the baby, I'm responsible?"

"No. It just means that while Theresa's in your care, we're not responsible."

"Oh," he said and signed his name.

"Theresa's in a therapy group right now. It's almost over. If you don't mind waiting in the lounge, I'll go get her."

In a hospital room—one that had no beds—musical group therapy was in full swing. Ten patients sat in a circle singing along with Sam, who was strumming a Bob Dylan tune on his guitar. Rose and Theresa were among them but neither were participating. When Sam came to the end of the piece, he looked over at Joanna in the doorway and smiled. Then he began to sing "Old Man River" with a young male patient whose face was marred by acne.

"Ol' man river, that ol' man river, he must know sumpin', but don't say nothin', he just keeps rolling along..." The rich timbre of the young man's voice was astonishing, and Joanna thought, given the right circumstances, he could have a future in the entertainment sector. Perhaps his presence on the ward was only a blip on his journey to old age.

Although the singing seemed to elevate the mood for many of the patients, Theresa sat rigid in her chair like a model for an artist doing her portrait.

Had Sam consciously chosen this song—one that seemed to speak to Theresa's condition—or was it one of those synchronous things that happens in life? A few more joined in the singing; even Rose was perched on the edge of her seat, rocking out of sync to the music. Though Rose wasn't singing, her face had a calmness to it.

Sam and the young man sang boisterously, "He don't plant 'taters, he don't plant cotton, but them that plants 'em is soon forgotten..."

Joanna took a seat by the door and watched as every patient except hers participated. The group was surprisingly harmonious.

"You an' me, we sweat and strain; body all achin' an' racked wid pain."

There was a smattering of applause at the end of the lyrics, and a few patients even broke out in laughter.

Sam clapped. "You all did great." He laid his guitar down on the floor and came over to Joanna.

"You're a man of many talents," she said.

"You don't know the half of it," he teased.

There he was, flirting with her again. Uncomfortable, she looked over at Theresa to see whether she was interacting with others or not. "I hope this visit of Theresa's works out well."

Rose started chanting, "Sam's got a girlfriend, Sam's got a girlfriend."

Sam smiled.

Joanna threw her hands up, doing her best to ignore Rose's chants. "I better get this show on the road."

◇◇◇

When Joanna and Theresa got to the lounge, Eugene stood up abruptly and tried to hug his wife, but she remained stiff—unrelenting. His face contorted in frustration as he finally let her go.

Joanna gently touched Theresa's arm. "Do you still want to go home for a short visit?"

Theresa nodded.

Even though Theresa was willing, Joanna began to have doubts about her decision. Eugene's parents would only be home long enough to hand the baby over to their daughter-in-law, but they were a factor to be considered when it came time for Theresa to return permanently. Was Joanna rushing the young mother? Would she be able to handle a brief visit without incident? If she was depressed, how depressed was she? Depressed individuals were known to not only hurt themselves but also others when life became unbearable. Joanna tried to allay her fears by reasoning that Theresa would only be gone a few hours and that she wouldn't be left alone with her baby; Eugene would be there. Before the couple left, Joanna scheduled a marital therapy session for the following day to deal with any

THE RUBBER FENCE

fallout.

Maybe psychoanalysts had it best. They just dealt with the individual lying in front of them on the couch. Once or twice a week, they probed their patients' unconscious minds and determined the forces that made their lives difficult. Usually they dug for what the patient's mother had done. Though she wasn't a mother, Joanna roiled at that. Why did psychoanalysts always blame the mother? All the key players in the sick person's life had to be part of the puzzle.

As Eugene walked away with Theresa at his side, he kept throwing sideways glances in her direction. His anxious looks made Joanna think the wrong marital partner was in the hospital.

NINETEEN

THERESA'S SOJOURN HOME was strained from the beginning. With the curtains drawn in their room, she sat on the bed, eyes fixed on the floor while Eugene hovered above her trying to get eye contact. She still hadn't forgiven him for what she now regarded as a series of betrayals.

"Please, baby, say something," said Eugene.

What did he expect her to say? Did he want to hear that she'd had it? That life wasn't worth living anymore? Is that what he wanted to hear?

Exasperated, he tried again, this time grabbing her by the shoulders and shaking her. That only annoyed her more, and her body went limp like a rag doll's.

"Don't do this, please," he said, letting her go. "Theresa, honey, they're going to shock you if you don't start talking."

Startled, she looked up.

"They do that, you know."

His persistence didn't pay off. She kept her head down and played with a thread on her shirt, twisting and untwisting it around her finger. Since she had walked through the door that evening she had found it impossible to regain even a smidgen of the composure she'd had before her breakdown. Breastfeeding was a nightmare. She refused to nurse Marlene in the nursery because that would be giving in to the memory of the scene that had taken her away in the first place. When she'd tried to feed

THE RUBBER FENCE

her baby in their bedroom, she'd failed. She wasn't at ease with her back against the hard headboard no matter how many pillows she slid behind her. Her anxiety over having to leave in a few hours prevented her from relaxing and bonding anew with Marlene. Instead, she sat rigid as a post and watched her infant struggle, mouthing her mother's right nipple first and then her left, searching for the liquid promise every baby expects.

They must have made an odd family portrait. Eugene had adopted a begging posture, and Marlene had curled her body in an awkward arc in her mother's arms. If anything, their positions underlined the tenuous hold each had in the family.

Though Eugene's parents were out playing cards with friends, Theresa could not settle down. Any sound upstairs put her on high alert as if she anticipated her mother-in-law's arrival in a rage downstairs.

When Mr. and Mrs. Boychuk returned a few hours later, it was time for Theresa to leave. She walked by the older woman in the hallway without any acknowledgement; she refused to admit the older woman was even there. Eugene and his father exchanged looks but that was as far as the men went in their comments on the impasse. Though Theresa was anxious to leave, she buttoned her coat as if she had an hour to complete the task. Perhaps it was the thought of Marlene being left in the care of a woman Theresa despised that slowed her movements. Eugene, who had been pacing by the door, couldn't wait any longer and left for the garage, saying, "I'll meet you in the car."

Theresa stood at the back door and fastened her last button. She heard Marlene crying in her room, and Mrs. Boychuk's footsteps quickening down the hall to attend to her. A tear threatened to fall but she brushed it away. She strained to hear her baby again, but when she heard no crying, she figured that she'd settled in her grandmother's arms. Clenching her fists, Theresa felt like punching the wall but instead exhaled deeply, unclenched her hands, and opened the door.

Eugene was bent under the hood of his Pontiac when she entered the garage. Without looking up, he said, "I'm going to need your help. I'm having trouble with the engine."

She glowered at him, but he didn't notice. Why couldn't he stand up for her, just once? Seeing her mother-in-law again was like having a sliver under her skin—an irritating one that couldn't be removed without some help. *Eugene's a coward. He'll be sorry.*

"Theresa, are you listening?"

Why should she listen? What did he have to say that meant anything?

"Theresa, if we don't get this car started, we're going to have to go back in the house. I'll have to get my Dad's car."

Back in the house. That jarred her. The last thing Theresa wanted to do was go back in the house and face the battle-axe. She nodded and joined him by the hood.

"When I start the car, I want you to pull these leads off one at a time."

After he had rehearsed it with her a few times, Eugene got in the driver's seat and started up the engine. He motioned for her to pull the lead, mouthing "okay" through the windshield.

She yanked it at first and then managed to pull it off, as he had instructed. A terrible shock ran through her body throwing her off. "Aagh!" she yelled.

Eugene rushed over. "Theresa, are you all right?"

She wasn't. Her body trembled as if an earthquake had shaken the ground beneath her.

"Oh baby, I didn't mean to hurt you. Not that much. I just

wanted to show you what you'll have to go through if you don't talk."

When she realized what he had done, her body froze. Eugene tried to rest his head on her rigid shoulder, but she abruptly moved away. He had tricked her. She'd been right not to trust him. Well, it wouldn't happen again. *No chance in hell!*

TWENTY

FROM THE WAY the young Boychuks entered the room, Joanna could tell the evening had not gone well. She glanced at the one-way mirror, knowing that Myron was observing from the viewing area behind it. He had put on a mike so that he could give her direction through the earpiece she wore if her meeting became bogged down. She'd heard of his hands-on approach, but was apprehensive, given that her work with Theresa had been moving at a turtle's pace. She didn't want him interfering—not when she still had some cards to play. She also knew that Bryce and Jerome would be observing out of interest but she hoped that they were there to support her and not there to judge.

Eugene and Theresa sat apart on the sofa as if they were leaving room for a third party to arrive. After a few pleasantries, Joanna explained that her supervisor would be watching, and how he'd be communicating with her in case there was something to add to the session. With that out of the way, Joanna adjusted her earpiece and said to Theresa, "The nurses told me you were very restless when you came back last night."

Tight-lipped, Theresa focused on the freshly painted wall beside her while Eugene, visibly anxious, threw looks at his wife and therapist. His left foot shook, creating the impression he might bolt at any moment.

Turning to Eugene, Joanna said, "Were there any problems with the home visit?"

THE RUBBER FENCE

Eugene reached for Theresa's hand, which was curled in a fist on her lap, but she refused to open it or allow her husband to hold it.

Joanna said, "Theresa? I gather the visit didn't go well?"

The young mother lowered her head, her long hair covering her face.

Joanna waited patiently and was momentarily distracted when her stomach grumbled. She'd overslept and had missed breakfast again.

"I tried everything," said Eugene. "I even set up a situation where she got an electrical charge, but she still wouldn't talk."

"You did what?" said Joanna, wondering if she'd heard right.

Eugene appeared sheepish as he said, "I wanted her to know what it would feel like. I wanted to show her what she was going to get if she didn't start talking."

"Eugene, there is no shock therapy prescribed for Theresa. Where did you get that idea?"

"I just thought... I read..."

Joanna put her hand up to stop him talking because Myron's voice was coming through her earpiece. She heard his frustration as he said, "Don't be so quick to discount ECT. Tell them you don't know yet what it'll take, and it may be prescribed for her own good."

For her own good. Right. When her grandmother got it, was it for her own good? She was no good after that. So whose *good* was it for? Joanna took a deep breath to calm herself. She knew that ignoring Myron's directions could hurt her later, but she could see no other way. She carried on as if there had been no interruption.

Folding her hands in her lap, she said, "I'd like to try

something with both of you. It's called family sculpting. It's a way that helps couples understand their relationship better."

Myron's voice boomed through the earphones, "Now what are you doing?"

Joanna took another deep breath, and looked at the mirror. She wished there were drapes she could pull to block out Myron's view. She touched her ears, indicating that she was having trouble hearing him. She then turned back to the young couple. "Right now, the way I see the two of you, Eugene has been taking charge and asking you to do what he and his parents would like."

Myron yelled in her ear, "Joanna, did you hear what I said?"

She'd heard all right, not only what he had said but the harsh tone in his voice, too. She pulled the earpiece out and put it down on the table. "This doesn't seem to be working. As I said, I want to try something here. Theresa, would you please stand?"

The young mother wavered but stood.

"Eugene, I'd like you to kneel."

Eugene hesitated long enough to make Joanna doubt he would comply. But then he took in Theresa's determined look and knelt. When he looked up at his wife, she smiled. Joanna could see that her patient was enjoying her exalted position.

"Great," said Joanna. "Now you're in charge, Theresa. Tall and strong."

The young mother nodded, encouraging Joanna to go further.

"Eugene, how do you feel?"

"Uncomfortable."

"Anything else?"

"Alone. Scared."

"It's natural to feel that way when you're in a submissive

THE RUBBER FENCE

position. It's natural to feel vulnerable. Now, let's try the reverse. Theresa, I'd like you to get down on your knees, and Eugene, you can stand now."

Eugene was only too happy to oblige, but the young mother didn't budge.

"Theresa," said Joanna gently, "it's your turn to kneel."

She remained standing, straight as a pillar.

"Theresa, I knelt," whined Eugene. "It's not fair. It's your turn."

Joanna asked Eugene, "What do you think is happening here?"

"I don't know," he said, glancing at Theresa, "but I don't like it." The lines on Eugene's forehead had deepened while he stood pleading with his wife to kneel. Theresa stared right through Joanna, clinging to her vertical status as if any downward movement would jeopardize her chance at some undeclared prize.

Joanna had expected as much, but wanted to try this controversial technique anyway. It was another way to discover what was at stake for the couple.

She had learned about this therapeutic strategy during a workshop the year before. It had been led by the flamboyant family therapist, Virginia Satir, who had become renowned for her ability to move patients who appeared unmovable. At the time, Joanna had questioned the validity of the guru's approach, but in this instance, her ideas made sense. To have patients act out their roles in a physical manner drove the message home more than any talking therapy could. And since Theresa wasn't speaking, what did Joanna have to lose by trying family sculpting? Only her superior's confidence in her. With that in mind, she half expected Myron to knock on the door, putting a halt to her session.

Joanna said to Theresa, "I understand. You're afraid to give up your power. I know this is hard, but I'd like you to try it, just once. As Eugene said, he kneeled. Now, it's your turn."

Theresa locked eyes with Joanna. Then, guardedly, she knelt down on one knee.

Eugene was thrilled. "That's great, honey. The sooner you do what they say, the faster we can get you home."

On hearing this, Theresa stood up and any possibility of her kneeling further was apparently over.

Eugene had jumped the gun, and there was nothing more Joanna could do. Frustrated, she said in a sharper voice than she would've liked, "Eugene, it's not about doing what others say." His brow furrowed and he looked puzzled. "It's okay." Her tone softened. "You can both sit."

It took a few moments for Theresa to settle back on the sofa. Once they were both seated, Joanna said, "When a relationship is unbalanced, whoever is one-down will fight to re-establish their identity. Most of us come from families where healthy ways of fighting are often missing. But in a healthy relationship, the power shifts back and forth, so there's a balance. One time, one partner will give in; another time, the other will. You learn over time how to support without compromising what you want and what you need. You learn where to give and how to be respectful in your communication."

Eugene and Theresa stared back, their faces vacant, as if nothing that had been done or said in the session had registered. But then again, maybe they were digesting what had transpired. Joanna could only hope. She paused, then said, "I think we've done enough for today. Thank you. You both did very well."

THE RUBBER FENCE

◇◇◇

Joanna entered the observation room with apprehension, but to her relief, Myron was in deep conversation with Jerome and had his head down and his back to her. Maybe her technique with the young Boychuks hadn't been that bad.

Bryce was standing by the door and was the first to comment on her work. "What you did in there was masterful, but you have your work cut out for you, my dear."

She smiled. "I know." She was tempted to leave with Bryce to further discuss her session, but Myron's voice stopped her. "I'll be with you in a moment." She stood at the back of the observation room and waited. She could only guess at what Myron might say and none of it was appealing.

Jerome didn't hang around either. He flashed her a smile. "I'll catch up with you later," he said, walking out the door. She wished he'd said something about what he'd observed, but with Myron in the room, maybe he was reluctant. She couldn't blame him. All the residents were on guard when it came to Myron, who now waved her over. She sat down on a folding metal chair, which felt especially cold in a room of empty seats.

"Myron…" she started.

"Theresa just won't do what she doesn't want to do, just like her therapist!" His words landed like spit.

"You didn't think their posturing shed some light on their relationship?" She knew instantly she was being naïve in her boldness. Why would he consider anything novel after she'd ignored him?

"You're missing the point. The next time I instruct you to do something, do it." His bald head shone in the dim light of the observation area. She wondered whether stress made his skin oilier.

"I couldn't hear you; your voice kept echoing." She hoped the lie didn't show on her face.

"Strange, those earpieces are high end."

"I thought, given the fact she wasn't talking, some approach that didn't use words might open things up."

Myron grumbled, "Joanna, this isn't about being creative, which you were, I'll give you that. I'm more concerned that you elected to continue on your own even though you had explicit instructions to inform the patient about the other option we might try."

"ECT," she said with a frown.

His eyes narrowed. "You're forgetting you're a resident. You do not have the authority to do whatever the hell you want."

She nodded, but in her heart she felt she had done the right thing. Even Bryce had told her as much.

Myron pulled at his ear. She must have looked cowed, as he calmed down. "Granted, residents need a chance to explore and try out different techniques, I recognize that, but at five hundred dollars a day per patient and counting, you don't have a blank check to take all the time you want. We have to get the patients moving. Hospital beds are at a premium."

There was so much she wanted to say, but what good would it do? She had already done enough to irritate him.

He must've taken her silence as compliance, as he moved on. "What medication is she on now?"

"Nortriptyline." She was relieved to get off the topic of her insubordination. "Sam prescribed it before transferring her to me. I think he was on the right track. She does seem depressed, but I'm concerned it may be affecting her breast milk."

"The fact that she's still here and her baby's at home is

enough to affect her milk production."

"True, but she's also struggling with dry mouth, nausea, and some diarrhea."

"Maybe she has the flu."

"Maybe, but these are also known side effects of the drug."

Myron exhaled sharply. "Joanna, you can't have it both ways. If she's not getting ECT, she needs something for her depression. Once she gets adjusted to the medication, the side effects should settle down."

"And if they don't?" She hadn't planned on being combative, but here she was again, challenging her superior. It was like chess—point and counter-point. "I know I'm making inroads. I think we should give her more time before ECT is prescribed."

"Better watch those 'shoulds' Joanna," said Myron, standing. "They're an indication of an overactive conscience."

After hurling his parting shot, Myron left Joanna to review his rebuke over and over in her mind. Every exchange with Myron seemed to turn into a battle. Just like with Michael. Maybe it was her. She was beginning to wonder if she was too obstinate where men were concerned.

On her way down the stairwell to the cafeteria, Joanna heard the door above open and then Jerome's bellowing voice. "Hey, you did good in there."

She stopped and waited for him to catch up to her. "You think so?"

"Yeah, you did, but you got to be careful. You know Myron's a control freak. You know what kind of cats these guys are. They got to hold on to their spot in line."

"It's all so frustrating," she said as they continued their descent.

He hesitated at the door to the basement. "I'm not saying you shouldn't do what you're doing. I admire your tenacity, but you got to look out for number one. The key thing is to get through your residency first, right? Then you can fly like the birds." He flapped his arms to illustrate.

She couldn't help but smile. "I know what you're saying, but it's hard."

"I hate to say it, but it's probably harder because you're a woman."

She loved this man. He was honest, and he said it like he saw it. She wished that Sam had seen the interview so she could run it by him as well, but she knew there'd be time later as this case wasn't going anywhere fast. Eugene and Theresa seemed to listen, but Joanna couldn't tell whether anything she'd said had made an impression.

She grabbed a coffee in the cafeteria and took it back to the ward, where she updated Theresa's file. As she reflected on the young couple, her thoughts drifted to her relationship with Michael. They were both stubborn. Everything had changed after her miscarriages. To deal with her grief, Joanna had gone to a support group for women who'd miscarried. She went several times and came to the conclusion that adoption was the way to fill the hole in their lives. But when she'd suggested it to Michael, he wouldn't hear of it—said he didn't think he could love a child that wasn't his.

Perhaps there was something to that, but if you couldn't have one of your own, then surely providing for another was the next best thing. People adopted pets all the time and loved them like family. A child would be so much more.

TWENTY-ONE

THE STAFF PARTY was way overdue. It had been initially planned as an icebreaker for the residents, but Dr. Bryce Morley's wife Julia had come down with a summer cold, so it had been postponed for a few weeks.

Joanna was looking forward to it as she'd heard so much about Bryce's beautiful home in Tuxedo—a ritzy residential area in Winnipeg. Michael hadn't been keen on going, but Joanna had pleaded until he gave in. He hated functions where people talked shop—said they were boring. Still, she was relieved to have him along. Without him, staff were sure to ask questions or assume her marriage wasn't going well—an impression she wanted to avoid since she had plans to specialize in family therapy. A therapist with a broken or frosty relationship wouldn't have much credibility in the field.

They parked on the street amongst both luxury and functional vehicles, reflecting the disparity of hospital incomes. Joanna had no trouble spotting Myron's Porsche. It was red and immaculate and something Michael coveted right away.

He whistled, then said, "Someone's doing well. Is this what I have to look forward to when you graduate?"

"Yes." She smiled. That was something they both wanted. Not so much the extravagant items but the choices that good incomes could bring.

Michael spotted an older cream Mercedes sedan parked a

few cars down from theirs. "Who owns that one?"

"Dennis Williams. He's a resident. Told me he inherited the car when his dad died. Guess his family is loaded." Joanna walked up the circular driveway holding on to Michael's arm.

He gave her an admiring glance. "You look wonderful."

"Thanks. You, too."

She was glad she had gone out and bought a new dress for the occasion—a short, blue sheath in silk shantung. It was stylish, and its scooped neck showed off her cleavage to advantage without being too daring. Michael had opted for a navy herringbone sports jacket, grey pants, and a white shirt unbuttoned at the collar—a look that made her heart skip. She let go of his arm and gave his hand a squeeze. They walked the rest of the way hand in hand.

Bryce's house was more fabulous than she'd imagined. It was a sprawling, contemporary, architect-designed home of stone, stucco, and glass. He hadn't presented himself as a man with taste, so Joanna suspected his wife must've had her handprint on this one. The inside was just as impressive. A massive limestone fireplace dominated the living room, original art-work hung on every wall, and the thick cream stain-free wool carpet suggested if they had any children, they were long gone.

Michael and Joanna made their way through the crowd to the buffet table, which was by the patio doors overlooking the backyard pool. China plates of hors-d'oeuvres were spread out on a white linen tablecloth, and a floral arrangement including a bird of paradise flower sat in the center. While they filled their plates, Donovan's "There Is a Mountain" played on the stereo in a mahogany cabinet standing in the corner. Since the music wasn't from Bryce's era, Joanna assumed one of the staff had brought the record.

Going through a stack of albums by the stereo was a tanned blonde with sizeable breasts protruding above a low-cut magenta sweater. Her tight-fitting skirt accentuated the rest of her curves. Joanna saw Sam offer the young woman a drink, and although he disappeared right after, she gathered they were together.

Myron passed by Joanna with a filled wine glass in his hand. He turned and grinned. "Not much room to move."

"Who's taking care of the ward?"

"The patients," laughed Myron.

Joanna chuckled, too. "Myron, I'd like you to meet my husband, Michael. Michael, Myron." The men shook hands.

"I've been hearing all about 2B," said Michael. "Sounds like you have your hands full."

Myron leaned in and said something to Michael in a low voice. He grinned again and wove his way out to the patio.

"What did he say to you?" asked Joanna.

"When I told him he had his hands full on 2B, he said, 'no, you have your hands full.'"

"What did he mean by that?"

"How should I know?" said Michael, shrugging.

"What did you say?" She could hear the strain in her voice.

He looked back at her. "Nothing."

"Nothing?" Irritated, she said, "You didn't ask him what he meant?"

"No." He looked around the room, stopping when he noticed the young woman at the stereo.

Joanna frowned. "He probably meant me. He's got a lot of nerve. I wish you had said something."

"Oh, did I do something wrong again?"

Joanna rolled her eyes.

"I'm getting a drink. You want one?"

"Uh..." Joanna was momentarily distracted. She'd noticed Sam and Jerome outside by the barbecue grill.

Michael followed Joanna's gaze outside and saw the two men. "Well, do you or don't you?" He sounded annoyed.

"A glass of wine would be great."

She watched Michael manoeuvre his way to the drinks table by the buffet. A burst of laughter from the dining room grabbed her attention, and she saw Dennis, Carmen, and others gathered around Bryce. Deciding to join them, Joanna squeezed her way through the crowd toward the archway separating the two rooms. As she passed people she knew, she said, "Hi," or "Nice party," or "I just got here." And, "Yes, he's over there," pointing to Michael at the bar.

When she reached Dennis, who was in the corner of the dining room, she wanted to ask him about his mother—how she was doing—but with Bryce regaling the half-a-dozen or so guests about one of his cases, it wasn't the time.

Bryce's face was flushed—evidence of more than a couple of drinks. "I went into the waiting room to get one of my patients, and I saw him sitting there wearing my pith helmet. I used to bring it to work, more for show than anything else. I didn't know how he got it, but I was damned if I was going to let him keep it. So, I took it off his head and told him to come with me to my office. Well, the guy started pulling at my helmet, so I pulled back. We stood there, the two of us, yanking away at it, until I finally gave up. I told myself I would get it later, during the session."

Bryce's face puffed out as he stopped to take a deep breath. "Well, when we got to my office, I saw my pith helmet sitting on a shelf." He laughed. "We spent the next hour talking about trust issues. The patient had been so unnerved by my aggressive manner, he wasn't sure he wanted to come back any more. And who could blame him?"

Michael showed up with Joanna's wine but before she had a chance to introduce him to Dennis, he left, saying he was going to try to find a bathroom.

"My husband," said Joanna. "You'll have to meet him later."

Dennis nodded, not seeming to mind. It was then that Joanna noticed he seemed more subdued than usual. He didn't have the same spark he'd had when she'd first met him.

"I haven't talked to you much lately," she said. "How's everything going?"

"I've been better."

"How's your Mom?"

"Hanging on. My aunt said she's rallying."

"That must be a relief."

"Yeah."

He said it, but he didn't look relieved. Joanna wanted to find out more, but she didn't want to pry. Instead, she said, "Are you getting anywhere with Marty? Is he still rubbing that damn spot on his pyjamas?"

"No, he stopped rubbing because the spot's gone." He half smiled. "Laundry took care of that." He paused, then said, "You know, I think I'm going to head out. I didn't get much sleep last night, and I'm getting a massive headache."

"That's too bad. See you Monday then." She watched him go, troubled that he seemed so preoccupied.

Her wine glass empty, Joanna headed to the bar for a refill. While she was filling her glass, Sam brushed up against her. His touch and musk smell sent a shiver through her. He had cleaned up some from his usual attire on the ward. No suit jacket, but he wore a tan pullover shirt slit at the neck, and tweed pants that hugged his hips.

"Hey," he said with a smile.

She smiled back. "Are you having a good time?"

"I wasn't until I bumped into you."

"Ha," she said, trying to sound offhand, but Sam had a way of unsettling her. She took a sip of wine to calm herself.

"You look smashing by the way."

"Why, thank you." Michael had said as much, but it was the way Sam's eyes ran over her that made her blush. She may as well have been naked. She looked at the blonde, who was still by the stereo. "I thought you said you didn't have a girlfriend."

"She's the one I call when I need to have a date."

"You needed one tonight?"

"Yeah." He then said pointedly, "The one I'd like to have come with was already taken."

She blushed again and, not knowing what to say, looked away. She looked again at the blonde rummaging through Bryce's record collection. Michael had now joined her. *Wouldn't you know it?* He was chatting her up.

Although she was flattered by Sam's smooth talk, she was bothered by Michael talking with the blonde in the corner. Her imagination took her on a scary ride as she watched the young woman part her red lips and laugh at something he had said. Michael had always been attracted to the wild ones.

Sam glanced over at his date with Michael. "Is that your husband over there?"

"How did you guess?"

"I saw you come in together."

"Oh," she said lightly, trying to hide what she was feeling.

"He seems to have found my friend. I guess you're available for the time being."

Joanna laughed, but it sounded false. She hoped Sam didn't notice. "You know, I'm not very good at this."

"No one's asking you to do anything." He leaned in and breathed in her scent; she was wearing White Shoulders. "You smell good."

"Sam..." She was attracted to him, but her mind somersaulted—one crazy roll leading her to Sam, suggesting there could be more between them, and another roll taking her to Michael, who was over in the corner charming some stranger.

"You say you're not good at this, but you're too beautiful and intelligent to ignore." He stroked her back. She felt her knees go weak. She wanted to go to Michael and get some assurance that he wasn't making a play for the blonde, but something held her back. She didn't want a scene. Instead, she said to Sam, "Excuse me, I have to find the little girls' room."

Sam shook his head, underlining his disappointment.

She knew she was passing up on a flirtation that could soothe her bruised heart, but all she wanted was to go somewhere and have a good cry.

The rest of the evening was a blur. The barbecued chicken and pork skewers were tasty, but she was too preoccupied to enjoy them. She chatted with some of the staff she cared little about, all the while trying to monitor Michael's whereabouts. What was this need? And why was he doing this? He knew it bothered her. Maybe she should just tell him to go fuck himself.

TWENTY-TWO

MICHAEL AND JOANNA rode home from the party in silence. During the last few years, their evenings out never managed to live up to either Joanna's or Michael's expectations. This time, they'd both had too much to drink. She was a cheap drunk—two wines and the ground wobbled under her feet—whereas Michael had plied himself with more than a few, causing Joanna to worry about getting home without being stopped by the police. She had offered to drive, even though she wasn't in the best shape herself, but he'd insisted.

She sat in the front seat, half stewing and half staying alert in case Michael missed a red light or failed to notice an oncoming driver. Joanna kept hoping that he'd say something to ease the turmoil in her head, but he wouldn't even look her way. He turned on the radio to CBC, and some soft jazz piano played through the speakers at the back.

She waited a bit and then with a sigh lowered the volume. "Did you have a good time tonight?"

"It was all right." Michael turned on to Portage Avenue. The sidewalks were empty except for a few late night stragglers zigzagging down the street, broadcasting their intoxication.

Joanna hoped he'd say more, but when he didn't, she said, "Aren't you going to ask me if I had a good time?"

His eyes narrowed. "Did you?" There was a bite to his question.

"Kind of. I would have had a better time if I could have spent more of it with you."

Michael said nothing. They stopped at a red light.

She looked at his left hand resting on the wheel. "How come you're not wearing your ring?"

"We've gone through this before. When I work out, I take it off. I just forget to put it back on. What difference does it make? You know how I feel." When the light turned green, he stepped on the gas.

"Do I?" She paused, expecting him to reassure her. "I saw you talking with that blonde. What's her name?"

"I don't know. There were a lot of blondes there."

"C'mon, Michael, don't play games with me. The one by the record player."

Michael looked at her. "Danika."

She hated the way he said her name; it was like he was massaging it slowly. She remembered seeing him lean in close to Danika and whisper something into her ear as if they'd just shared some intimacy. "What's she like?" Joanna asked, knowing she was treading on uncertain ground.

"She's nice."

"I bet," she said with an edge. She had hoped for a different answer—a lie maybe. She wanted to hear that Danika had some fault, something that would make Joanna feel like she didn't have anything to worry about.

Michael's knuckles turned white as he tightened his grip on the wheel and went through an amber light.

The last thing she wanted was a heated argument while he was driving, so she changed topics. "What did you think of Myron?"

His hands relaxed, but his expression didn't. "He's okay, I

guess. I don't know. What's there to think? I hardly talked to him."

"Why didn't you stick up for me when Myron told you I was a handful?" She could hear the accusation in her tone. Again, she was crossing into dangerous territory.

"What?"

"You know, when he talked to you."

"Jesus, Joanna. Why is it that every time we go out, I get the third degree?"

"Why are you getting so upset? I was just asking you—"

Michael veered the car sharply, screeching to a halt by the curb.

"What the hell are you doing?" Shaken, she yelled, "You want to get us killed?"

"Fuck!" He banged the dashboard with his fist. "I know what the fuck you're asking. I'm so goddamned sick of it! I can't even open my fucking mouth without you telling me what I should say or what I shouldn't say." Michael's face grew into one of those carnival ones, where the big red smile turns sinister.

"You know how he's been riding me. I can't believe you would have just let that go."

"Every fucking time we go out…"

"Just forget it, okay?" She hoped he would. She realized she should've stopped her questioning sooner, but the damage was done. Nothing she could say would convince him that she was sorry now—Myron, the blonde, all of it.

After they'd been sitting for a few minutes, each consumed by their private thoughts, Michael started the car and they rode the rest of the way home without saying another word. Joanna stared out the side window to hide her tears.

When they got home, Michael went straight to bed. He fell

asleep hugging his side of the mattress. Joanna didn't understand how he could just leave their quarrel behind and drift off like that. Aware of his warm body so near, yet so far, she cried herself to sleep. It was like they were living in two different countries on opposite sides of the border, and for now, that border was closed.

TWENTY-THREE

THE WEEKLY WARD meetings—where patient progress was dissected and digested—took place in a barren room with a bank of windows overlooking the other wing of the hospital. In a circle of folding metal chairs, Joanna sat between Jerome and Dennis. Beside Dennis sat Sam then Myron, Bernie, and Bryce all in a row. The other chairs were filled by Roberta, Carmen, a few nursing students, a psychologist, a social worker, and the occupational therapist. With the shrinks together side-by-side, it was clear where the power lay.

"I have some good news," said Bryce, beginning the meeting. "We've reduced inpatient stays to an average of two weeks, but we need to do more." He scanned the room as if expecting some objection. "All right then. Let's move on."

Roberta read from the cardex on her lap. "Mrs. Kowalski is eighty-five years old and this is her first admission."

Myron said, "This is becoming an old folks' home."

"Welcome to the future of psychiatry," said Bryce. His remark was met by a few titters.

Roberta continued. "Mrs. Kowalski tells every nurse and orderly she sees that her son-in-law is planning to kill her. She says she hears digging in the basement at night."

"A paranoid schiz in full bloom," said Myron.

Roberta looked at her notes. "She's not responding to Mellaril."

"Why isn't she on chlorpromazine?" asked Bernie.

"Good question," said Myron. "We'll review her meds later."

Jerome leaned forward. "I've seen the son-in-law. He's rough looking. Maybe there's some truth to her complaints."

Joanna had seen him too. A tall, wiry man in a crumpled shirt and stained pants.

Myron said, "We all need to keep an eye out for any other signs of paranoia. You want this one, Jerome?"

"Sure."

Roberta made a note and checked the cardex again. "Theresa Boychuk. There's been no change in her. It's been two weeks since she stopped talking."

"She could be malingering," said Bernie. "Prison inmates often resort to mutism to avoid discussion of their crimes."

Roberta added, "In prison, they use sodium pentothal to loosen the tongue."

"She's not in prison," said Joanna with an edge she wished she'd kept better hidden. She was still smarting from the remark Myron made to Michael at the party a few days before. It had been a sneak attack as far as she was concerned.

"Not yet," added Roberta sarcastically.

Sam, who'd been sitting quietly, said, "Her mutism could be a hysterical reaction to something that happened."

"That's what I'm thinking," said Joanna. "She hasn't been charged, so I suspect her mother-in-law's claims were trumped up. But at the same time, I'm surprised that with the accusations levelled against her, she hasn't said anything in her defence."

"But if she's guilty," said Bernie, "as long as she keeps quiet, she doesn't have to deal with what happened."

Myron crossed his legs and cleared his throat. "This is a

good discussion, but no matter what, we have to get her moving."

Roberta said, "The family reported—"

"We can't always trust the family, can we?" interjected Joanna.

Myron said, "Have you met her parents?"

"No. Her GP told me on the phone that they live in the city but that there's been some kind of rift. They're Jehovah's Witnesses, and they basically disenfranchised her when she married Eugene. He's not of their faith."

"You wonder what her parents gained by that," said Dennis.

Joanna nodded. "I've tried to get Eugene's family to come in, but there's always some excuse. Mrs. Boychuk's arthritis acts up, or the baby has a fever. I've been toying with the idea of seeing all of them at home."

Myron scrunched up his face as if she'd suggested some dish that didn't suit. "Better leave home visits to the social workers. Can't do any treatment there; you have no control. If it's not the television playing that gets in the way, it's people rising to go to the bathroom. It's impossible to find out anything except how they arrange their furniture." His remark got a few smiles. "It's not only unproductive; it's also a waste of time."

"It may not be," said Joanna. "The literature suggests it might even save time. With a home visit, you can see the family in action—their dynamics in their own setting. If they're as disturbed as I think they are, it might give us some clues as to how to break the pattern."

"I could go with Joanna," said Sam.

Bryce nodded to Sam. "There's an idea."

Myron's smile faded. "Right. Instead of one practitioner off in the field, we'll have two." He met Bryce's gaze. "You're the one who's been bellowing about the shortage of beds. The longer we put off treating her with ECT, the longer she stays."

Joanna couldn't believe what she was hearing. "I know you brought up the possibility of ECT down the road, but we're a long way from that happening. I told her husband—"

"I know what you told her husband," said Myron angrily.

"Time is getting on," said Bryce, looking at his watch. "We can probably debate this 'till the cows come home. And since we have none of those," he said to a few snickers, "a conjoint home visit wouldn't hurt. Especially since Sam is so agreeable."

"Isn't he." Myron's voice dripped with sarcasm. He faced Joanna. "I expect you'll set up an appointment in the next few days. If nothing changes after your visit, we'll schedule a course of ECT and take her off her meds. She has to be clean. No drugs whatsoever."

Given her position, Joanna could only nod. It bothered her that Theresa could end up like Rose, and she, as her doctor, would not be able to stop it.

TWENTY-FOUR

THE EXPECTED VISIT to the Boychuks' home didn't materialize as now Mr. Boychuk was sick with the flu. With the cancellation, Myron reminded Joanna, as if she needed a reminder, that Theresa's status was skewing the statistics in a negative direction. Although Joanna had no idea of the severity of Mr. Boychuk's illness, she told Myron that it was probably a twenty-four-hour flu and that the home visit would take place in a matter of days. If it didn't, she had no other plan. Individual sessions with Theresa continued to be an exercise in futility. If nothing changed, Joanna would have no support in delaying shock treatment for the young mother.

As Joanna struggled with how to speed up Theresa's recovery, she was offered a distraction that she welcomed. Jerome asked for help with the Kowalski case, the old woman who believed her son-in-law was up to no good in the basement. Jerome was meeting with Mrs. Kowalski, her daughter, and her son-in-law in the interview room and he asked Joanna to observe through the one-way mirror. If she felt that Jerome was being thrown off track, she was to knock on the door and offer some suggestion or join him as a co-therapist.

Jerome was hardly seated when Mrs. Kowalski pointed her knobby finger at Frank. Her hands were gnarled and swollen—signs of arthritis. She said, "Ever since I signed the property over to him and my daughter,...ever since, he's been treating me badly." Her daughter sat beside her with a pinched expression on her face.

"I don't know what to do with Mom," said Natasha. "She tells me she can hear the shovel hit the basement floor at night. She believes there are other bodies buried there. She keeps telling me she saw fresh cement."

Joanna studied the accused. Frank Ruby had a craggy unshaven face, greasy black hair, and dirty fingernails. At well over six feet, his arms and legs stretched way beyond the borders of the chair he was sitting on. He looked like one man Joanna wouldn't want to meet in a dark place. What surprised her the most was that Frank didn't seem to be bothered by the grim accusations. If he was guilty, he might think no one would believe an old woman. He could always say she was demented.

"Ask him where my money went," said Mrs. Kowalski, pointing her finger again at Frank.

Instead of complying, Jerome said, "How did you decide to all live together?"

Nice segway, thought Joanna. Clever of Jerome to steer them back to the beginning to try to untangle the paranoid mess.

"My Dad died," said Natasha, "and Frank and I decided that it would be better to have Mom live with us. She sold her house soon—"

"You told me to," interrupted Mrs. Kowalski. "You said, 'Mom, you sell your house and then we can buy one big enough for all of us to live in.' Isn't that what you said?"

Natasha cringed at the wagging finger in front of her face.

"I remember you telling me that. You think I don't remember so well. You think I'm an old lady who knows nothing, but I know. I remember. I remember what you said. Don't you worry."

Before the meeting ended, Jerome made arrangements to visit the home with Joanna on Friday. At first, Frank and Natasha resisted, but in the end, agreed. They said they wanted to put a stop to all of the old lady's babbling. The way Frank said it gave Joanna the shivers.

◇◇◇

With the Kowalski case in overdrive, Joanna decided to push Eugene about getting someone other than his mother to take care of Marlene, especially if Mr. Boychuk was sick and needed his wife's attention. She told him on the phone that Theresa's recovery required a family meeting at home without delay, otherwise there was no guarantee that his wife would be coming home anytime soon. She further said, "The longer we wait, the more entrenched she'll become."

Eugene was hesitant at first, saying he'd check with his parents, but it wasn't long before he called back, proving Joanna's hunches were right. Mr. Boychuk had made a miraculous recovery, and they could meet with Joanna the following afternoon. It wasn't so much that Mrs. Boychuk wanted Theresa back home. It was more what she didn't want, and that was some stranger looking after her granddaughter.

TWENTY-FIVE

THE RELAXING EVENING Joanna had hoped for at home became anything but after she received another phone call with no one on the other end of the line. That was the second one she'd had in the past month. She suspected it was one of Michael's students wanting to talk to him, but when she answered, there was nothing but silence and then a dial tone. When she mentioned it to Michael, he looked blank for a moment and then said, "It's probably a crank call. I've had one of those, too."

She wanted to believe him, but instead went to bed mulling over the call and how Michael had reacted when she'd mentioned it. And in the morning, when she told Michael she'd make dinner that evening, he announced, "I'm not going to be home. I have a faculty meeting."

That sounded odd; faculty meetings didn't usually take place after hours. "So late?" she replied.

"If you must know," he said, sounding annoyed, "I'm on a committee to review the curriculum. It's been hard with everyone's schedules to organize it at any other time."

What could she say? *I don't trust you!* She drove to the hospital fretting about their exchange. She tried to recall when they'd last had a tension-free conversation. She couldn't let go the gnawing feeling that just below the surface of her marriage there was some kind of danger—something dark she could not see.

◇◇◇

A number of acting-out patients kept Joanna's mind off her marital worries for a while and then it was time to leave for her home visit to the Boychuks'. She went straight to Theresa's room, but she wasn't there, nor was she in the lounge or the women's restroom. Joanna hadn't expected any problems, but now her patient was missing.

Not ready to panic yet, she approached Annette, the ward clerk, who was in the midst of telling Roberta the latest hassles she was having with Axel, the hospital handyman. "I told him about it. He said squeaky wheels weren't his priority. Neither are lights, toilets, or taps. I'd like to know what the hell he thinks his job is."

"I think it's to bug you," said Roberta.

"Well, he's doing a good job of it."

"Annette," said Joanna, "have you seen Theresa? I've checked everywhere."

"I'm not sure, but she might be in the chapel. She usually goes there around this time."

"Thanks." This was new. The fact that Theresa was religious was an angle Joanna hadn't considered. But before she could give it any more thought, she was distracted by Dennis, who was standing nearby with Marty and a middle-aged couple who were possibly Marty's parents.

"Mrs. Feldman," said Dennis, "this is going to take time."

The pear-shaped woman with wavy black hair said, "Have you seen his hands? They're raw and red like fresh meat." She picked up one of Marty's hands and extended it to Dennis as if he couldn't see from where he was standing. "He can't stop washing them, can you dear? Mommy has some of that cream you like. I'll bring it next time we come, okay?" Marty withdrew his hand. His mother then patted his hair like a woman in love.

Mr. Feldman shook his head. "That's all he does. My wife calls him for dinner, and he can't get out of the bathroom. You should see our water bills."

As Joanna walked by them, Dennis gave her a look that said, Get me out of here. She smiled in sympathy.

Joanna found Theresa alone, sitting near the front of the chapel—a room with half-a-dozen pews and a large wooden cross, which hung on the wall behind the altar. While Joanna waited for the young mother to finish praying, Joanna sat down at the back and said "The Lord's Prayer". At the end of it, she mouthed, "Rest in peace, Granny." Since it didn't look like Theresa was going to finish anytime soon, Joanna went up to her and tapped her on the shoulder. The young mother followed Joanna out, soldier-like.

As planned, they met Sam by the exit to the parking lot and walked to Joanna's car. Theresa got into the back seat, and Sam and Joanna sat in the front. When Joanna caught Sam eyeing her legs, she tugged her skirt down and scolded herself for wearing one so short.

It was a perfect summer day, not a cloud in the sky. Joanna drove down William Street to McGregor and then over to Burrows Avenue with its wide, welcoming boulevard. When she saw Theresa through the rear-view mirror, her hair blowing wildly across her face, she shouted over the sound of the traffic, "Do you want me to roll up the window?" When her query got no reply, she rolled up the window anyway. Next, she tried some small talk with Sam but gave up when it started to feel awkward

THE RUBBER FENCE

with Theresa sitting silently in the back.

The Boychuks' home was a neat-as-a-pin bungalow on a street of other well cared-for homes. A row of red geraniums bordered by white alyssums was in full bloom under the living room window, and the weedless lawn had been neatly trimmed on each side of the front walk. Glancing at the other houses nearby, Joanna could see that the Boychuks were the most compulsive of the lot.

Eugene greeted them at the entrance, swinging the door open before they'd even reached the threshold. At first, Joanna thought he looked pale, but then concluded it was probably the lighting. The dimly lit interior would give anyone a grey look.

"I see you've found the place," said Eugene. His eyes flitted from the therapists to his wife, who stood frozen in the doorway. Rather than hug her, he turned abruptly and went into the living room with its plastic-covered furniture. On one side was a sofa, and across from it, a love seat, where Mrs. Boychuk, with her tightly curled salt and pepper hair, was already seated. Dressed in a sleeveless flowered shirt and plain skirt, she made an obvious display of cooing to Marlene, who was nestled in her arms. Mr. Boychuk, a thin man with hollow cheeks and closely cropped brown hair, sat stiffly beside her on a dining room chair.

Visibly distressed, Theresa entered the living room as if it were a house of horrors with something—or someone—ready to leap out at her any moment. She looked askance at her mother-in-law and hesitated before sitting down beside her husband on the sofa. Eugene sat forward, his knees bouncing up and down as if he had to go to the bathroom but wouldn't dare leave for fear of missing something. On a library table behind the young couple were photos of Eugene at different stages of childhood, a few of baby Marlene, and one unflattering photo of Theresa that looked rather recent. It must've been taken near the end of her pregnancy, because it showed her with very fat cheeks.

Joanna was about to sit down on the love seat beside Mrs. Boychuk but decided against it. She said to the older woman, "Do you mind if we move a couple of dining room chairs into the living room so that we can face the whole family?"

"Go ahead," said Mrs. Boychuk, unsmilingly. Once the chairs were arranged, she added, "I prepared some tea and cookies. Please help yourself."

Joanna poured herself and Sam a cup from the teapot on the coffee table and said, "Thank you for this meeting. I know—"

Suddenly, Theresa rose and crossed over to Mrs. Boychuk. She tried to pick up her baby, but her mother-in-law resisted.

"Mom, please," said Eugene, putting his hand on his forehead.

"Here you go," said Mrs. Boychuk sweetly, as if there hadn't been an issue. She then said, "Another migraine, Eugene?"

Looking anguished, he nodded while Theresa returned to the sofa cradling Marlene. The baby was barely settled in her mother's arms when she began to fuss, whimpering and kicking her legs. Mrs. Boychuk immediately jumped up and tried to grab the baby back, but Theresa held fast. As they struggled, Marlene's cries grew louder.

The only one in the family seemingly unaffected by the dispute was Mr. Boychuk. For all the emotion he showed, he might as well have been a statue.

Afraid the baby would get hurt, Joanna said, "Would it be better for the moment if I took her?"

Theresa looked surprised but Mrs. Boychuk ignored Joanna and said to Eugene in Ukrainian, "Talk to your wife. Tell her to

THE RUBBER FENCE

give me the baby. She's more used to me."

Joanna wondered whether or not this would be a good time to let the family know that she understood Ukrainian, having learned it from her grandmother. But before she could say anything, Eugene whined, "Theresa, let Mom take her. Marlene doesn't like the way you're holding her."

Theresa's chin quivered and she relaxed her grip, allowing her mother-in-law to take the baby without any further trouble. Slumping back on the sofa, Theresa averted her eyes from everyone.

Mrs. Boychuk paraded her granddaughter before them, kissing the top of her head from time to time, the sounds of it punctuating the air like so much static. "That's Grandma's little girl." Marlene's cries soon switched to soft whimpers.

Joanna said, addressing Eugene, "Now-a-days, it's rare to see young couples living with their parents. How is that working?" She then scanned the family, communicating that the question was open and any of them could answer.

Still on her feet, Mrs. Boychuk said, "We stay out of their way. I make the dinner; I do the wash. All she has to do is take care of Marlene. I don't ask for much. Eugene can tell you that." She zeroed in on Eugene's face, but he pretended not to hear her. He picked up his china cup and inspected the bottom, as if he were an antiques peddler.

Joanna said to Mrs. Boychuk, "I'm sure Theresa appreciates your help, but I'm sure it's difficult—"

"Why should it be so difficult?" interrupted Mrs. Boychuk. "She has all of us to help her. She doesn't know when she's well off." She sat down on the love seat and rocked Marlene in her arms.

Joanna glanced at Sam and could see from the way he raised

his eyebrows that they were on the same page.

With a grim face, Mrs. Boychuk said, "We could have lost this little one, oye, oye, oye."

Her husband looked over. "Don't get yourself so worked up."

"Why shouldn't I? You see what's happening."

"Mom, she didn't hurt the baby."

"You weren't there, Eugene," said Mrs. Boychuk. "If I hadn't come into the room, who knows what would have happened."

Joanna was about to ask another question when Theresa got up so quickly that the photos behind her rattled. She stomped out of the room and, seconds later, slammed a door down the hallway. Marlene wailed upon hearing the noise.

"My God," said Mrs. Boychuk, her eyes bulging and her face reddening. "One of these days, she's going to break one. She's nothing but a spoiled woman. See what we have to put up with? Eugene, you go tell her she's got no business slamming my doors."

Eugene left on command, whereupon Mrs. Boychuk stood up and rocked the baby some more. "Shh. Shh."

Joanna was beginning to think Myron was right. It was insanity to conduct a family interview in a patient's home. With Theresa and her mother-in-law jumping up and down, it was impossible to maintain control of the session. She looked to Sam for support, but since they'd decided beforehand that she would lead, he sat back and said nothing.

Joanna sighed. "Mrs. Boychuk, Theresa's slamming the door has to do with her frustration over not being able to take care of her own baby. It's just natural that she would be upset."

"Natural? You think she acts natural?" Glaring she said,

THE RUBBER FENCE

"I'm not standing in her way." She glanced at her husband but he was looking elsewhere. Irritated, she shook her head and cuddled Marlene even closer.

Joanna said, "I believe that her not talking also has to do with the way she handles her anger. At the moment, she doesn't know any other way."

"You think that's right? Banging the door that way? I don't know if you were raised that way—I certainly wasn't. If I had acted like that, my father would've kicked me out a long time ago."

"I understand, but when people get upset, sometimes their emotions are so large they spill out in unfortunate ways. It happens most often when they feel powerless. Theresa feels that way right now."

"What a bunch of hooey! What does she have to be angry about? What? You tell me. She doesn't know what it is to suffer, really suffer. Young girls today have no idea of what hard work really is. You ask my husband how we worked, how I didn't have any help—no help at all! You ask him. I didn't have any parents around to help me. They were too sick themselves. I had to help *them*." She shook her head and noisily puffed out some air. "Such a life I had."

"Mrs. Boychuk," said Joanna, "I'm sure you mean well, but she needs to have time alone with her baby."

"Are you crazy?"

Joanna was about to answer when Eugene came back into the room.

Mrs. Boychuk said, "Did you tell her to stop slamming doors like that?"

"I did."

"See? She doesn't even come back and apologize. This baby

would be dead if I hadn't come along. That girl needs a good kick in the ass. She should get on her knees and thank God she has it so good. Spoiled, that's what she is. Spoiled."

Joanna regarded Mr. Boychuk, whose head was bent. She then looked at Eugene. His quick trip down the hall to blame Theresa—as his mother had commanded—must've been a bad choice as he looked as if he'd been whipped. *Like father, like son.* Joanna sat forward. "I was wondering, Eugene, if you and Theresa were thinking of getting a place of your own?"

Eugene's right eye began to twitch and he looked at his mother as if she might answer for him.

Mrs. Boychuk said in Ukrainian to her son, "Is she going to pay?"

Eugene shrugged.

Joanna debated her next move, but time was of the essence and this wasn't a chess game. "Mrs. Boychuk, my grandmother lived with us when I was little. I understand Ukrainian."

"How nice for you," Mrs. Boychuk said with an attitude that refused to give any ground. She said to Sam. "Do you understand Ukrainian, too?"

"No, unfortunately I don't."

Mrs. Boychuk grunted and then said to Eugene, "Do you agree with her? Do you want to leave? If you want to leave, go. Go with my blessing."

"Mom, I'm not going anywhere." His voice sounded like that of a child pleading with his mother for forgiveness. "Theresa and I appreciate all you and Dad have done for us. We like it here."

"Sophie," said Mr. Boychuk. "They're fine here."

Joanna frowned and again exchanged glances with Sam.

Mrs. Boychuk got up, making a crackling sound as the

plastic peeled away from her bare legs. She said angrily to Eugene, "Suit yourself. I told you this therapy shmerapy was a bad idea." Without waiting for an answer, she marched out of the room with Marlene.

"What's happening?" said Sam.

Joanna couldn't help rolling her eyes. "I think we've worn out our welcome."

"I'm sorry," said Mr. Boychuk. "This has been a very hard time for all of us."

"I know," said Joanna. But did she really know the extent of it? She knew that Eugene was incapable of standing up to his mother, and Mr. Boychuk may as well have been a non-player. She also knew that Theresa didn't have a chance of mothering if there wasn't a change at home. Now that Joanna had a clearer picture of how the family operated, maybe she could light a fire under Eugene. One he couldn't afford to put out—not if he wanted his wife back.

Joanna's mind was still reeling as she stood on the boulevard. She said to Sam, "That's enough to shut anyone up."

"Don't know what kind of shape Theresa will be in when he brings her back."

"She can't get much worse."

"You ever hear of suicide?"

"I don't think that's her style. She's getting too much mileage out of not talking." Joanna glanced back at the house. "I really think this is more to do with a battle between two strong women and the impotence of their men."

Sam nodded. "You want to grab a java or ice cream and we

can kick it around some more? Nothing like analyzing a case when things are still fresh."

Joanna checked her watch. Michael wouldn't be home waiting for her. "Sure. Why not?"

TWENTY-SIX

IT WAS ONE of those warm summer evenings—the kind that Winnipeggers appreciated and thought they were owed after surviving a long winter. Sam and Joanna decided to buy some ice cream at a grocery store and take a walk through St. John's Park off of Main Street. Heading down the main path, they found the park empty except for a few families gathering their blankets off the lawn after an outdoor picnic, and a couple of older men sitting on a bench, catching up on one another's news.

Joanna licked her Revel and said, "I know we agreed for me to handle the session, but I was surprised you were so quiet during the meeting. Didn't you see I was floundering?"

"You did fine on your own. Of course, if Mrs. Boychuk had stood up and attacked you with a machete or something, I would've been there."

Joanna laughed. "Right. You would have taken the blow for me."

"Sure. I wouldn't have let her do any injury to our junior resident. I mean, if you were senior, that would be different. You'd be competition, and of course I'd welcome any help getting rid of you."

"Good to know. Now, how do I cure the ills of this family? What can I do when they don't even believe in the process? They were fighting me every step of the way. You saw that. Should I have gone to Mr. Boychuk and said, 'Hey, you ineffectual twerp, do you know what part you play in this mess? Do you see what your wife is doing to your son and his wife? And you just sit there, like a lump of lead. Can't you see the destruction? She's killing them.'"

"That would've gone over big," said Sam, folding down the wrapper on his Fudgsicle.

"Of course, the fact that he's so impassive—he's her accomplice. How can he just sit there like a robot, as if he doesn't even live there?"

"Maybe that's how he survives. There are many families like that all over this planet."

"Yeah, sad to say." She kicked a pebble on the gravel path.

"You know, the men are there, they pay the bills, but they keep one foot out the door, just in case they have to run out when it gets too hot for them. They work long hours, come home tired—it's their excuse. Besides, if you ask them about what goes on in the house, they'd say it's woman's work. And they'd appease their women by saying You do it best, honey."

She looked at Sam sideways before taking another lick of her Revel. He was describing her father, who kowtowed to her mother whenever there was an argument.

"You women are a strong bunch. Hard to deal with at times. I don't think you're the weaker sex, not by a long shot."

She glanced at him again. "Is that why you never got married?"

He didn't answer, and she knew better than to push. Maybe she had pushed enough already, given his silence. The dying light of the day did nothing to illuminate what he was hiding. It was obvious he was his own man and planned to keep it that way for whatever reason.

They passed a father throwing a football to his son while the

THE RUBBER FENCE

mother took pictures. It seemed that they had left the Boychuks far behind.

Sam followed her look. "Nice, huh?" Sam took another bite of his Fudgsicle, which was almost gone.

"Yes, it is. Good to clear the head after a session like that."

"Speaking of clear heads. As your senior…"

Joanna laughed and licked some ice cream that had dripped onto her finger.

"No, wait a second. It's one thing speaking out, it's another cutting your own throat."

"What do you mean? You thought I was out of line back there?"

"No. I'm talking about Myron."

"Oh. Jerome said the same thing, not in so many words."

"Myron could be numero uno one day." Sam raised his eyebrows to underline the point. "Bryce has a weak heart, so you never know."

"Hmm. You remember that day we were coming out of the cafeteria and Myron said, 'you be a good boy and you can get one too'?"

He looked at her quizzically. "You do ruminate on things, don't you?"

"You were talking about his new Porsche."

"Myron thinks I don't look out for myself enough. He thinks altruism died out a century ago, not counting Gandhi and a few more like him, of course. See, there's this little relationship we have with the drug lords—the legal drug lords. If we play cool with them, they play cool with us. And sometimes we get some nice toys."

"Dinners, golf games…" She ate the last bit of chocolate.

"Paid conferences in exotic places, front seat tickets to big events. It's a good life."

She wasn't surprised. Myron's quickness to prescribe drugs or shock treatment benefited him.

"Those pharmaceutical companies will come courting, and then you can decide whether you want to go to the prom or not. You think it's about saving lives, but you learn that to get ahead—whatever the fuck that means anymore—you need to publish, and for that you need money for research, and who's got it?"

"The drug companies," said Joanna. "There's so much at stake. How can you win against all that capital?"

"And with the pressure to get those patients out, it's just easier to give a pill than to admit you don't know what to do. Plus, the pills work. Most of the time."

Joanna said sarcastically, "And if they don't, there's always hydro, right?"

"Bingo. The truth is, there are big bucks in ECT."

"Why not for psychotherapy?"

"Takes too long to see results. Economics 101."

Sam threw his Fudgsicle wrapper in a garbage can; Joanna did the same with hers.

With grand arm movements, Sam pretended to twirl a fake handlebar moustache. "Ladies and gentlemen!" he said, pretending to be a travelling medicine man of pioneer days. All that was missing was his costume. "Don't be too quick to dismiss this amazing cure. I have before you the most amazing apparatus for all those wackos that are a social pox in our community!"

When Joanna guffawed, Sam smiled and said, "Just set the dial to the age of the patient, and press the button. Painless, fast, and when they wake up, they won't remember one bit of the pain that troubled them in the first place. That, my friends, is the

THE RUBBER FENCE

marvel of this contraption."

"Marvellous," she said clapping.

Sam then said in a serious tone, "And if you're lucky, really lucky, you'll manage to help a few, and if you're not, you'll bruise a few once-gentle souls."

The thought quietened them both, and nothing more was said as they walked down the hill to the shore of the Red River. Overhead, the leaves of oak and poplar trees darkened in the fading light. They stood on the bank and watched a few canoes pass. The paddlers' laughter floated up to them. On the other side of the river, a few house lights came on, signalling the late hour. Joanna wondered what Michael was doing at that moment.

"It's such a nice evening," she said.

"Magic hour. How did you decide to enter this noble profession?"

"I guess I always liked helping. I used to take my grandmother to the doctors and to church. She spoke little English, so she counted on me to interpret for her." Joanna stared at the water, which was getting blacker by the minute. "There came a point when life became too much for her. She just drifted away. I wasn't happy with the treatment she got."

He nodded. "I'm sorry."

"It wasn't your fault." She paused, then said, "What about you? What drove you to choose psychiatry?"

"Not much to tell. I grew up on the border of Minneapolis and St. Paul. Half the time I didn't know which city I was in. And my old man was bipolar, so I come by my craziness naturally." He said it quickly, running over the fact of his father's mental illness.

"That must've been hard."

"I didn't hang around much when I got to a certain age."

Sam found a spot on the grass. "This okay?"

He lay his denim jacket down for Joanna. She sat down on it, careful with her skirt. He stretched out beside her, his thigh almost touching hers. It was too close, but she made no effort to move. Sam took a joint from his shirt pocket, lit it, and offered it to her. She hesitated at first, but then took a drag, holding in the smoke, savouring its warmth. It was her first time and she was surprised she hadn't coughed. When she passed the stub back to him, he inhaled deeply, held it for a bit and then let the smoke weave a grey ribbon through the air.

He handed the weed back to her. This time, when she tried it, time slowed. She felt the heat between them and broke the connection first by pulling at her skirt and then taking in the river as if she were trying to see something that had earlier caught her attention. A motorboat went by in the dark; the chatter of the folks and music on board advertised a party in progress. The sounds coming from the water were pleasantly amplified, making Joanna realize she was high.

He said, "What are you thinking?"

"Nothing." She stared at the boat and made out a couple on the deck, their arms around one another. She wondered what it would be like to be Sam's girl.

"You got somebody?" she asked.

"Not since a week ago, give or take a day. That's when she married my old roommate from my days at boy scout camp."

"Oh, that's too bad."

"No, it's all right. I actually got over her fifteen years ago when she had her braces taken off. Couldn't get used to kissing her without feeling the pain."

Joanna chuckled. She wasn't any wiser. She couldn't tell if anything he'd said was true. Sam rolled over to her and rubbed her cheek. "Some chocolate," he said.

His lips looked wet and welcoming and his eyes, a blue she hadn't seen before. They were the color of periwinkle flowers, sky blue tinted with mauve. When he leaned over and kissed her, she was tentative at first, but then he kissed her again. This time, she didn't hold back. Her body trembled against his, and she let out a gasp. Shortly after, she pulled away, even though her body was aching for more.

"Sam, I..." She straightened her skirt. "I can't." They regarded one another, both saying with their eyes what Joanna was unwilling to do with her body. He took another slow drag, and put the joint out. The possibility of more vanished with the smoke.

When Joanna got home, Michael was already asleep. He looked so vulnerable, his body curled up like a fetus in its mother's womb. Her heart went out to him, and she wished he would let her in again. It had been awhile since they'd made love. Was it two weeks already? It wasn't that long ago they wouldn't let two days go by without coupling—immersing themselves in hot, passionate sex.

She gargled with mouthwash to cover any trace of marijuana, took her clothes off, and got into bed, cuddling her naked body next to his. She kissed him tenderly at first, on the back of his neck. He stirred. She continued to kiss his back, each kiss moving lower down his spine, and then moved her hand from his chest to the warm soft hair around his hard member. She wondered if he was dreaming of her or someone else. He turned and sleepily pecked her on the cheek.

He began caressing her breasts. She drifted in and out, enjoying the feel of his hands on her body, but her mind also drifted back to Sam, and what they had done by the river.

Michael stopped touching her and said, "Where are you?"

"Nowhere. I'm right here with you." Could Michael tell she was lying? He fondled her breasts again. She stayed with him this time as he stroked her belly and the inside of her thighs. She moaned with pleasure as he found her sweet spot.

Afterwards, she wondered if she had come because of her evening with Sam or because Michael was still able to arouse her.

TWENTY-SEVEN

JOANNA WAS RECORDING her notes on the Boychuk home visit when a grating sound interrupted her thoughts. She looked up as Carmen wheeled a gurney up to Annette and said, "Can't they do something about fixing these things?"

"I can tell Axel to oil those wheels again, but you know Axel. He keeps telling me they're not a priority. I'd like to know what is."

Joanna winced upon seeing Rose lying semi-sedated on the gurney. The elderly woman's drawn face and frightened eyes were unsettling. Every patient that went down for shock treatment wore the facial expression they'd been backed into a corner with no exit. As Carmen wheeled Rose away, Joanna remained fixated on the receding figures. She couldn't help feeling she'd let Rose down.

When Joanna walked into the doctors' lounge—sparsely populated with one doctor stretched out on a sofa and two others reading in the corner—Myron was already seated at a table by the window. She was late and scolded herself for not paying more attention to the time. She knew that lateness was considered to be a passive-aggressive habit, if not downright rude. As she crossed the floor toward Myron, she was aware that he was watching her. She had always felt self-conscious in a large space—vulnerable and exposed. She assumed it was because there was no place to hide, and this time, there really wasn't, not with Myron watching her every move.

"I was beginning to wonder if you were coming."

"I'm sorry I'm late. I got carried away with my recording and lost track of time." He nodded. It was good of him not to object.

"So, Sam's already told me about your bomb of a home visit. This mother sounds like the mother from hell." He laughed. "I have to admit though, you may be on the right track. Maybe Mrs. Boychuk is doing a number on Theresa."

Joanna smiled but cautioned herself to go slow, not to get too excited about his favorable reaction.

"But we still have a problem. You can't undo all the damage in the short time we have to work with her, but I will give you a little more leeway."

"Good." She was grateful but still wary. She suspected he wasn't just being charitable.

He cocked his head. "How are you doing with Rose?"

Swallowing, she said, "I'm planning on setting up a family interview."

"Your home visit with Theresa was informative, but I wouldn't try it with Rose. It would be too traumatic for her. You'd best see her sister alone."

"Behind Rose's back?"

"Rose is seventy years old! Her siblings are older still. What do you think you're going to do, revolutionize the family? You'd have an easier job climbing Mount Everest!"

"I'd still like to try."

"You're very stubborn."

"I know."

"Just remember who's in charge."

She held his gaze, barely, as Myron's eyes showed a steely resolve—one she'd best not ignore. At least she hadn't backed down. She congratulated herself on that much.

After that, their conversation veered to what had just happened in Munich. Five Arabs had scaled the fence of the Olympic village and, together with three insiders, managed to kill eleven Israeli athletes and one German policeman. It was all over the news and on everyone's mind. Joanna fell silent when Myron told her he had visited a kibbutz in the past year and had seen some of the victims in training. At least, this was one area they could agree on. There was no excuse for that kind of slaughter.

In some ways, Joanna envied the Jews and their solidarity. They appeared to have a lock on excellence no matter what they tried. She knew it had to do with their shared family values and common history of global persecution. It was as if there was an unspoken understanding amongst them, that no matter what, as long as they stuck together, they could conquer the world. Or at least stand out in their chosen professions. All of that was certainly evident in Myron, Bernie, and Sam. Each one said what was on their mind without fear of being judged. It was the kind of confidence that Joanna envied. She, on the other hand, had come from farming folk, one of whom had emigrated from the breadbasket of the Ukraine—good people who were content to live off the land and not expect much more. With her medical degree, Joanna had gone far beyond that, so why did she still feel she wasn't measuring up.

TWENTY-EIGHT

WHEN MICHAEL SUGGESTED they have one of his fellow instructors and his wife over for dinner, Joanna knew it was about his desire to smoke grass. Gary and Donna weren't potheads, but they indulged often enough and knew where to get good weed.

Michael's craving to get high had been sparked a few months back when they had gone for a walk to Memorial Park. It was where the hippies who traversed Canada stopped to play their music, swap stories, buy weed, or just hang out.

At the park that day, they'd seen a hundred or so young vagabonds sprawled on the lawn that surrounded the water fountains and the red geranium flower gardens. Their clothes were ragged and the hems of their bellbottoms soiled. Their feet were bare or encased in weathered brown leather sandals. The girls were braless, the shape of their nipples pushing at the rayon fabric of their tie-dyed T-shirts. Peace sign necklaces, long beads, and broad leather wrist wraps signalled the deeper changes ahead. The war in Vietnam was still on everyone's mind even though it wasn't Canada's war. And with all the draft resisters who had come across the border, the protests on both sides were only getting stronger.

A guitarist with a paisley headscarf played and sang "Hey Jude" on the south side of the park to a crowd of listening youth. After Joanna and Michael had passed a few discreetly smoking

THE RUBBER FENCE

pot, its sweet smell wafting through the air, Michael said, "You know Gary? He and Donna toke up regularly. I wouldn't mind trying it some time."

That was over two months ago, when it had been the start of summer.

Now, Joanna's brow tightened. Since trying marijuana with Sam, she was no longer worried about handling it, but there was something about Gary she didn't trust. "I don't know," she said to Michael. "It can mess with your head."

"Naagh. That's bullshit. The most it'll do for a little while is make you forget your troubles."

It was the Sunday evening after her visit to the Boychuk home. Gary and Donna brought over some marijuana, a bowl of magenta hibiscus flowers, and an electric color wheel that threw a rainbow around the room. Joanna had been apprehensive about their visit, but she went along with it, mostly because she wanted to please Michael. She was also feeling guilty about her feelings towards Sam. She reasoned that if her relationship with Michael improved, she wouldn't lust after someone else.

At the beginning of the evening, Gary told them that he had left his home in England at thirteen and had travelled through France and Morocco before heading across the ocean to Canada. He admitted to being wild, and though he'd been married to Donna for fifteen years and had had three kids with her, it hadn't been easy for him to settle down. Donna, petite and pretty, didn't say much, just looked adoringly at him while he told his story. Like him, she was knowledgeable about motorcycles and auto mechanics. Together, they were an experimental, gutsy—and therefore dangerous—couple, at least that was what Joanna thought. Some of that danger came from the way Gary looked at her, the way his eyes travelled her body, that kept her off balance.

She would've been more comfortable if she knew where Michael stood. In the early years, he had been insanely jealous, questioning any study groups she was in that contained men. But as time went on and Michael became more confident with his own career, he stopped making jealous comments. Joanna couldn't put her finger on when that change had taken place. All she knew was that other men's attentions didn't seem to bother him anymore.

Gary lit the first joint. Joanna hoped the sweet smell wouldn't waft through their walls to the other tenants in the building. Smoking weed was against the law and therefore risky for both Michael and Joanna. Neither the hospital board nor the university would look kindly on what they were doing. But Michael had reassured her that the concrete walls and the fact that their apartment was an end unit would keep their marijuana party secret from the other residents in the building.

Michael was the first one to get high. Being a novice at marijuana but a former smoker, he went up quickly, like dry timber with only a spark to get it going. Time slowed; it seemed that more than a half-hour had gone by. She watched Michael stand up unexpectedly, walk over to the mirror, stare at himself, and then return to their group. On his face, some unidentifiable fear.

"None of you looked at me," he said. "I went over to the mirror and you didn't even notice."

Joanna had heard that marijuana could make one paranoid. She felt out of control herself. When the pot started to hit her, she was stirring her tea. The sound the spoon made in the teacup startled her. It was like a church bell, clear and musical, not the quieter clinking sound she usually heard. She marvelled at the

THE RUBBER FENCE

spoon's musicality and the rainbow coloured spots the wheel threw on the wall. Then she blanked. She didn't pass out, but there were moments that later she couldn't account for. Michael, Gary, and Donna carried on, passing the joint from one set of lips to another. She refused when it came to her again. Her stomach churned, not with the kind of torment that comes from digesting the wrong food, but rather with the feelings that come from an upset mind petering on the edge of the unknown.

Then great hunger came and they ordered pizza. That was followed by apple pie that she'd made for dessert. Gary and Donna left soon after their meal; it seemed late, but it had only been three hours since they'd arrived. As for great sex—which many said came as a result of smoking grass—both Joanna and Michael felt too weird to have any and went straight to bed. She should've fallen asleep quickly but instead her brain was on guard. She worried about Gary coming back and raping her. Even with Michael next to her, she felt unsafe. When she got up to go to the bathroom in the middle of the night, the hallway seemed unusually dark. She listened for sounds of anyone else in the apartment, and just to make sure, she checked the lock on the apartment door one more time. She even pulled aside the living room drapes and looked down onto Roslyn Street to see if Gary's car was parked out front.

In the morning, she decided that marijuana wasn't for her. The paranoia it had unleashed was too much to handle. Especially her crazy thoughts about Gary.

Though they made no plans to see the couple again, Gary's name came up over dinner a few evenings later.

"Gary called," said Michael with a smile on his face. "You'll never guess what he wants to do."

"He wants to do it again?" She took a bite of chicken.

"No," said Michael, wiping his mouth. "He wants to swap wives."

"What?" she said, nearly choking on her food. "You've gotta be kidding. He has some nerve." She had read that wife swapping was spreading. It was called swinging. Married couples got together, threw their house keys into a circle, and swapped partners for a night of wild sex.

"You don't have to get so upset." Michael took a swig of beer. "I didn't say yes."

"As if that was an option."

"I thought you'd be flattered."

"Right." She stood up and took her half-eaten chicken dinner to the sink. She had lost her appetite. Scraping the remains of her meal into the wastebasket under the sink, she said, "I don't want to see them anymore."

Michael didn't say anything. They never saw Gary and Donna again.

TWENTY-NINE

AT THE NEXT rounds, Myron and Bernie discussed the ongoing dilemma of keeping a few beds open for adults suffering from an acute psychotic attack. Once the oldsters were on the ward, it was nearly impossible to remove them. Myron was spending more and more of his time yelling at social services to hurry up and find homes for seniors with dementia. It was this latter part that they all said they hated as the problem was discussed ad nauseam.

Sam agreed to follow up with the ward social worker on her backlog, and the meeting progressed to discussing the patients they were following. Myron glanced at Joanna, and for a moment she panicked. But instead of asking her to report on Theresa or Rose, he said to Sam, "Have you seen Dennis?"

As if on cue, Dennis opened the door and came into the room. "I assume you slept in," said Myron sarcastically. "You're up first."

Although Joanna had escaped scrutiny for the time being, her heart went out to Dennis. His greasy brown hair, dark circles, and rumpled clothes screamed troubled nights. The way staff traded looks around the room, it was obvious to Joanna that she wasn't the only one who'd noticed a change in his demeanour.

"Okay, Dr. Williams. Tell us what's happening with Marty Feldman. You do know that any contact you have with a patient or his family has to be recorded?"

"Yes. I'm a little behind," said Dennis, stumbling over his words.

"I wouldn't have used the word 'little'." The veins in Myron's forehead stood out. "We can't afford to have any gap in our records. The nurses rely on our analyses. What's the point of seeing patients if we keep the information to ourselves?"

Humiliated, Dennis shrunk.

Myron scowled. "I assume you won't leave until it's done today."

There was tension in the room that left no one free of its mark.

Dennis took off his glasses, wiped them on his shirt, then put them back on again. Maybe he wanted a moment free from all the faces staring at him.

Joanna wanted to give Dennis a reassuring smile to let him know he wasn't alone, but he didn't look her way. He fumbled with some papers on his lap.

"Since the record has holes, Dr. Williams…" said Myron, pausing until Dennis lifted his head. "Fill us in, if you don't mind." It wasn't a request; it was an order.

Dennis exhaled sharply. "I've seen Marty a number of times. I've noticed, and the nurses have as well, that he's constantly washing his hands, obsessing about them, closing doors repeatedly whether it's his room or his closet or his drawers. The fact that he's socially isolated, all of this together, makes me suspect he…I believe he has an obsessive-compulsive personality disorder."

"Exactly," said Myron with a slight smile.

"He could be dangerous," said Bernie. "He did threaten to kill his mother."

"According to his parents," said Dennis, sounding a bit more confident, "it was a misunderstanding. He was just waving a knife around."

"Yeah, for no reason," said Sam.

Dennis looked at Sam. "I'm surprised they even want him back, especially after he told them he never wanted to see them again. They were very upset. It's taken him thirty years to get it out—to say what he really feels, and they won't accept it." Dennis paused and then said to the team, "Maybe if he didn't laugh hysterically every time he tried to put his foot down, they'd believe him."

Jerome chuckled. "Double message. Maybe home was where he learned that."

Joanna said, "It'd be interesting to study their communication patterns."

"If only we had time," said Myron, sending her a 'not this again look'. He said to Dennis, "What are your treatment plans?"

"I'm not sure what to do next. Marty has no other place to go. I don't know how he'd function in a boarding home or whether his parents would even allow it. They keep blaming me. Said if it wasn't for me putting ideas in his head, he wouldn't be talking that way."

Joanna said, "Sounds like you're doing a great job helping him express his feelings. Any time we shake up a family system, there's bound to be resistance. Bateson, the anthropologist, talks about homeostasis—how if any member of a family tries to move in a different direction, the rest conspire to maintain the status quo."

"Good point," said Sam.

Dennis frowned. "The Feldmans say I don't understand their customs."

Myron snorted. "That's a nice way of dismissing you.

They're Jewish, so letting their son go to a strange place like a boarding home is not acceptable, not to their community. It would look like they were abandoning him."

"Marty's mother still reads him bedtime stories."

Jerome said, "I saw Marty walk backwards into his room the other day. What's up with that?"

"He doesn't want to face the bogeyman. His parents also told me he's never had psychiatric help before." Dennis shook his head.

Bernie crossed his legs and sat back. "I wouldn't be surprised if there's more to this than what we're seeing. I think he's a funny boy."

Before Joanna could figure out what Bernie meant, Myron said, "I agree. Dennis, have you considered the impact of his sexual orientation?"

Dennis blinked more than usual. "I…I don't think it has any relevance. Besides, we don't know if he's homosexual."

"No, but consider his behaviour and the possibility he might be. Check the DSM II. Homosexuality is right up there.

Sam said, "There's a lot of debate about that diagnosis."

"There's debate about all of them," said Myron. "But at the moment it's all we have. The DSM II gives us a standard language that we can all use in confidence, and in this case, it would be irresponsible to overlook Marty's sexuality."

"That makes sense," said Joanna.

"Well, thank you, Dr. Bereza," said Myron with more than a hint of sarcasm.

"What I meant was, it makes sense if Marty is gay, then it could be a factor in his illness, especially since it's hard for gay men to feel completely at ease in a society that's homophobic."

Myron looked askance at Joanna. Dennis squirmed in his

THE RUBBER FENCE

seat.

Sam said, "So in other words, you're suggesting we need to take Marty's sexuality into account when we're making treatment plans?"

"My, you're a bright group," said Myron.

"You're so kind, Myron," replied Bernie. "Your analysis must be going very well." The residents laughed, dissipating some of the tension in the room.

Myron folded his arms. "Sexuality is always a factor. For example, if he's socially isolated, how does he relieve himself? If he masturbates, does the obsessive washing have to do with feeling dirty?"

"It would be interesting to know if he masturbates," said Jerome, "and how often he does it and where and when."

Sam said to Jerome with a twinkle in his eye, "Are you volunteering to follow Marty around and graph his movements?"

Everyone laughed except Dennis.

Myron turned to Dennis. "Try to get a sexual history from him and from his parents. Like, was he ever interested in girls; did he try to date; did they try to hook him up? What was his reaction? Did he have any disappointments? And look up Sexual Dysfunction Not Otherwise Specified. Do all of that before you draw any conclusions, all right?"

Dennis made notes, but his hand wasn't steady. Seeing the tremors, Joanna hoped that whatever was bugging him wasn't drug-related.

THIRTY

JOANNA SAW THERESA with Eugene again, but it was as if the record player they were using to play their tune was on repeat. Same old, same old. Nothing had changed. As for the family interview with Rose, it had to be postponed because her sister, Mrs. Marks, had gone to visit a friend in Virden—a three hour drive from Winnipeg—and planned to stay there for a few days. It was a disappointment for Joanna, but it did afford her the opportunity to help Jerome once again.

Mrs. Kowalski had been diagnosed with dementia. Paranoid features of her mental illness were being considered as she continued to make allegations about buried bodies in the basement. Jerome wanted to make sure he was on the right track, and given the creepiness of her son-in-law, decided it was best to humor her and go see for themselves. A more complete assessment would also help in discharge planning.

Joanna felt flattered when Jerome said, "You're the one who's made a practice of studying family dynamics. I don't even know where to begin."

Her reputation for having combed the literature on family therapy had preceded her. Professor Peterson, her mentor at the university, had even encouraged her to publish an article on her research, but she hadn't yet found the time to write one.

The Kowalski home was situated on Balmoral Street in west end Winnipeg—a street lined with stately elms and two-story houses built in the 1940s with wood siding and glassed-in verandas. Joanna and Jerome arrived at the house a little after the dinner hour on a cloudy night. Unlike the other well-kept houses on the avenue, this place was an eyesore. Situated on a narrow lot covered with weeds and tall grass, the wooden structure with its peeling white paint and cluttered porch had deteriorated over the years from neglect. And to add to its grimness, the house was in darkness except for a small light that appeared to come from some room in the back.

"It looks spooky," said Joanna.

"I did tell her it was this evening," said Jerome. "She went home this afternoon with her daughter."

They walked up the cracked sidewalk toward the house; the last concrete slab of the walk was tilted and with the dim light, Joanna almost tripped. The porch steps were worn and the rubber treads that had been nailed down the middle of them were torn and in need of replacement. The open veranda had a rusty bedspring on it, a baseball bat, a box of odds and ends, and an old red bike with only one wheel.

The front door creaked open, and Mrs. Kowalski's daughter, Natasha, welcomed them in. At first it was hard to see, but Natasha turned the hallway light on, exposing the dirty walls and the bare light bulb overhead. She ushered them into the living room, which opened off the cramped front entrance and immediately went over to an end table by a chesterfield where her mother sat, and switched on a table lamp. Joanna wondered whose idea it was to have the old lady sit in the dark. Were they saving money, or were they just peculiar? Mrs. Kowalski huddled at one end of the worn and soiled brocade sofa, and Natasha sat down at the other. Above them hung a black velvet picture of Elvis in his white rhinestone-studded suit, and on the opposite wall, hanging high was an unframed mountain landscape done with a paint by numbers kit. In the middle of the room, under a chipped laminate coffee table that had a bottom shelf littered with old newspapers, lay a weathered British Indian rug that had seen more than its share of spilled dinners.

Joanna and Jerome sat opposite the Kowalskis under the do-it-yourself painting in easy chairs covered with wrinkled throws faded from too many washings. A chrome airplane ashtray full of butts stood on the floor between the interns, its propeller missing. In the corner, a TV cabinet showed its age through its scratched wood top where a ceramic black panther lamp with a lime lampshade had been placed on top of a doily.

Joanna couldn't pin down the smell of the place, but the odour seemed to be a mixture of stinky feet, fried onions, and old newsprint. She did her best not to wrinkle her nose in disgust. She wondered where Natasha's husband was and looked to her left, where an archway separated the living room from the dark table-less dining area with old wood floors.

Mrs. Kowalski propped her cane against the sofa. "Ever since I signed the property over to them, I get no respect. I may as well not even be here."

"Mom," said Natasha. "That's not true."

"I told you, Natty," said Frank Ruby, coming out of the gloomy dining room carrying a chrome kitchen chair in one hand—its stuffing showing through the rip in the green leatherette seat—and a bottle of beer in the other. His oily black hair brushed the back of his neck. The shadows behind him underlined his sinister appearance. His dirty undershirt exposed a tattoo of a buxom mermaid on his right arm with the inscription LOVE CHILD. He was also drunk. He set the chair down at the edge of the light, straddled the seat, the chair back facing them,

THE RUBBER FENCE

and took a long guzzle of beer. Then he belched.

The old woman muttered. Natasha's eyes narrowed in anguish as she avoided her husband entirely. Joanna couldn't help but stare at him. His intense gaze was intimidating as he rocked in and out of the dark.

Jerome prodded Mrs. Kowalski to go on. "You were saying, Mrs. Kowalski?"

Frank leaned forward and said to Joanna, slurring his words, "You're not going to believe this ol' crackpot, are ya?"

Natasha said quietly, "Frank, please."

Frank burped and then released a hideous laugh.

Joanna and Jerome exchanged concerned looks. What good could come out of a session where one of the key players was inebriated? And if Mrs. Kowalski was right, he could be dangerous.

"Mrs. Kowalski," said Joanna. "Your daughter loves you very much. Even so, it's difficult for seniors to live with their children."

"Now you're talkin', girlie," said Frank.

Joanna ignored him, angling her body toward the old lady. "You're not as strong as you used to be. You need more help, and it's not good being scared in your own house." She hesitated. She could see that Natasha was agitated, but she wasn't sure if it had to do with the subject they were discussing or whether there was something else Natasha was afraid of.

"Not my house anymore, I told you," said Mrs. Kowalski. "They were good to me when the house was in my name. Oh, yes." She looked accusingly at Natasha and Frank. "But things changed soon as I signed on that line."

"Mom," said Natasha. "You know Frank and I would do anything for you."

Mrs. Kowalski harrumphed. "That'll be the day."

"She's sick in the head is what she is," said Frank. "Needs to be locked up somewhere."

"You promised," said Natasha. "You promised me you'd behave."

"For her own good, Natty. Thass all I'm sayin'."

"Frank, no."

"Well, I'll be a son of a gun. Hear that? The little woman wants me to behave. Jump up and bark like a dog." Frank made some barking sounds. At Natasha's scolding look, he stopped and took another swig of beer, spilling some on his undershirt.

Jerome moved forward in his chair. He said to Mrs. Kowalski, "Your comfort needs to be considered. We'll have to talk more about this. We can set up a family meeting on the ward."

"Not with me, you won't," said Frank, slurping his words like his beer.

Jerome said, "If you're not there, decisions might be made that could affect you. I would strongly suggest you come. Sober."

Frank sat up straight, but a moment later, jumped up and disappeared into the dark. Mrs. Kowalski followed him with her eyes.

The old lady said in a hushed voice, "He's probably thinking of going down to the basement. Do you want to see it?"

Jerome traded looks with Joanna. They also looked at Natasha, who shrugged as if to say, Whatever you like.

Joanna scanned the dining area again trying to see where Frank had disappeared to. If she was apprehensive about being in the same house with that man, how did frail Mrs. Kowalski feel? She took a deep breath, but it didn't allay her fears. Her wild imagination had her discovering Frank waiting for them in the

THE RUBBER FENCE

basement with an axe.

Mrs. Kowalski led the way to a painted cream door that needed a good scrubbing. Joanna hadn't asked what kind of work Frank did, but she wouldn't have been surprised if he was a mechanic of some kind, given the dirt that was embedded in his fingernails and on the basement door. Natasha went ahead of her mother and turned the loose brass doorknob. On the landing above the basement stairs, she pulled the chain for the bare light bulb hanging from the ceiling. Then they all trudged down the creaky wooden steps.

The damp concrete floor was cracked in places around the sewer, and the musty smell suggested some forgotten rags or unwashed laundry. Natasha said apologetically, "I know it stinks. I'm having problems with my washer. I've called a service man, but he can't come until tomorrow."

Although the floor's wet spots didn't look like fresh cement—the kind that would suggest some recent work had been done—Mrs. Kowalski pointed to some rough spots on the concrete. "That's where he's been digging."

Jerome bent down to examine the area, more to appease Mrs. Kowalski than anything else. "It's rough all right."

"It's always been like that," said Natasha, "ever since we moved here when I was ten."

"What are you talking about?" Mrs. Kowalski said, her face scrunched in frustration. "He's been digging here for the past few months. Haven't you heard him digging?" She shook her head, as if she were trying to get rid of a fly that had landed on her forehead. "Of course not. You sleep like a log, you always have. It's me he keeps awake at night with that shovel of his."

Jerome patted her on the shoulder. "Well, I appreciate you showing us, Mrs. Kowalski. We can talk about this more tomorrow."

She nodded, apparently pleased that there would be further discussion, and gave Natasha a look suggesting she'd been right all along about her concerns.

Natasha said, "Is it okay if I bring her back tomorrow morning?"

"I'm sorry," said Jerome. "We need her back on the ward tonight. We're trying to establish some routine, make sure she's taking her medication."

Natasha took a few steps back and glanced around as if she expected Frank to show up. Not finding him, she whispered, "Frank has never liked my mother. He makes it very hard for me when I want to do anything for her."

Mrs. Kowalski, who was right behind her, said, "Speak up. You know I can't hear."

"I was just telling them it's hard for you here."

"Of course it's hard for me to hear. You're always mumbling."

"Mom, that's not true."

"You want to put me away, I know that. Now that you have everything, you can just throw me out."

"No, Mom," said Natasha, sighing. "No one wants to put you away."

Mrs. Kowalski shuffled away, leaving Natasha to escort the interns to the front door where she said, her face lined with worry, "I've thought about leaving him, but Frank's not a bad man when he isn't drinking."

Natasha looked so earnest that Joanna was at a loss for words. She half-smiled. *Why was it that so many women put up with so much for so little in return?*

THE RUBBER FENCE

◇◇◇

It felt good to step outside the blackness that flowed through the Kowalski home. Joanna took a whiff of the crisp fall air and marvelled at the golden elm leaves, their edges marked in red, beginning to make a blanket on the ground. She wished she could jump into a pile of them just to rid herself of the nasty feelings she had gathered in the past hour.

Getting into Jerome's Chevrolet sedan, she said, "I'd be scared, too. Did you see his mermaid tattoo? What does that tell you?"

"He used to be a fisherman?" Jerome smiled and started the car.

"Can't imagine that. He doesn't have the patience for it. What did you make of that whole basement scene?"

"Weird. The cement *was* wet. Maybe there are a half-dozen bodies buried there."

Joanna gave him a second look.

Unable to remain serious, Jerome guffawed. "You should have seen your face."

She playfully punched his arm.

"I don't think Natasha would have taken us down there if there was anything to worry about."

"You're right."

Their home interview was no therapy session but it had shed light on subjects that were even more obscure in sterile hospital interviews. It wasn't that long ago that it was common practice for physicians to call at home. She remembered doctors coming over at all hours when she was a child. They seemed more like distant relatives than outside professionals. And now, she'd done the same thing, for the second week in a row. By doing so, she was sure they'd gained the confidence of Natasha and her mother. But Frank, at this point, wasn't having any of it.

THIRTY-ONE

MRS. MARKS WAS back from her trip to Virden, and a family session with her and Rose's brother was scheduled for that afternoon. It hadn't been easy convincing Rose of the need. Joanna had to reassure her that when it came time for her to leave the hospital, she wouldn't have to go live with her sister and that the family interview was only needed to gather more information.

On the way to the interview room, Rose was tighter than a wet knot. She said to Joanna, "I don't know why the hell you need me. Just go ahead and talk to those turkeys yourself."

"I'd like to know the kind of support you have. I don't want to talk about you behind your back."

Rose swallowed and said no more.

Mrs. Marks and her brother were already seated in the interview room when Joanna and Rose walked in. When Mrs. Marks stood to greet her sister, Rose said, "It took you long enough to come."

Mrs. Marks frowned and said, "Oh, Rose." She sat back down in a chair by their brother, Tony Andalucci, who nodded to Rose as if she were a stranger he'd just met.

Joanna and Rose sat across from them. As Joanna reviewed the rules of confidentiality, she noticed how different the two sisters looked. Although Rose was younger by a few years, she appeared much older with her short salt and pepper hair and lined face. Her baggy sweater and pants did little to camouflage her gaunt figure. In contrast, Mrs. Marks, with her frosted hair in a fashionable layered style, was dressed in a Jackie Kennedy-type dress and high heels that showed off her still fine legs. As for Tony, he hadn't inherited either of his sisters' lean frames. He was squat and bulky, and the underarms of his T-shirt were wet, revealing that Rose wasn't the only one who was nervous.

After Joanna explained that their meeting was confidential and that any information obtained would be used to help Rose, she said, "I was hoping you could give me a little background on your family. So…" She looked from one to the other. "Who wants to begin?"

"What do you want to know?" asked Mrs. Marks.

Joanna wasn't surprised to hear Rose's sister speak first; she seemed to be the one in command. "I'm wondering what's still troubling Rose. From your perspective. Was there something in her past?"

Rose looked warily at Joanna, as Mrs. Marks mentioned that they grew up in a boarding home in the north end with a mother and father who were too busy trying to make ends meet to give them any time. There were eight of them altogether. A few had moved to Ontario, but they were long gone before Rose started falling apart, as she phrased it. This was helpful information, but not what Joanna was looking for.

The brief family history was followed by an uncomfortable silence. Joanna allowed the silence to reign, hoping one of them would disclose something that might've triggered the onset of Rose's illness.

She didn't wait long before Tony rubbed his upper left arm and said, "Rosie here, she got in the family way. She was seventeen, and you know, times being what they were, well, our priest, he told us—he told my mother—that she'd have to go away. That's right. That was pretty tough back then. People talked. It nearly finished our mother."

"You had to bring that up," said Rose, more irate than nervous now.

Tony ignored her and whispered to Joanna as if she sat next to him, "And then, the baby. The baby was given—"

"What the hell you whispering for?" said Rose. Agitated, she got up and began to pace.

"Rose, sit down," said her sister.

"I'll sit down if I feel like it. You don't have to tell me to sit down."

"It's all right," said Joanna. "They're just trying to help."

Rose stared at Joanna as if she'd just woken up and was getting her bearings. After a moment, she sat down again.

Tony played with his hands for a moment and then said to Rose, "We're telling her this for your own good, Rosie. She's gotta know everything if she's gonna help you." Rose made a face but that didn't deter her brother. "After that, she dropped out of school. Went to work in a home several hours away. We didn't see her for about a year."

"We never did find out who the father was," added Mrs. Marks.

"And you never will!" shouted Rose, rising again. With a shake of her head, she added in a low tone, "Christ, you people…"

The strain of the session was becoming too much for Mrs. Marks, who said to Tony, "Tell her about Vincent." Her brow furrowed, casting a gloom on what was about to be revealed.

Rose's hands trembled and her eyes darted from her brother to her sister. Joanna suspected she was dying for a smoke, but there was a no smoking policy during interviews.

"Vincent lived down the street from us. Rosie liked him, but you know boys," said Tony with a shrug of his shoulders.

"Boys are boys," said Mrs. Marks.

"When he found out about Rosie, well, he stopped calling. And after that, she kinda went wild."

"You goddamned busybodies! Puritanical horse-shitters!"

"Rosie," said Joanna. "I mean, Rose."

"They never liked him," said Rose. "None of my family liked him."

"That's not true," said her sister. "Papa liked him."

Rose rushed to the door and started banging on it with her fists. "Let me out of this goddamn hell hole! Open this goddamn door!"

Tony and Mrs. Marks exchanged anxious looks.

Joanna nodded to the mirror. "The door's not locked, Rose."

"Rosie, don't—" said Tony.

"Rosie, don't. Rosie, don't. Rosie, don't." Rose continued to strike the door.

Joanna went to her and laid a hand on her shoulder. "This wasn't easy." Rose wrenched her body away so hard she almost hit Joanna in the process. She opened the door to find a nurse and a hospital aide, who grabbed her arms and took her away.

Joanna sighed. Mrs. Marks and Tony looked like they'd just lost a championship match that should've been theirs.

THIRTY-TWO

JOANNA CAME HOME to find Michael in the living room reading *Open Marriage* by the O'Neills. The book had become a bestseller in the last year. She sat down beside him. He continued to read, barely acknowledging her presence.

She glanced at the page he was reading and saw something about love getting stronger if couples allowed one another to move outside the relationship, to have intercourse with someone other than their spouse. A feeling of dread swept through her body. Why was he reading this? They'd had an argument about this very thing when Gary had proposed wife swapping.

She steeled herself and said, "What do you think about what they've written?"

"It's all right."

"I can't believe you think it's all right. It's ridiculous." Her voice had a tremor in it; it sounded whiny.

"If it's so ridiculous, why are so many people doing it? The O'Neills think an open marriage can stimulate a stagnant relationship. What's wrong with that? It's just sex; it doesn't mean anything."

"What do you mean, it doesn't mean anything?"

"It's not love. Look at Europeans. It's common for them to have other lovers. Maybe they know something we don't."

"You mean to tell me that you can have sex with someone other than your wife, and if you do it without loving them, it's supposed to be okay?" This time she made no effort to hide the strain in her voice.

"Yeah," he said, shrugging. "It shouldn't be a big deal." He smile an upper hand smile that made her feel like she had to claw her way back to some kind of stability.

"Are you sleeping with someone?"

He stared at her for a moment as if weighing what he was about to say. "No. Why would you say that?"

"The way you're talking, I thought you might be." She wished she knew what he was really thinking. A friend of hers had once said, "How do you know what's going on with him? Still waters run deep, you know."

Later when he stepped out to get some milk, she sat down to skim the book but was interrupted by their phone ringing. She picked up the black receiver in the kitchen and recognized the woman's voice. It was one of Michael's students; she had called a number of times before.

"Yes, I'll tell him," Joanna said at the end of the call.

After she hung up, she leaned against the wall, growing more anxious with each passing thought. Why did she let them get to her? She knew the games students played. Michael was an attractive man, and she had come to expect some rivalry for his attentions. But lately, this young student had been calling too often for Joanna's comfort.

When Michael returned a half-hour later, she said, "Cindy Bell phoned. She said to tell you she can't make the meeting tomorrow morning." Joanna checked his reaction. When there was none, she took a deep breath. "She also told me I was lucky to have you."

He grinned. "I've been helping her out with some of her papers. Her husband's an asshole. I guess she likes the fact that I

THE RUBBER FENCE

listen to her."

Joanna couldn't help the biting sarcasm that laced her reply. "Did you tell her that I like when you listen to me, too?"

Michael glared at her. "What the hell is that supposed to mean?"

She wished she could retract what she'd just said and how she'd said it, but the damage was done. "It's just that you don't seem to have any time for me anymore."

"I don't have time? You're the one who's jammed up with rotations, your courses. Your schedule is all over the map."

What he'd said was true. She couldn't deny it. Frowning, she said, "Yeah, I know. I just…" She just what? Did she want to say "I don't trust you"? How would that go over?

"You knew it would be like that when you enrolled." He went into the kitchen and she followed. He put the milk in the fridge. "It's never good enough, is it?" His jacket was still on, and he looked like he was ready to bolt.

"Stop, please. She calls you at home, for God's sake! Since when do students call their profs at home? What am I supposed to think?"

"Think what you want," he said with a scowl. "You do anyway." With that, he left the kitchen. She hoped it was to hang up his jacket.

Why had she said anything? It was probably the book. That and Cindy. She had wanted him to understand it wasn't easy being married to a man exposed to so many young, available women. They were single and only too eager to please and worship their mentors. It wasn't fair. She knew she still looked good—in fact, very good—but after a few miscarriages and busy schedules, it was hard to find any romantic time to keep their love kindled. She imagined Cindy searching for every opportunity to get Michael alone…and winning. Now, all he'd be thinking about was how bitchy his wife was, and there was nothing she could do to take the words back.

Fighting back tears, she went into the living room where he was back reading *Open Marriage*. She grimaced when she saw it. "I'm sorry for snapping." She waited for a response but he ignored her and returned to his reading. "I said I was sorry."

"Okay," he said without looking up and with no hint of forgiveness in his voice.

She knew it wasn't okay. She knew he'd be blaming her for their quarrel. He didn't know that she was just trying to get some reassurance—reassurance that she was the one, his only one. That was what she was trying to get to earlier, when they'd talked about what the *O'Neills* were saying in their book. But he didn't understand. It was as if she were speaking a foreign language that had no existing translation. All she wanted was to feel his warm, strong hands around her, desiring her as he had when they'd been so young and so in love. She believed the love was still there, but now it was coloured by time and many disappointments. How many more arguments would it take before their love completely withered like the last leaves of summer?

She went into their bedroom to prepare for sleep. Before she shut the blinds, she looked outside. The night was black, the stars just peeking through. Somewhere, some mother was showing her child the big dipper. Somewhere, a young man and a young woman were discovering one another for the first time. Somewhere, an old woman was reviewing her life and regretting her choices.

THIRTY-THREE

SHE SAT THROUGH intake and went on rounds, but her mind was elsewhere, struggling to figure out the next step with her patients' lives and her own.

Finding the ward claustrophobic, Joanna took her lunch break on the front lawn of the hospital. The day was mild and the blue cloudless sky calmed her mind. On a bench shaded by a giant oak, Joanna took a bite out of her peanut butter and banana sandwich, opened the book *Conjoint Family Therapy* by Virginia Satir, and flipped to a chapter titled "Accepting Differences". She was about to read when Myron's voice pierced her fragile tranquillity. "As you can see, Bill, our residents never stop working."

Styrofoam cup in hand, Myron came toward her accompanied by a tall man in his early forties. The man's red hair was slicked back with grease of some kind, and he was dressed in a navy designer suit, white shirt, black and navy striped tie, and black loafers. He swaggered as he walked, giving the impression that he thought of himself as a prize catch.

"Joanna, this is Bill Gilroy, a drug rep with Kaleidoscope. Bill, Dr. Joanna Bereza."

"Nice to meet you," said Joanna, putting her sandwich down. She shook his hand, passing on a touch of peanut butter. "Sorry."

"No problem." Bill laughed and took a handkerchief out of

his pants pocket to wipe his finger. He then gave her an appreciative look and said to Myron, "If you ever find me going loony tunes, set me up an appointment with Dr. Bereza here. I'd get cured just looking at her."

"You'd be the easiest patient in history," said Joanna.

He grinned. "Do you golf? I'm looking to fill a foursome. You could be my guest on the best greens around."

"No, I don't, but thanks anyway. I went golfing once at Falcon Lake. The horse flies were so thick my arms got bloodied with bites. I scored two hundred and twelve. Impressive, huh?"

He arched his eyebrows. "Too bad, but lucky horse flies tasting a pretty thing like you."

Joanna bit her lip, wanting to tell him to buzz off.

"Well, maybe something else. Theatre? Concerts?"

Annoyed, Joanna shook her head. Myron didn't seem to be bothered by Bill's pushiness.

"If you change your mind…" He winked at Joanna before patting Myron on the shoulder. "I'll send you that report you were asking about when I get back to the office."

As Bill walked confidently away, Joanna said quietly, "Smarmy little guy."

"It's part of his job. Wooing doctors."

"Dumb job." She frowned. "Tell me they're not all like that, are they?"

"No. Some of them are more polished." Myron sat down on the bench beside her and pulled up his pant legs. "What's happening with Theresa?"

"I feel I'm on the verge of cracking through that silence." She didn't believe that but didn't know what else to say.

He shook his head. "I meant it when I said you only have a little more time. It's about to run out."

Her body stiffened. She could no longer justify her approach with Theresa. They sat there for a few awkward moments without saying anything. Then Myron said, "What about Rose? Any headway there?"

"You were right. Rose lost it in the family meeting, but I did learn some things."

"Like her illegitimate child and her running around?"

"You knew about that?"

"It's all in the file."

"Sort of. But she's had no psychotherapy to deal with her loss."

"Maybe she did. Not every exchange that takes place is recorded."

Joanna thought about that for a moment. "Maybe she still feels guilty or ashamed. You should've seen her. She was fighting for control with her brother."

He raised his eyebrows. "Interesting choice of words, Joanna. Control. I suggest you get some and then we'll talk." Myron stood, crushed the Styrofoam cup in his hand, and threw it in the bin by the bench in a way that suggested this was only some of the trash that stood in his way.

THIRTY-FOUR

MYRON'S "LITTLE MORE time to work with Theresa" was like a ticking time bomb Joanna had to figure out before it exploded. She had been meeting with the young mother daily in one of the offices. They sat opposite one another but on the same side of the desk to eliminate the doctor-patient barrier.

The sessions were plodding as Theresa kept her head down and hid in the long hair that covered her face. There was little eye contact, and with each interview, Joanna felt more and more doubtful about her ability to get through. She had to admit that Myron had been good enough to cut her some slack, but even she could see that Theresa was at a standstill.

Joanna was at the point of giving up when she said, "Theresa, I know that your life with your in-laws is difficult. I know that Mrs. Boychuk is critical of your mothering, but I need you to help me here. If you can't talk to me about what's going on inside of you, what you're afraid of, then I can't see how I can help you."

Theresa looked intently at Joanna, who hoped once again that this time the young mother would utter something. But hope vanished when she lowered her head again and Joanna went back to staring at the untended dandruff in her patient's hair.

Joanna wondered if one of the new alternative therapies would be better. She had read of primal therapy, where patients were put in padded rooms and given free license to release the

THE RUBBER FENCE

pain by screaming at the top of their lungs and pounding the walls to their heart's content until they were spent. Anything was allowed as long as the patients didn't hurt themselves or anyone else. But Joanna also knew that in the wrong hands, those undergoing primal therapy could snap and never come back. It would be risky with someone like Theresa. Her elastic band had already been stretched to the breaking point—the point where she'd given up her voice. What else would go if she were pushed any further?

Joanna deduced that it wasn't just the dynamics in the Boychuk home that had led to Theresa's hospitalization. Theresa had severed her ties with her own family, who were Jehovah's Witnesses. Or had her parents severed their ties with her? Either way, these wounds were buried deep and would need to be exhumed before they could be healed.

"Theresa, how did you meet Eugene?"

Theresa peered out from under her hair. Joanna met her gaze for a few moments, then took a sheet off her note pad and passed it to Theresa along with a pen. "Please, tell me how you met Eugene."

Theresa fingered the pen, and then began to write. When she was finished she passed the paper back to Joanna, who read: *I met him through a friend of mine. We were bowling, and he showed up. He was her brother's friend.*

Joanna held her breath. She regarded the note as a major breakthrough. Why hadn't she thought of having Theresa write before? She wanted to jump up and clap to acknowledge the forward movement. Afraid her exuberance might stop any further revelations, she contained her glee and said, "Was it love at first sight?"

Theresa took the paper back and wrote, *No.*

"Do you love Eugene?"

I don't know. Maybe.

"You've been here for three weeks. Marlene must miss you very much. I know you miss her."

Theresa put the pen down, which let Joanna know that Marlene was not someone Theresa wanted to discuss.

Not to be deterred, Joanna tried again. "If you could change one thing about your life, what would that be?"

Theresa picked up the pen, hesitated, and then began to write. *I wouldn't have married Eugene if I knew we were going to live with his parents so long. It's been BLOODY HELL!* Theresa underlined the last two words several times before writing, *And now she's after my daughter.* She drew a devil beside the word HELL then pushed the paper to Joanna.

"Now, we're getting somewhere."

Theresa looked surprised.

"I have an idea, but before I say anything about it, I will need to work out the details."

Theresa pulled the paper back, wrote, and once more handed the sheet back to Joanna. *I don't know if he loves them more than he loves me. If he had to choose, would he choose me? If he wouldn't, what's the point of trying anything?*

"We'll see." Joanna could barely contain her excitement at the prospect of what she had in mind.

THIRTY-FIVE

THOUGH ELATED BY her session with Theresa, Joanna saw no record of any forward progress in the nurses' notes. Though the young mother hadn't spoken yet, Joanna expected some change in her on the ward. People always said the pen was mightier than the sword. Hadn't the last session opened up anything?

From her vantage point in the nurse's station, Joanna observed Theresa in the patient lounge cuddling a baby doll. The two patients seated nearby were carrying on their conversation as if her behaviour was appropriate. She appeared to be holding the doll too tightly. Joanna couldn't tell whether Theresa was trying to hurt the baby, or squeezing the pretend infant out of fear that someone would come along and yank it out of her arms. She looked scared. Had she shared too much with her therapist and now regretted it?

Joanna couldn't wait to propose her new strategy at rounds. She hoped to present it in such a way that Myron couldn't possibly say no.

As for Rose, Joanna didn't expect much. Her elderly patient was sliding downhill. The nurses charted that Rose was now mumbling more to herself and had doubled the time she spent pacing the corridor. Had the family meeting opened up old wounds? But what if the family intervention hadn't been a failure? What if Rose had to go backward before she could move forward again? Joanna sighed heavily. Or maybe the situation was such that no matter what she tried, nothing would change as long as Rose continued to receive ECT. That alone could account for the elderly patient's backward steps.

It was at times like this that Joanna wished she'd been content to stay in general practice. At least there she could measure a patient's progress with less ambiguity.

The ward meeting began with Roberta informing the others about the new admissions. She read from the charts, "Mrs. Tantini showed up in emerg last night, unable to move her lower body. She rambled on and on about her husband coaching young female swimmers."

"What some women won't do to get attention," said a young male nurse. A couple of the female staff shot him a dirty look.

Myron said, "What we have here folks is hysterical paralysis."

"Jealousy?" asked Sam.

"In full spades," said Myron. "The kind our mothers warned us about."

Joanna caught Sam's eye, and they smiled at one another. Having been the last staff member to enter the room, she was now sitting with the nurses opposite the shrinks. Sam looked particularly appealing in a fitted white shirt, open at the collar and tucked into his jeans.

Myron said, "Jerome, how about you handle this one?" Roberta recorded the assignment.

Bryce cleared his throat. "Speaking of mothers, how's our young mother doing?"

"The poor thing," said Roberta in an uncharacteristically soft tone. "She walks around all day clutching a doll. The woman's almost catatonic."

Joanna was taken aback by Roberta's description. She didn't want Theresa labelled as some kind of psychotic, at least not until all avenues were exhausted. A patient that was catatonic was sure to get ECT.

As if Myron had heard her thoughts, he said to Joanna. "I know you're not in favour of hydro, but now there appears to be no other choice."

"I don't think we've tried everything yet." She could feel her heart racing as she prepared to present her idea.

Bryce cleared his throat again. "Myron is right. There's been enough time to—"

"This woman has a baby she can't hold in her arms," interrupted Joanna. "It's not surprising that she's playing with a doll. What if…what if we gave her some time to practice here on the ward, with her baby?" Her new plan was out there, hanging in the air by an invisible string.

"Bring a baby on the ward?" asked Myron, his voice rising.

"Her baby?" questioned Roberta in her usual clipped way, as if Joanna had said something stupid. "Tell me I'm dreaming. Do you know how much supervision that would require? We have a lot of deranged souls on this unit, in case you didn't notice."

Bothered by Roberta's rude tone, Joanna ignored her and directed her response to the senior shrinks—Bryce, Myron and Bernie. "Theresa desperately needs some time alone with Marlene, which every young mother needs. It would give us the opportunity to see what kind of mother she really is without the interference of her in-laws and her husband."

"It's impossible," complained Roberta, her brows knitted in a frown. "We're not a nursery."

Joanna looked at Bryce. "You said yourself that she wasn't the only one who was crazy. Eugene exhibited some strange behaviour when he tried to shock Theresa at home and yet he's not on 2B. She is. In a way, her escape from reality gave her a haven from her interfering mother-in-law, but what's missing is her baby."

Sam piped in. "I think Joanna's showing some creativity. Maybe we can afford to loosen up the rules a little. We can handle a lot of fruitcakes. Surely we can handle a little baby."

Joanna shot him a grateful look.

Roberta said to Myron, "You know how short-staffed we are."

"You're right," said Myron, nodding. "Let's not forget we have some seriously acting-out patients on this ward. Who knows what the presence of a baby could instigate. It could be risky. The nursing staff can hardly cope as it is."

Joanna could feel her support waning. "I can appreciate that it won't easy, but what about on the weekend? It's quieter then, with some of the patients going home."

"It may be," said Roberta, "but I only have two nurses on then."

"I can come in a few times and you can page me if things get rough."

"I'm on call then, too," said Jerome. "I can help out in a pinch."

Pleased with Jerome's unexpected offer, Joanna mouthed a thank you in his direction.

"Wait a second," said Bernie, who had been quiet up until

then. "You're all assuming she's innocent of any abuse. Can she be trusted? This is a woman who was admitted because her family said she tried to kill her baby."

"Since they haven't pressed charges," said Joanna, "seeing her with her child could help us determine whether there was any fabrication on their part. So far, we haven't seen this young mother with her baby alone. This would be an excellent way to assess whether she's capable of taking on that responsibility.

"It's too big a gamble," said Myron.

Joanna pursed her lips. "How about a video camera? Video surveillance along with the staff should ease any concerns."

Bryce's eyebrows went up. He folded his arms and said, "That could work. What do you think, Myron?"

"I don't know. I have my doubts, but that would definitely help."

"What if there's a problem?" asked Roberta. "God forbid any of my staff call in sick."

"I said, I'd—" said Joanna, but before she could finish, Myron intervened.

"If there's a problem, we'll stop immediately. If there's any hint of any kind of disturbance, any kind," he emphasized, "this experiment will be over. Agreed?"

"Yes. Of course." Although Myron had tried to pierce her balloon, he hadn't succeeded. Still, she knew what she'd suggested was a long shot—one that could miss its mark.

THIRTY-SIX

MYRON HAD BEEN on edge since the last ward meeting two days before. Standing in the cafeteria line-up with Sam, he didn't mince words. "The shiksa's married, you know."

"You're wasting your lecture on me," said Sam, pouring himself some coffee from the carafe. "There's nothing happening."

Myron looked him in the eye. "Keep it that way."

"Since when did you become my mother? I thought the whole idea of Jews not coupling with gentiles was passé. You've got your feet in the wrong decade."

"In my circles, it still counts. Besides, she's not that stable." Myron paid for his coffee and led the way to a table. Sitting down, he said, "I feel sorry for her husband."

"Why do you say that?" said Sam, taking the chair beside Myron.

"She's opinionated and willful."

"I thought those were good qualities for a doctor."

"Listen, you have a brilliant future ahead of you. Don't tamper with it by chasing some skirt that will take you nowhere but down."

"Is it because she's a woman? Is that what's bothering you? I've never known you to give much credit to female doctors."

"You know me better than that."

"I know. That's why I'm saying it."

Myron leaned forward. "Be careful. That's all I'm saying. Don't wade into a swamp you can't get out of."

Later that day, Myron did wonder if he held a bias against women entering the profession. He still thought they were too emotional to handle the work, and their seductiveness could be a problem in transference—notably someone like Joanna. Her long legs and great smile hadn't escaped his notice.

It troubled him that every time he saw her, he found her more and more beautiful. The rose sweater she wore the other day accentuated her fair complexion and soft-hazel eyes. Her breasts were small but enticing and in proportion to the rest of her slender body. Even though he'd cautioned Sam against getting too close to her, he felt the pull himself. He recognized some of that had to do with Diane being so frigid. Of course, these were excuses that men often made for their illicit affairs, but he couldn't help wondering if Joanna was as aggressive in bed as she was with him in her arguments about her patients. He pushed those thoughts away. That kind of thinking compromised his objectivity and nothing was more important than that if he wanted to continue to climb the hospital ladder.

THIRTY-SEVEN

PREPARATIONS FOR MARLENE to join her mother on 2B were in full swing. Joanna had some resistance from Mrs. Boychuk, who initially balked at the plans and did some fear mongering of her own but in the end gave in and agreed to help Eugene bring in the necessary clothing, receiving blankets, and a change pad for the baby. The grandmother wasn't happy about the disposable diapers that would be used, underlining that all they did was give babies unnecessary rashes, but as with the other demands, she relented and understood the practicality of the decision.

After reviewing the weekend plans with Theresa, Joanna entered the nurses' station, where Annette had just hung up the phone. "Maternity is sending a crib down."

"Great," said Joanna. "I'll also need baby powder, zinc ointment, and some wash cloths. Eugene is supposed to bring those from home, but I want backup just in case something is forgotten."

With Annette working on the baby supplies, Joanna contacted the video technician who set up a camera in Theresa's room and a corresponding monitor in the nurses' station. With the hard objects in place, there was nothing left to do except wait for the baby to arrive. Joanna hoped it would all go according to plan—meaning that Mrs. Boychuk would continue to cooperate.

She re-examined Theresa's record for anything that could

THE RUBBER FENCE

cause a problem until the squeaky wheels of a gurney got her attention. It was Carmen pushing an empty one toward the nurses' hub.

Annette looked up from her work. "I begged Axel to oil those wheels. That man will be the death of me yet."

"I bet if you tried to do it yourself," said Roberta, who had arrived just behind Carmen, "he'd be up here faster than you know what."

"You know it. He's a real union man," said Annette, smiling.

"Roberta," said Carmen, "I can't find Rose."

"She's probably hiding in the men's room again."

"I wouldn't be surprised," said Joanna, thinking the old woman was doing what she could to avoid being strapped down once again.

Roberta said, "If I find her, I'll personally recommend a higher dose."

Joanna's forehead creased. "Not while she's my patient."

"Were you born without a sense of humor," said Roberta, "or does it just look that way?" She walked off in a huff, leaving Joanna startled for a moment.

"Don't let her bug you," said Carmen.

"I could lighten up."

"She's one unhappy lady."

"How come?"

"Her husband left her for a man about five years ago, and her son's a drug addict. She has trouble herself with alcohol and God knows what else, always has. I probably shouldn't be telling you this, but she was threatened with suspension years back, but somehow she pulled herself together. Got to give her credit for that. And now her mother is dying. Some people walk through life with black clouds hanging over their heads. I think she's one of them."

"That's awful," said Joanna. "Thanks for letting me know. It explains a lot. Still, I hate being on the wrong side of her."

"Don't we all."

Hearing about Roberta's challenges did little to soften Joanna's feelings about the head nurse. She interpreted Carmen's divulgence as a warning. Roberta was not to be trusted.

Joanna had never been in Myron's office before. It had an airy feel with its tall ceiling and large window overlooking the front lawn of the hospital, but its lack of personal decoration suggested a very private man. One characteristic did stand out though: he was meticulous. Books on his shelves were lined up like soldiers in a parade, each one the same distance from the shelf's edge. Various documents were stacked neatly on his desk. There was, however, a half-eaten sandwich and a cup of coffee that'd been pushed to the side of the papers he was working on.

She sat opposite him in a leather club chair and took a deep breath. "Rose is hiding again. It's obvious she doesn't want ECT. I feel I make some progress, and then it's all wiped out with these treatments."

"Joanna, if we don't give it to her, she'll stay depressed and won't eat. She could die."

She hadn't thought of that, but she had her doubts that would happen. "She's never attempted suicide and has never talked about it."

"There is a lot she doesn't talk about. Killing herself could be one of those things. You want that on your conscience?"

THE RUBBER FENCE

Joanna sighed. "I don't think that's a consideration yet." She hesitated, then said, "I checked her file. She's never consented to ECT."

"She is unable to make that decision. This is a mentally ill woman. It's your duty as a physician to treat the illness."

"So we play God?"

"Isn't that what you're doing? You're wanting to stop the only thing that can save her. Would you rather she suffer than get the life-saving treatment she needs?"

"Of course I don't want her to suffer."

"There's your answer. You're taking this much too personally." He paused, then said, "I know about your grandmother."

"What?" Joanna reeled. *What does he know?*

He sat back, all the while playing with his pen. "Your undergraduate paper on an elderly woman. You submitted it with your application for further studies."

"How did you know it was my grandmother?"

"It couldn't have been anyone else. You wrote it with such heart that, well, it was obvious."

How could she have been so stupid? She had included that assignment as evidence of her compassion and her desire to find out more about the human mind. But that was at the university. How could Myron have had access? Maybe because he was her supervisor they had opened up her file to him. She looked at Myron, who was studying her reaction.

She felt trapped. "My grandmother...she was involuntarily given shock treatment. It ruined her life. And it affected mine. She lived with us, raised me in my early years. When she changed, I was a teenager by that time—it was too much. She may as well have been a stranger. We'd visit her, and she'd sit there, rigid. Didn't know us, or if she did, she was no longer interested. It was hard to tell what was going on with her. She no longer knew me..." Close to tears, Joanna didn't finish her statement. The wound opened every time she talked about her grandmother.

Myron said gently, "How long ago was that?"

"Twenty-three years ago."

"It was different then. We didn't have the drugs back then to keep the patients from hurting themselves during the procedure."

Yeah, right. As if it's much better today. Joanna avoided his scrutiny by looking out the window. Visitors were coming up the front sidewalk to see their loved ones, who they hoped were getting good care.

She exhaled heavily. "I can't see how the treatments are helping."

"You have to give it time."

"She doesn't want them. I need to show her that her voice is important. If I don't have her confidence, I can't work with her."

"You knew the conditions when you took the case." He was abrupt but then adopted a kinder tone. "Perhaps you should talk to someone, a therapist, you know, about your grandmother."

For a moment, she didn't know how to read him. Was he saying this to disarm her?

"A word of advice, Joanna. You're going to have to distance yourself if you want to survive in this profession." Myron's words were like an echo in her ears. Sam had said more or less the same thing.

"Maybe it's easy for you, but I don't have a shut-off valve."

"Too bad," he said. "You'd better figure out how to get one."

Distressed, Joanna stood up. "I'll...I'll think about it," was all she managed to say.

"I suggest you do more than that. This kind of attitude could affect your whole career."

She nodded. "What about Rose, then?" She knew she was acting like a dog with a slipper. She couldn't let go no matter how hard Myron tugged.

He put his pen on the desk and leaned back in his chair. "Joanna, don't think that I haven't weighed everything you've told me. I've given serious thought to your dilemma, and what I've decided to do for the time being is to take you off the case. It will be better if I took over Rose."

"But I can handle it."

"It'll be less disruptive for Rose," said Myron, coldly. "You're not happy with the way things are going, and patients can read that kind of ambivalence. Besides, she knows me. You still have Theresa—a very demanding case. More than enough for now. You need to learn to think more like a psychiatrist and less like a granddaughter."

Her chest ached. She left feeling as though she'd been punched. She had let him get to her, and what was worse, he knew it. She was also infuriated with herself for having written that paper. Had she thought that no one would make the connection? Her grandmother's depression had happened so long ago, but Joanna's hurt over it was as strong as if it had happened yesterday.

After her grandmother had discovered that her youngest son had been hit and killed by a truck while crossing the road, she sunk into a deep depression—one that led to shock treatments, the primitive kind. Administered more than a dozen times, she received enough jolts to wipe out a few lifetimes.

Now, Rose was travelling down the same path. Whatever

fire she still had was about to be extinguished for good.

THIRTY-EIGHT

THE WEEKEND FOR the baby visit was shaping up to be a quiet one on the ward with more patients out on family visits than expected. For that, Joanna was grateful. The only stumbling block now was her confidence. After losing Rose as a patient, it was hard to present a brave front.

On Friday night, Joanna checked the charts and double-checked them. Everything seemed to be in order. Eugene and a strained Mrs. Boychuk arrived at the nurses' station with Marlene, dressed in a pink nightgown and a white crocheted sweater and bonnet.

"Right on time," Joanna said.

"I hope this is everything she needs," said Eugene, holding what looked like a well-stocked diaper bag.

Mrs. Boychuk gripped Marlene like she was a football destined for a touchdown, and no one was going to pry her loose. The baby peered around like she understood that something momentous was about to take place.

Joanna asked Mrs. Boychuk, "Do you mind waiting over there while we get her settled?" She pointed to the patient lounge where a patient was counting dust in the air. Mrs. Boychuk looked as though she did mind and shot Eugene a bitter look. Eugene took the baby from his mother, and Joanna could tell by the way he fumbled that he rarely held his child.

When Joanna and Eugene walked into Theresa's room with

the baby, they found the young mother watching news about a robbery somewhere. Theresa looked momentarily startled, as if she had been expecting someone else.

Marlene's legs kicked at the sight of her mother, at least that's what Joanna imagined. She said to Eugene, "You can give her the baby now."

Theresa took Marlene and cradled her in her arms. Her face lit up as she took in her daughter's tiny hands and mouth. For a moment, the mother and child seemed as normal as any.

Shuffling from one foot to the other, Eugene gave the impression he was unsure about this experiment. Joanna wondered what tales his mother had told him on the way to the hospital. He said to Theresa, "Do you think you'll be able to manage?"

Trembling, Theresa tried to give Marlene back to her husband, but Joanna shook her head at Eugene. She placed a reassuring hand on her patient's shoulder. "It's hard at first, but you can do it. I know you can. We'll let you spend some time with her alone. You have the whole weekend, and the staff will be here to back you up. If there's anything you need, all you have to do is ask, okay?"

Theresa's forehead furrowed, but she gave Joanna a half smile. Before Eugene could do anything more to discourage his wife, Joanna ushered him out the door.

That evening, Joanna and the night nurse, Beverley Wong, a petite woman in her twenties, manned the station. There was another nurse on the floor tending to a patient down the hall who was moaning about stomach cramps. An orderly and a few aides rounded out the rest of the skeleton staff.

Beverley stared at the monitor and shook her head. "Don't you think the baby should be in the crib?"

THE RUBBER FENCE

Joanna checked the monitor. Theresa was sleeping soundly in bed with her baby. "No, it's fine. It's good for both of them."

"What if she rolls over on her?"

"That's a risk I'm prepared to take. That kind of accident is such a rarity that there's no need to worry." Though Joanna tried to reassure Beverley, underneath, she was just as anxious.

The young nurse said, "It's going to be hard for the baby. She'll get used to sleeping with her mother."

"Not in two nights. She's not going to form a habit in two nights."

"Well, what if when Theresa gets home and wants to sleep with her husband, what's she going to do then? The baby will scream, and no one will get a good night's rest."

Exasperated, Joanna said, " Look, they'll deal with it then. Our job is to help this young mother get close to her baby again. Do you have any problem with that?"

That settled the argument. "Hmm," was all Beverley said.

The nurse's questioning gave Joanna pause. Did she appear that weak? Beverley had showed no qualms about criticizing her actions. It wasn't that long ago that a doctor's word was respected without question, not that that was a good thing.

Checking the monitor again, Joanna found the image calming. A few hours had gone by, and Theresa and her baby were still asleep. Yawning, Joanna put her book in her bag and asked Beverley to call her at home if there was any change.

When Joanna opened the apartment door, she was surprised to find the place in darkness except for the stove light in the kitchen. She then remembered that Michael had mentioned he'd be home late as he had some meeting. The stove clock read past eleven. He should've been finished by now. She had hoped to talk to him, to share her excitement about the baby on the ward, but it had been hard to stay awake even on her drive home. She went to sleep smelling his scent on his pillow and wondering where he could be at this hour of night.

THIRTY-NINE

THE YELLOW MORNING light streaming through the bedroom window woke Joanna and she felt for Michael beside her. He wasn't there. She glanced at the radio clock. Six a.m. Unsettled, she dragged herself out of bed, put on her terry cloth robe and moccasins, and went into the kitchen.

The coffee was already on and Michael was making toast.

She poured herself some apple juice. "I didn't hear you come in last night."

"I didn't want to disturb you, so I slept on the couch."

Taken aback, she stared at him. "You never do that."

He took the toast out of the toaster and began to butter it.

"You wouldn't have disturbed me." She didn't like the idea of him sleeping in the living room. Once that started, there was often no turning back. Her aunt and uncle had separate bedrooms, a habit that had no doubt started by one of them snoring or during some argument that got out of hand. "I didn't know what to think. You could have called and left a message."

"I was going to call, but we were into this heavy-duty free for all on Fidel Castro and Cuba, and you know me, a few beers and I'm *el fasto* to the wind." He smeared some extra jam onto his toast.

She watched the red strawberry jam spread as if in a trance. "Where did you go?"

"Salisbury's."

She knitted her brow. "I thought they closed early."

He seemed intent on eating his breakfast and didn't say anything. Was he lying to her? She couldn't tell.

"Was Cindy Bell there?"

"What is this, the third degree?"

"Well, was she?"

"Yeah." He studied her now. Was he expecting a big reaction?

She noticed his luggage by the door. "You going somewhere?"

"Conference in Gimli."

"What? I thought you were passing on this one."

He ignored her and took his dishes to the sink.

She placed her empty glass by his dishes. "It's Saturday morning. Hasn't the conference already started?"

Barely looking at her, he said. "I've heard the main speaker before. They have the workshops in the afternoon. It goes to Monday, and then I thought since I'm already there and there are no classes on Tuesday, I'd take an extra day, do some fishing, and come home late that night."

Her body was on high alert. A feeling of dread swept over her. "An extra day? Fishing? Since when do you fish?"

"You know Barry?"

She rummaged her brain but couldn't remember Barry.

"He's in the department. He invited me to go fishing with him, so I thought I'd take the opportunity."

He was slowly giving her pieces for a puzzle, but none of them fit. "Were you just going to leave? Not say good-bye or anything?" He continued to clean up. She whined to her own annoyance. "Can't we at least have breakfast together?"

He looked at her accusingly. "When was the last time we did

THE RUBBER FENCE

that?"

"I know. That's why I was hoping we could have some time this morning, give us a chance to talk."

"About what? Your work?"

"Michael, don't do this."

"Do what? I'm tired of competing with your goddamn patients. I'm tired of waiting for the doctor to show up."

"Great. I get dumped on at the hospital. I come home, and you're not here. I don't know where the hell you've been and now you're yelling at me about my work!"

"Somebody has to." Grabbing his khaki sports jacket from the chair, he headed for the back door.

"Michael, don't walk away like that. You always walk away."

"You don't own me. Nobody owns me." He slammed the door on his way out, leaving Joanna dazed. She sat down and the tears trickled down her cheeks like a brook that had been dammed up for too long. He hadn't even kissed her goodbye.

FORTY

SO FAR, THERE had been no cries for help from the ward even though she was on call. Still, she was anxious to find out how Theresa was doing and was tempted to leave for the hospital at once. Instead, Joanna decided to tackle the rising panic in her chest—some to do with Theresa, some with Michael—by cleaning out her closet. They had moved into the apartment just before she returned to her studies, and she hadn't had a chance to organize it properly. Winter clothes were mixed in with summer things, pants with skirts, shirts with sweaters, it was a wonder she was able to find what she wanted even when she had time. She started by emptying the lower rod and throwing her clothes onto the bed. As soon as she'd done it, she felt a knot in her stomach. Was this how she was going to deal with Michael's cold treatment?

She sat down on their bed and looked out the window at the boulevard. The trees were rapidly losing their colour; leaves had already fallen on the ground. Normally, she loved this time of year—a time to take stock before the winter winds came roaring into the city. But with her marriage in turmoil, it felt like a blizzard had already arrived.

From the kitchen, she could hear the radio she'd left on playing Peter, Paul and Mary's "Leaving on a Jet Plane". She sang along as she began to separate the pants from the skirts. As she mouthed the words, they caught in her throat and the tears started to flow, rocketing down her cheeks.

Staring at her reflection in the dresser mirror, she told herself to stop crying or she'd end up like one of her patients. Was this where it started, with the feeling that nothing they did made a difference? That the love they wanted was out of reach? Bawling was one thing, but when it went on for days and days, and then went underground, well, that was the definition of depression. Like what those women profiled in the book *Women and Madness* went through. Some seed of loss was planted and grew until nothing mattered anymore. They became dead inside.

Why wasn't she enough? Why did Michael have to look elsewhere? He was as "bold as brass," wasn't that the expression? Look at how he'd been at Bryce's party. He didn't care where she was or who she talked to.

Maybe if she just up and left, he'd have more respect for her. It was too bad that they hadn't had children. With children, there was some kind of glue. But then again, why put children through this kind of mess? She whispered to the trees outside her window, "Dear God, please help me."

Joanna showed up on the ward in the early afternoon. She kept her coat on as if she might need some kind of shield. All the way to the hospital, her mind had been on Michael and Cindy Bell. She imagined them having a wonderful time in bed. She couldn't go on like this. Something was going to crack, and she hoped it wouldn't be her.

Entering Theresa's room, Joanna found Carmen and a changed young mother. Marlene was restless and wailing, but Theresa responded like any mother would—walking her baby while cooing to her at the same time. Even so, it seemed that whatever was going on with Marlene wasn't going to be resolved that easily.

Carmen said to Joanna quietly, "Theresa's been good."

Joanna went over to the young mother, who was rocking Marlene by the window. "If you want a break, Carmen can take over. It's okay. Babies can wear out the best mothers."

Theresa hesitated, looking from Joanna to Carmen and back again.

"Sometimes it's hard to tell what's bugging them and harder to know what to do about it. It could be gas or an earache or…God knows what." Joanna had delivered enough infants and supported enough mothers through their trials to know that much. "All mothers go through this some of the time, wondering how to help their little one."

Carmen laughed. "Some? You mean all of the time." She said to Theresa, "Don't be afraid. You don't have to hold her so tightly. She won't fall."

Theresa relaxed her grip as Carmen suggested. Marlene's cries slowed and became quieter, more like birds calling for dinner rather than squawking about an oncoming attacker.

"She's got your eyes," said Joanna.

With Marlene's cries reduced to a whimper, Theresa sat down on a chair and positioned her right nipple between her infant's lips. Carmen folded a receiving blanket and placed it under Theresa's left arm for support, before leaving with Joanna.

Afterward, Carmen said to Joanna, "Roberta was being a cow this morning. When Marlene started hollering, she lost it. She said to me, 'Would you go shut that damn kid up? If I wanted to work with kids, I would have applied for the children's unit.' Thank God she didn't." Carmen made a face.

THE RUBBER FENCE

"I'm glad you're here," said Joanna. "I can't tell you how thrilled I am to see Theresa handling her baby so well." She then reviewed her patient's file, where she found nothing out of the ordinary.

With her patient managing on the ward, Joanna went home. There, she made some tea and called Sam to share her excitement. "You should've seen her. She was just like the Madonna in a Raphael painting."

"Isn't that stretching things a bit?" She could almost hear his smile.

"Ha. If she can keep this up…"

"Myron will have to stop riding you."

"Wouldn't that be nice?"

"Are you going to the poetry reading tomorrow night?"

"What poetry reading?"

"R.D. Laing's works," said Sam. "There might be some by Sylvia Plath as well."

"I didn't know about it, but it sounds interesting. I'd ask Michael to go but he's out of town. He's working out his demons. He thinks I'm one of them." She snorted and then wondered why she'd shared her husband's absence in that way. It sounded so offhand, so uncaring.

Sam's voice grew softer. "Last time I looked, I didn't see any horns on you. Why don't you come with me? I could pick you up at seven?"

"I don't know…" She hesitated. It would be nice. It wasn't exactly a date; it had to do with work. R. D. Laing was a Scottish psychiatrist who had voluntarily spent time as a patient in an asylum in order to study the mentally ill. Because of that and the way he presented his material—sometimes breaking down during his lectures—many shrinks worldwide viewed him as insane and ignored his findings. But there were many who regarded him as a guru, a genius—someone who had penetrated the muddled minds of psychotic patients and then made sense of it through his poetry and other writings.

"Joanna, are you still there?"

"Sorry. I was thinking. That would be nice."

She hung up, uncertain of whether she should've agreed to go, but with Michael leaving the way he had, she was still angry. Why should she stay home and brood over what her husband was doing?

Michael was right about one thing though. She hadn't made time for him, and she did talk about her work too much. But how could she not? If he saw what she witnessed, would he act any differently?

Uncomfortable with her decision to go with Sam, she decided to call Dennis to see if he'd go too, but all she got was his answering machine.

"You've reached the Williams residence. Please wait for the beep and leave your name and number and I'll get back to you as soon as I can."

She wondered if there was more than one Williams in the household. "Dennis, it's Joanna. Sam and I are going to Granada's tomorrow night. I would love for you to meet us there. Quarter to eight. Don't be late or I'll think you're an ingrate. Just kidding. But please come. Would love to see you. Bye."

She was glad she'd thought of asking Dennis as he hadn't been looking good this past week. Maybe he could use an evening to take his mind off of his troubles, too. And he'd be a good support for her if things didn't improve with Michael. Of the three residents, he seemed the most sensitive and the least threatening. Even if Dennis didn't come, at least she had called.

Her date with Sam didn't seem real now that a third party had been involved.

◇◇◇

On Sunday, she got to the hospital early. While she was reviewing the young mother's chart, Carmen came into the nurses' station with the biggest grin. "This'll knock your socks off. I caught Theresa mouthing the words to *Goodnight Moon*. She was reading to Marlene."

"She spoke? You heard her?"

"Yep. Goodnight moon, goodnight brush…"

Joanna beamed at the monitor beside her. On the screen, she could see Theresa nursing Marlene. It should've been a joyous moment but an uneasy feeling swept over Joanna. "The Boychuks are picking the baby up this evening."

"Don't worry. Roberta and I are both on again, and Beverley comes in a little later to spell us off."

"I could stay."

"Are you crazy, girl? If you hang around too much, you're going to look like them."

Joanna smiled. "We wouldn't want that. Annette's already complaining that she's having a tough time identifying who's staff and who's not. She's suggesting we start wearing our uniforms again."

"She was just being sarcastic about the lighting on the ward. The way she battles it out with Axel…who knows? Those two might get married some day."

"Her and Axel?"

"We tease Annette," said Carmen. "We tell her he's a phantom. He comes in and out of here when no one's around.

Does his little thing and whoosh, the man disappears. That's what gets Annette's goat these days."

"Well, if you're sure you can manage, I'll see you tomorrow. You're a doll to do this."

"Get out of here," said Carmen with a wide smile.

"I'll pop into Theresa's room before I leave."

Joanna found the young mother changing her baby's diaper. "You're becoming an expert at that."

"Thanks. She ate well, too."

Stunned to hear Theresa's low voice, Joanna could barely contain the joy that swelled up inside her. "What did you say?"

Theresa grinned. "I said she ate well. My baby.."

"Yes, she is! She's yours, all right." Joanna gave her a big hug.

Theresa stiffened up, seemingly embarrassed by Joanna's display of affection.

"Sorry. I'm just happy for you."

"It's okay." Theresa picked up Marlene from the change table. The baby's tiny fist curled up in her mother's palm.

Joanna said gently, "Now tonight, when Eugene comes to get Marlene…" She paused as she saw Theresa's shoulders arch. "You're going to be fine. Try not to worry. It won't be long before you're back home."

The young mother nodded, looking as if she wanted to believe.

FORTY-ONE

IT TOOK HER awhile to figure out what to wear for the poetry reading. As Joanna went through one outfit after the other, she thought about Michael. There had been no word from him yet, and she knew that if she didn't go out, she'd end up sitting at home stewing, waiting for the phone to ring. She was tempted to call him, but it might look like she was checking up on him, and she didn't want to give that impression. Not after he had accused her of giving him the third degree. And what if she did call and found out something that she'd rather not know. What then?

She remembered another time when he'd gone away. She had phoned his hotel room, and he hadn't picked up. She learned later that he'd had a few people in his room for drinks, including some women, and he had just let it ring. What must they have thought? That was the thing that embarrassed her—what other people thought. She was smart enough to know that that was what she'd brought into the marriage—a need to have everything look right. Just like her mother.

◇◇◇

Considered one of the hot spots for entertainment, the Granada Club was in the warehouse district, between Adelaide and Princess Streets. Sam and Joanna had driven over on his Harley, a ride that had given her a sense of freedom she hadn't had for awhile. It felt strange putting her arms around his waist and breathing in his musk scent at such close range. Though that's all it was, it felt illicit. With Michael away and acting aloof, she felt vulnerable, especially with a man like Sam, who was surprisingly unattached. But then again, maybe he was saving himself a lot of heartache.

While Sam secured his motorcycle, Joanna combed her hair with her fingers, unbuttoned the top button of her white, long-sleeved, ruffled shirt, and patted down her jeans that had ridden up above her short suede boots. Straightening up, she could see in Sam's eyes that he approved.

They sat away from the crowd of mostly young medical professionals at a round table for two in the dimly-lit room. She pulled up a third chair in case Dennis showed up late. On the stage was a pretty woman with granny glasses reading a number of R.D. Laing's poems. She read for about ten minutes and concluded with a quote from *Knots*. *"They are playing a game. They are playing at not playing a game. If I show them I see they are, I shall break the rules and they will punish me. I must play their game, of not seeing I see the game."*

Joanna had read the psychiatrist's works before, but now they touched a personal chord.

The woman took a stilted bow, and the audience clapped with enthusiasm. After the applause, the host, a tall skinny man in black stovepipe pants and a black T-shirt, helped the presenter off the stage. "That concludes our readings from R.D. Laing's work. And now, it's open mike time."

Sam and Joanna listened to a couple of men who got up and read from their own works. There was nothing remarkable, but their courage and creative attempts were appreciated by the crowd. They were followed by the host's announcements of other

THE RUBBER FENCE

shows to come, and then he said, "This week, we have a new face, a new voice—Gabriella Oslow." A gangly female with long, unkempt blonde hair jumped onto the stage wearing a flowing gauze skirt over long red underwear and army boots.

"Interesting group of people here," said Sam. "Have we left the ward yet?"

Joanna laughed. The wine was starting to do its trick, and she'd almost forgotten that Michael wasn't at home waiting for her.

Gabriella cleared her throat several times and adjusted the mike. "Here goes. I've tentatively called this, 'Crazy Nights'."

Sam whispered in Joanna's ear. "I told you. Why don't we get out of here? I know a better place."

"What if Dennis shows up, and we're not here?"

"It's been over an hour already. I doubt he's coming."

"I guess you're right." Joanna wasn't sure if she was relieved or disappointed. And where did Sam have in mind?

Out of politeness, they waited until Gabriella was finished before making a move for the door. The young poet's words, like Laing's, resonated: "It's crazy now / I lie awake / his body's near / it used to soothe / and be enough to put at rest / a mind too swift / a mind at work. Making love was all it took / ecstatic bliss and wails at night / his flesh on mine / our limbs entwined. The desire was there / the love was strong / yet the body aches for stillness now."

The rest of the poem blurred in her mind as she struggled with the thoughts that emerged. Where was Michael now? Was he alone? Was he being faithful? It was a given he was fooling around.

Sam nudged her to leave. As they filed past the tables and out the door, Joanna glanced back at Gabriella. Was the universe trying to tell her something through this strange woman? And was she that strange, or just another sister coping with a universal problem?

FORTY-TWO

THERESA WAS SETTLED in an armchair with her baby sleeping nestled in her arms when, unexpectedly, Carmen popped in. "I have to leave early tonight. My little girl is sick, and I can't find anyone to be with her. I think Eugene should be here soon. I'll see you tomorrow." Carmen gave a reassuring smile and waved before disappearing out the door.

Theresa hadn't expected to be alone when Eugene came. Sure, there were other nurses around, but no one she trusted like Carmen. The prospect of having to send Marlene home to a woman she hated was uppermost in her mind. She reminded herself of what Joanna had suggested: Try not to worry. *Easier said than done,* thought Theresa.

By the time the Boychuks reached Theresa's room, Marlene had awakened and Theresa was in the middle of another diaper change. She had put her anguish aside and was enjoying her daughter, who was kicking her chubby legs and gurgling her pleasure out loud.

Upon entering, Mrs. Boychuk took one look at Marlene's red bottom and said with a voice laced with venom, "You better put something on that!"

Ignoring his mother, Eugene gave Theresa a peck on the cheek and showed no concern that his mother had sliced the air with her sharp tongue. Theresa couldn't even respond to her husband's warmth because she was still dealing with her in-law's order.

Eugene said, "How's it going?"

Theresa gave him a sour look and then spread zinc ointment on her baby's bottom. She finished the change, fastening the diaper expertly without any problem.

"Eugene, pack the diaper bag," said Mrs. Boychuk, icily. "As usual, we have to do everything ourselves."

Theresa again tried to overlook her mother-in-law's snide remark and opened her robe, exposing her right breast.

"There's no time for that," said Mrs. Boychuk, not bothering to hide the disgust in her voice. "We're in a fifteen minute parking zone."

"We didn't want to walk far with the baby," Eugene added.

Theresa disregarded the two of them, wishing she had a magic wand to make them vanish. Her movements became deliberate. She slowly sat down and guided Marlene's mouth to her nipple.

Eugene packed the bag with one eye on Theresa and the other on his mother. In went the diaper cream, the undershirts, and the diapers that had been neatly stacked on a little tray table by the crib. Theresa felt the loss already, just from seeing Marlene's necessities disappear from the table.

Mrs. Boychuk stepped into the corridor and then quickly returned. "Okay, Theresa. That's enough. We have to go. We're going to get a ticket."

Theresa didn't budge. She continued to nurse as if she were alone with Marlene. Mrs. Boychuk raised her eyebrows at Eugene and then put out her arms as she walked toward her daughter-in-law and grandchild. The women exchanged looks like two boxers sizing each other up before a fight. And just when Mrs. Boychuk was about to grab Marlene, Theresa took her

THE RUBBER FENCE

baby off her nipple, stood up and pushed her mother-in-law to the side with her elbow.

"How dare you!" said Mrs. Boychuk. "You knew it was just for the weekend. Time's up, Missy."

Theresa glared at her mother-in-law. "No. How dare *you*!" Then she began to sing, "Daisy, Daisy, give me your answer do. I'm half crazy all for the love of you. It won't be a stylish marriage, I can't afford a carriage…"

"Do something, Eugene," said Mrs. Boychuk. "You remember what happened the last time she was singing."

Theresa saw Eugene's face turn to horror the same way it had the morning of her breakdown. She turned away and snuggled Marlene inside her robe as she kept on singing. "But we'll look sweet, upon the seat, of a bicycle built for two."

"Theresa, let me take the baby," said Eugene. "Please, honey. We have to go. I'm going to get a ticket."

Theresa's voice grew louder as she made her way to the door. "Daisy, Daisy, give me your answer do…"

The veins in Mrs. Boychuk's forehead stood out like trees in a forest.

Singing at the top of her lungs, Theresa walked out of the room with Marlene secure in her arms. An elderly patient standing outside her door joined in, her voice cracking as she sang.

Eugene, clutching the diaper bag, followed with his enraged mother close behind.

Theresa sat down in the lounge beside an old woman mumbling to herself and continued to sing. "It won't be a stylish marriage, I can't afford a carriage…"

Beverley rushed over with Roberta saying, "C'mon now. It's time to let go."

The head nurse tried to take the baby, but Theresa refused to give her up. "No! She's mine!" Marlene burst out screaming, as if someone had stabbed her with a needle.

"So you can talk when you want to," said Roberta, frowning. To the Boychuks, she said, "Would you please wait in her room?"

Eugene said to his mother, "You go ahead. I'll move the car." He gave Theresa a pleading look but all it did was annoy her. Why couldn't he for once be on her side? Caught up in her thoughts, she relaxed her arms. It was then that Roberta seized Marlene.

Theresa let out a piercing wail. What encouraged her to keep yelling were all the other voices that joined in. At least the patients understood what was happening.

Roberta called for help, and from down the corridor a man built like a fridge came running with a hospital aide. There were now four of them—three to restrain Theresa and one to hold the baby. Theresa kicked and bit as hard as she could when they tried to pull back her arms.

"I guess this is your initiation, Crosby," said Beverley. "I'm glad you're on my shift."

The orderly held Theresa firmly while Beverley jabbed a needle into Theresa's hip. She struggled a bit and then went limp. While Crosby and the aide pulled her back to her room, she saw Roberta pass an overwrought Marlene to Mrs. Boychuk.

"She's a hellfire, that's all I got to say," said Mrs. Boychuk. "I don't know why my son picked her."

Theresa overheard and wanted to tell her mother-in-law to go to hell, but she couldn't. Her body, her thoughts, and her will had slowed to a crawl. Everything began to blur. And then, it went black.

FORTY-THREE

SAM'S RENTED APARTMENT was in one of the classic three story buildings built in the 1940s on Morley Street in Riverview. The red walls in his low-lit living room were covered with watercolours of Chinese villages and farmlands. Some wood planks with bricks in between held all manner of books—the expected texts on psychiatry as well as classical literature, like Dostoyevsky's *The Brothers Karamazov*, and contemporary fiction like Heller's *Catch-22*. Joanna also noticed a book titled *The Kama Sutra*, which she recognized as an ancient text on love and sex. She'd always been curious about the practice of intimacy in other cultures, but this wasn't the time to whet her appetite in that department. Sitar music on the record player made her feel as if she were in a far-off country with customs she had yet to learn.

She stood at his living room window and looked at the full moon and wondered if Michael was looking at it at that moment too.

"How are you doing with that wine?" asked Sam as he came out of the kitchen. He walked up to her and ran a finger lightly down her left cheek, as if he were seeing her for the first time. She thought he was making a move to kiss her, but instead he took her wine glass and went to fill it from the half empty bottle on a side table. Joanna, feeling tipsy from two glasses of wine—one at the club and another one here—followed him to the corduroy floor cushions against the wall. They sat down next to one another.

She could feel herself falling for Sam, but her logical mind dismissed it as a reaction to feeling cut-off from Michael. While she gazed at the candles placed on various surfaces around the room, she reminded herself she was married, and given her somewhat inebriated state, she'd best be careful.

The brief warning in her mind was quickly forgotten when Sam's feet began to play with her toes. She fingered the rim of her wine glass and said, "Round and round we go, where we stop…"

The candle on the coffee table was burning low. Sam took a joint from his shirt pocket, toked up, and then passed it to Joanna.

This time she didn't hesitate and took a puff, inhaling the weed deeply. It was too much, and she coughed like she was going to choke.

Sam laughed. "Easy."

"I'm not a smoker. It's hard to get used to."

Sam took another drag and the smoke swirled up like a serpent trying to come up with some new moves.

Joanna's thoughts kept returning to Michael. She loved him, but what was the point if he didn't love her? She took another toke and let the smoke stay in her mouth for a bit before exhaling. This time she didn't cough.

"Well done."

"Oh, fine, now I'll be craving Mary Jane."

"I doubt it."

She examined one of the paintings on the wall. A Chinese man was pushing a wheelbarrow up a roadway. "That's what I feel like sometimes—like I'm pushing a heavy load. You know, I suspect Michael might be seeing someone. One of his students. I

THE RUBBER FENCE

feel so fucking stupid."

"He's probably just trying to find himself. Just trying to be true to himself."

"Great," she said sarcastically.

"I'm a man. I know how we think."

"Good for you," she said. "I thought it was perfect."

Sam gave her a look, like 'give me a break'.

"Okay, not perfect, but at least a good marriage."

Sam put what was left of the weed down on a metal ashtray, leaned over, and gently kissed her on the forehead, then around her ears, neck, and lips. Sam's foot moved slowly up her leg, arousing her. His blue eyes twinkled as if to say, Come on, you want this as much as I do.

"Be wary of what you start," she said. She wasn't kidding. She didn't want to be played with, not now.

"I don't scare easily." He kissed her softly on the lips.

She responded, tentatively at first, and then she softened in his arms. He lowered her on to the faded Persian rug, and began unbuttoning her cotton shirt, all the while kissing her around her ears, creating havoc in her heart and a delicious desire between her legs. He put his hand inside her shirt and began to fondle her breasts. As he undid more buttons, her pager went off, twice. Unfazed, Sam moved his hands to her back and undid her bra, unleashing her breasts. He took off her shirt and she did the rest, leaving her chest bare. Bending down, he sucked her nipples, causing her to moan with pleasure. His hand moved lower, and she arched her body toward his. He played with the zipper on her jeans. She'd just reached down to help him when her pager beeped again. Startled, as if from a deep dream, she realized she could not ignore it. Untangling herself from his arms, she sat up.

"I have to get this. It might be Theresa." As she dialed the ward, she became self-conscious about her bare breasts and picked her shirt up from the floor. She covered herself, and as she did, she saw Sam's disappointed face.

Speeding to the hospital, Joanna noted the moon shining through her windshield window, reminding her of what she had just left behind. In some ways, she felt relieved that her pager had halted her tryst. She didn't think she'd have been able to forgive herself if she had gone all the way, but she knew in her heart that, given the right man and the right moment, she could easily be swayed. Is this what Michael was experiencing, the freshness of someone new? Yes, it was exciting, but where did it lead? With free love being vocalized by hippies, it wasn't surprising there was a rise in marital breakdowns. Taking care of a marriage was like tending a fire. If you neglected it, it died.

By the time she got to 2B, it was a little after midnight. The janitor was washing the floors and seemed annoyed when she traipsed past him making wet footprints all the way to Theresa's room.

The young mother lay on her bed, her back to the door. Joanna tiptoed over for a closer look. The other patient in the room squirmed with the intrusion. Though fast asleep, Theresa did not look at rest. Her hair was matted from sweat and her brow lined, as if her dream made her work harder than necessary. Something had happened, but what?

Joanna went to the nurses' station, where Beverley was engrossed in a paperback. "I got here as fast as I could."

Without looking up, Beverley said, "It's all in the charts. Better read that first."

THE RUBBER FENCE

"Where's Carmen?"

"She had to go home. Her daughter came down with a fever."

Joanna's stomach lurched. "What about Roberta?"

"I told her you were coming in, and she left after Theresa was settled. She had one of her migraines."

Joanna frowned. Did Roberta really have a migraine, or was she still upset over having her wishes overruled? Joanna settled down at the table and read the detailed report.

Joanna looked over at Beverly, who had returned to reading her book. "You know, I would have fought too if someone was trying to take my baby away from me. I consider that progress."

Beverley's face was blank. Joanna wasn't sure the young nurse had heard anything she'd said.

"I love your attitude." Joanna slammed the chart down with a bang and left shaking with fury.

Joanna sat immobilized in her car. The hospital parking lot was empty for the most part, which underlined the loneliness and frustration she felt. Nothing seemed to be working out. Not Michael, not Rose, not Theresa. If she had gotten to the hospital sooner, could she have stopped the staff's aggressive handling of her patient? She knew the answer, but still felt horrible when she thought of what Theresa had gone through. At the moment, Joanna didn't think she had anything left to give. But she couldn't give up. She hadn't come from a family of quitters.

FORTY-FOUR

THERE WERE SO many snakes to fight—big long ones, one on top of the other, twisting toward her. One had the face of her mother-in-law. Theresa punched and kicked, but the old woman came closer and closer to where the baby lay.

Theresa yelled at the snakes, "Stand back. No! Get Back! Back! Don't eat my baby! Oh God, no, please don't!"

Theresa hit something that hurt, waking herself up. She was disorientated at first, but then felt the throbbing in her right hand. Her knuckles were red and puffy. She must have hit the metal headboard behind her.

On the other bed, the patient stared at the ceiling. "You were having a nightmare."

Theresa was wet with sweat and threw off her covers to cool down.

There was more yelling, but this time by someone in the corridor. It was Marty, whose room was next to hers. "Bogeyman on 2B! Going to get you!"

Theresa could hear Crosby trying to settle him. "Whatcha doin' up? Do you know what time it is? It's way past your bedtime."

Marty was now outside her room. "I…I…I'm not, not going back in there. No, no. They're co…co…coming out of the bogeyman. The bogeyman's here. Keep him away. You got to keep him away from me."

THE RUBBER FENCE

Theresa got out of bed and went to her doorway, where she saw Crosby in the corridor talking to Marty. "No, Marty. There's no bogeyman here. You heard Theresa screaming. She was just having a bad dream, that's all. That's all it was. I'm going to tuck you in, you got that? We can keep a light on for awhile, just so you get settled. A little night light. We'll just plug it in, so you can see there's nothing there. Nothing at all."

"I don't want to see what's not there."

Crosby laughed. "I know you can't see what's not there." He laughed again. "You'll be okay. Yes, sir. You'll be just fine."

Theresa went back to her bed, but she heard Crosby talking quietly to someone just outside her room. "He wet his bed. Better have them call Dr. Williams first thing in the morning. There's a whole lot of something going on with that boy."

Joanna's mind shifted back to Marlene. What was she doing right now? Was she in her crib or in her grandmother's arms while her mother was in a hospital with strangers.

As soon as Myron heard about the calamity on the ward, he arranged for a meeting with Theresa's husband. He should have contacted Joanna, but given her obstinacy, it was better this way. She was in classes on Mondays and this couldn't wait.

Sitting across the desk from Eugene and Roberta, Myron listened along with Eugene to Roberta's review of Theresa's horrible night. He wondered what this simple man was trying to do with his life. How could he tolerate being under his mother's thumb and dealing with a wife whom he couldn't please either? But was his own situation any better? He had married a Jewish princess. He'd been warned, but he'd admired her spirit back then. Now that spirit was destroying him bit by bit. What was worse, he was letting her.

"I don't understand," said Eugene. "Dr. Bereza said she was moving along."

"We were hoping for a breakthrough," said Myron, "but it didn't happen."

"She started talking. I thought—"

"Yes, she did, but then there was that altercation with your mother. It's obvious she's not ready to leave yet. Whatever troubled her when she came in is still troubling her. We are confident that with electrotherapy, she will make a quick recovery."

Myron could see Eugene struggling. The young man's eyes darted as if he were the one about to undergo ECT. "I can assure you," said Myron, "we wouldn't be recommending it, if it was going to harm Theresa in any way." He slid the consent form across the desk. "The thing is, Theresa is not of sound mind. You saw that for yourself—the way she screamed and fought the staff who were trying to help her." He tapped the consent form for emphasis. "It's up to you to make the right choice."

"Aren't there any other pills?"

"I wish there were."

"I'd like to talk to Dr. Bereza about this."

"She's at the university today." Myron handed him a pen.

Eugene glanced at Roberta, who nodded for him to sign it.

"You're doing the right thing," said Myron. "I've already talked to her family doctor, and he's prepared to be the second signature. We need two doctors to authorize this treatment. We both want her to go home with you as soon as possible."

With a shaky hand, Eugene signed the document.

FORTY-FIVE

THERE WAS NO one in the psychiatric residents' room when Joanna walked in after the day away at classes. She welcomed the opportunity to collect herself before facing the pressures of the ward. And Sam. The intimacy they'd shared the night before crowded her mind. She hoped it wouldn't change their working relationship.

She opened the side drawer of her desk to get some paper and was surprised to find a gold box of chocolates with a card on top. She opened the card and read what someone had written with a blue fountain pen: From Someone who cares for you more than you think. She smiled knowingly, put the card in her pants pocket, and left the room carrying the box.

She strode by a few loitering patients and an elderly woman who was wandering aimlessly down the corridor. Carmen grabbed her by the arm and escorted her back to her room. The woman's blue gown was open at the back exposing a frail, naked body. Carmen said to her, "When is your husband bringing you some clothes?"

"Husband? I have a husband?"

Joanna smiled, though the woman's state was far from comical. She was thinking about that when she entered Theresa's room and found her thumbing through a *Chatelaine* magazine without looking at it.

"Good morning, Theresa. I hope you slept well." Theresa

didn't answer. It was as if she hadn't made any progress—as if the talking and bonding that had taken place over the weekend had been only a dream.

"I heard what happened. Things will get better, I promise."

Just then, Annette popped into the room. "I thought I saw you come in here. There's a phone call for you."

"Okay. I'll be right there." She saw Theresa eyeing her box of chocolates. "Would you like one? Take a couple."

Theresa looked unsure as she examined the sweets in their brown paper cups.

"Take your time. It's hard to know which one to pick. I'll be right back."

When Joanna returned about ten minutes later, Theresa was eating a chocolate. She handed the box back to Joanna.

"The nurses said you did very well with Marlene. I wish I could've been here when your mother-in-law came. The staff over-reacted. I'll make sure it doesn't happen again."

Theresa stared out the window.

Joanna sighed deeply, as if she were trying to expel the young mother's anxieties for her. She tried to reassure her patient but could see that whatever progress had been made had since fizzled and stalled. *One step forward, three steps back.*

Placing a hand on Theresa's shoulder, Joanna said, "We'll talk more about it when we meet at four today." This time, Theresa nodded, and Joanna left feeling that the door had opened a smidgen again.

Back in the residents' room, Joanna laughed when she opened the box of chocolates to find that seven were gone. She hadn't realized that Theresa had a sweet tooth. Perhaps that sweetness could come back in other ways as well.

THE RUBBER FENCE

◇◇◇

The phone call that interrupted her time with Theresa had been from Sam asking her to meet him for coffee in the cafeteria. His voice had sounded tentative...or was she reading too much into it? It was only one night at his apartment, but it may as well have been a week the way she worried. What had she been thinking to let him go so far? What must he think of her?

She found him already in line, looking appealing as usual. He had his hair pulled back in a ponytail and was dressed in jeans and a pressed khaki shirt. She was about to apologize again for rushing out the night before when he said, "Was everything all right?"

She raised her eyebrows. "I guess you haven't heard. Theresa had a rough night. I saw her this morning and she's gone silent on me again. It's so damn frustrating."

"Welcome to psychiatry."

She considered a blueberry muffin then put it back. "They put so much sugar in these things, it's like eating cake."

"When you didn't come back last night..." he said as he filled his cup with coffee.

"I thought about it, but it was late." Joanna grabbed an orange juice.

"Don't worry about it." He said it in such an offhand manner that she relaxed. Maybe for Sam, this was no big deal, just another missed opportunity.

She looked at him and said, "I was also in such a foul mood by the time I left Theresa, you wouldn't have wanted to see me."

"Don't be so sure about that." Sam added cream and sugar to his coffee.

"Actually," she said, "my pager going off saved me. I

shouldn't be telling you this, but I was pretty weak. You're a very charming guy. Any further and—"

"That's what I was counting on." His smile was delicious, in fact, too tempting. "Maybe we can pick up where we left off."

"You're a rascal, aren't you?"

"No, just human."

They paid the cashier and looked for a table away from the others in the cafeteria. She was aware of how their relationship had changed. If they became serious, there would be no end of entanglements to deal with. No wonder so many marriages didn't endure, not when the husband or wife saw more of their coworkers than their spouses. Was that what had happened to Michael? Temptation right in his classroom, too hard to resist, especially when his wife was so unavailable?

Seated, Joanna took a sip of juice and said, "After last night, I'm beginning to think I need help."

"I have this couch," Sam said in a thick German accent.

"You're crazy," said Joanna, cracking up.

"True." He continued in his thick German accent. "But it's *gut* the patient's humour is still intact. Lady doctor still most beautiful woman in hospital. All's *vell vit da vorld*." Then Sam said in his normal voice, "Why don't you come over after work tonight? We'll finish what we started. I have a new mattress. You didn't even get a chance to try it out."

"Do you always solicit your prospective patients?"

"Very interesting," he said, again in his German accent. "She answers a question *vit* another question."

She laughed. "How did you know I love chocolates?"

"I don't. Do you?" He looked puzzled.

"Sam, don't play coy with me. I found this lovely box of chocolates in my desk."

"Lucky you. Maybe I've got some in mine, too." Sam picked a serviette up from the metal dispenser on the table and wiped his mouth.

"You mean...they weren't from you?"

"I wish they were. If they were, would you come over?"

She laughed again. "Then who put them there?"

"*Ze* elves? Maybe some other secret admirer? There must be more of us out there."

Joanna loved this man, though not like she loved Michael. No one could match Michael, but with the way things were going, whatever love she had with him was waning as quickly as the light at sunset. And if that continued to happen...well, she shouldn't be thinking that. But Sam was appealing, she had to admit that. His sense of humor alone was worth the trouble.

Sam said, "By the way, did Dennis call you back?"

"No, why?"

"Marty acted up last night. The nursing staff want his meds increased or changed, but they can't seem to reach Dennis."

She frowned. "Maybe he turned his pager off."

"He's supposed to be on call."

"There's probably some emergency with his mother again."

"Or his sister," said Sam.

"I didn't know he had a sister."

"He's been looking after her. She's pretty slow. She's in a group home somewhere. I only found out because I saw the two of them in a park one day and asked him later about it."

"Funny, he never said anything about her to me." But then again, they hadn't spent that much time together. And everyone had secrets.

"So, are you coming over or not?"

"No."

"Okay, you're missing out. Just so you know, it's a nice mattress."

She laughed easily again. "You're incorrigible." She suddenly felt hungry and realized she had left home without eating breakfast. "You go ahead. I think I'll get that muffin after all."

FORTY-SIX

JOANNA FLIPPED THROUGH the stack of charts a few times but was unable to find what she was looking for. She turned to Annette, who was at her desk doing paperwork. "Have you seen Theresa's chart?"

"I saw Roberta looking at it," said Annette in such a strained voice that Joanna wondered what stress the ward clerk was under. "It's probably on her desk."

Joanna found Theresa's chart on top of Roberta's binder and took it back to the work table to read the latest recording. Her eyes widened when she came to this morning's notes. Her stomach heaved, as if the blueberry muffin she'd just eaten had been too much to digest. She quickly got up and pulled the ECT schedule from the pile of papers beside Annette. Her pulse quickened as she read, marked in black ink: *Theresa Boychuk*.

Livid, she said to Annette. "Why in the hell didn't you tell me?"

"I walked in this morning and there it was."

"But why didn't you call?"

"I didn't think there was anything you could do." Annette's face turned red, and she began to stutter, "And…and…I didn't know what to say."

"I can't believe this. Carmen recorded the improvements, same as me. Mother and baby: fine. You know that. But Roberta, damn her! She wrote 'Theresa continues to be mute and unresponsive'. Why did she do this?" Joanna took a black marker from Annette's pencil holder and crossed out Theresa's name. "Well, I'm cancelling it. This is not going to happen."

Sam arrived at the unit and said to Joanna, "I was looking everywhere for you."

"Did you know about this?"

He looked at the schedule. "No." He shook his head. "I didn't know anything about it until I saw Carmen wheeling Theresa down a little while ago. I was surprised you hadn't mentioned it over coffee."

"What? Omigod!" Joanna tore out of the unit with Sam right behind her. The ECT room had never felt so far away before.

Joanna and Sam burst into the ECT room, where the procedure was well underway. Myron and the anesthesiologist stood around the gurney where Theresa lay pale and unconscious. Carmen and Roberta stood nearby but off to the side.

Joanna fought back tears as she watched the shock jolt Theresa's body. First her head and heels went up, then her toes pointed and her fingers turned inward. Her eyelids and mouth twitched like a mouse's whiskers when a cat comes into sight. A moment went by and the room was quiet. It felt like the stillness before a lightning strike.

Theresa struggled, coughed a little, and then she started to choke.

"Something's wrong!" exclaimed Roberta. "She's choking!"

Myron barked at the anesthesiologist. "What did you give her?"

The anesthesiologist double checked the syringe and

THE RUBBER FENCE

medication lying on the side table. "Looks good."

"We're picking up some dysrhythmia," said Roberta as she quickly grabbed the Ambu bag. But before she had a chance to apply it, Theresa vomited some brown and yellow liquid. Some of it landed on Roberta. "Oh, shit!"

"Suction!" said Myron. Carmen worked the tube, and with a damp sponge, cleaned Theresa as well as she could under the circumstances. Myron was sweating now. "Is she clear?"

Roberta nodded, but didn't look hopeful.

All eyes were on the young mother. Joanna's heart raced like she'd just run a mile.

Then Theresa stopped breathing.

Roberta checked the patient's air passage then her pulse. The monitor showed all signs were down.

"I'm not getting anything," Myron said. He sounded like he'd gone into shock and was now operating on remote. "We need to intubate!"

Shaking, Roberta inserted a tube down Theresa's throat. "C'mon, c'mon!"

"Did she eat anything?" asked Myron.

Roberta shook her head and applied the Ambu-bag.

Joanna's mouth went dry at the realization that her patient could die. She held Theresa's clammy hand.

"Would you stand the hell back?" shouted Myron, pushing Joanna away.

"She's still my patient."

"Goddamn it! Would you follow directions for once in your life?" Myron glared at Joanna then began manual compressions. His hands worked feverishly, up and down on Theresa's chest. The veins in his forehead protruded with the pressure.

Sam gently pulled Joanna back, whispering, "You can't do

anything right now."

She stood immobile, as if her breathing had something to do with her patient's. The room spun as she took in what was happening.

The electrocardiograph went flat.

"It can't be!" Myron stared at the monitor, demanding it to show something different. He reached for the defibrillator to kick start Theresa's heart.

"She's going down," said Roberta, watching the patient's chest heave with a jolt and then subside.

"Code Blue!" said Myron.

"Sweet Jesus." Carmen picked up the emergency phone and dialed.

On the verge of tears, Joanna found the scene surreal. Her throat was raw, and she struggled to find saliva to swallow. She mumbled, "Dear God, please."

The room was beyond tense as they all waited for Theresa to breathe. Roberta worked the Ambu bag while Myron kept up the manual compressions. Twin emotional and physical fatigue weighed them down, but they continued to apply what they knew.

Theresa's body lay motionless. Myron checked the ECG. There was no sign of life. Fifteen seconds had gone by, but it could've been five times as long. Time meant nothing.

Sam tapped Myron on the shoulder and shook his head. Joanna stroked Theresa's hair. She said, "I'm so sorry."

Moments later, Sam pulled Joanna away, and Roberta drew a white sheet over Theresa.

FORTY-SEVEN

IN THE HOURS that followed, a pall settled over the nurses' station. There was a lot of soul searching as the staff combed Theresa's chart, looking for clues—anything that could explain the tragedy. The patients, aware that something was up, milled around the lounge; their nerves running on overtime.

Carmen had gone to check Theresa's room for any clues and had returned with a bunch of gold wrappers in her hand. "I found these in her room. There were seven of them."

"The chocolates. Oh, no." said Joanna, her mind reeling with the realization that she may have played a part in Theresa's death. "I forgot about those. I gave her some this morning."

"You did what?" said Myron.

Her words tumbled out like a confession pried after much interrogation. "When I went to her room, I offered her a chocolate, then I left. Afterwards, I noticed there were a number missing. I didn't think much about it; I thought she was saving some for later." Joanna glanced toward Theresa's room half expecting her to appear and explain why she took so many.

"You gave her something to eat?" Myron shouted. "What the hell were you thinking?" Roberta shook her head in disgust.

"What I was thinking?" she shouted back. "When I left yesterday, there had been definite progress. I know she had a rough time giving up her baby but that was *no* reason to schedule her for shock treatment. None. What happened to teamwork?"

Everything in her body vibrated, as she said, "This was *my* patient!"

"We couldn't wait until you came in," said Myron.

"You couldn't wait to—"

"For God's sake, Joanna. You're a resident. You have classes. What did you expect you could do from across the city?"

"I had a right to know. I could've filled you in on what I saw."

Myron said coolly, "We had an agreement. If nothing changed, we were to proceed with ECT. We had to get her moving for her sake and the baby's!"

"Oh, you got her moving all right!" Her eyes flooded. "Is she moving now?"

The colour drained from Myron's face. It seemed as if everyone around stood still. A few patients in the lounge took sideways glances at the arguing staff. Annette—who had been listening at her desk—lowered her head and pretended to read the requisition sheets in front of her.

"This is not the place to do this," said Myron, lowering his voice. He took Joanna by the arm, ushered her into Roberta's office, closed the door, and shut the blinds.

Joanna braced herself against the head nurse's desk, as if some unexpected blow was about to be delivered.

"You've pushed your luck too far this time," said Myron, standing less than two feet away, his face red with anger. She considered various responses in her defence, but his glare blistered any words she was conjuring up to fight back. She was saved from telling Myron to go to hell by Sam, who knocked on the glass door and entered the room.

"What is it?" snapped Myron.

Sam gave Joanna a sympathetic look before saying, "I talked

THE RUBBER FENCE

to the anesthesiologist. He's questioning whether she had any drug allergies that could have precipitated a cardiac arrest."

Myron said to Joanna. "Do you know anything about this?"

"No."

Sam said, "He also took the chocolates into account and doesn't think she ingested enough to kill her. That small amount of food wouldn't have done it."

Joanna absorbed this news, and although she felt relieved to hear that her part in Theresa's death was questionable, it didn't change the fact that the young mother had died.

Myron took a deep breath and rubbed his forehead as if trying to soothe a pounding headache. "I'll talk to you later when you've calmed down."

Joanna wanted to add, When we've both calmed down, but didn't. She recognized that he was beyond hearing anything she might say.

As she exited the room with Sam, she heard Myron say, "Sam, you need to be involved..."

Wanting to escape, Joanna rushed down the corridor toward the exit stairwell. The high white walls on either side closed in on her, and her breathing became shallow. She struggled to catch her breath, as if she were having an asthma attack.

"Wait up!" said Sam.

She couldn't slow down. *How could it have happened so quickly? People don't die of shock treatment anymore, or do they and no one knows?*

Sam grabbed her arm, and instinctively she hit him on the chin.

"Whoa. I'm just trying to help," he said rubbing his jaw.

His face showed concern, but she kept walking. She slowed down enough to say, "I'm afraid if I stop, I'm going to start bawling."

"Hold on," said Sam, taking her hand. He guided her down the corridor to the laundry room. The room was crammed with soiled clothing and sheets in blue metal bins stacked by the washers and dryers, which were presently quiet. He shut the door and switched on the light. "You didn't know she was on the list. You did everything you could. Everything."

"I wish I could believe that."

"You have to. It's the truth."

Joanna leaned against a washer with a pile of dirty laundry on top, her body collapsing against its hard surface. "I hate this fucking business!" A pair of green cotton hospital pants fell from the top of the machine and Joanna kicked them.

"I know." He took her in his arms, and she let go. Her tears showed no sign of stopping. Her body shook as she continued to sob into his shoulder. He caressed her hair. Then after what seemed like an eternity, her cries abated.

"Thank you." Her voice was muffled against his shirt. He smelled good—a mixture of musk and manly sweat.

FORTY-EIGHT

JOANNA WOKE UP completely disorientated. Dreamland had taken her to a place surrounded by water and garbage. A place where there was no way out. She saw herself climbing a mountain of trash, falling over herself as she tackled one mound after another, each one taller and deeper than the one before. It seemed that no matter what she did, she couldn't make a dent in the nightmare assignment of cleaning it up.

She realized her bad dream had parallels to the mountain of trouble that surrounded her in her waking hours. She tried to clear her head by thinking about what she had to do next. Her illuminated watch showed that two hours had passed. She had been so strung out that she'd fallen asleep in one of the interview rooms. After getting up from the couch and stretching, she smoothed the wrinkles from her skirt and made her way to the nurses' station.

There, she began a detailed search of all the medical records that had to do with Theresa, even the ones compiled on the maternity ward. Given what the anesthesiologist had said, maybe she could find some mention of a drug allergy that had been overlooked. She was engrossed in the files when Roberta came by.

"Joanna, have you contacted Eugene yet?"

Stunned, she said, "No. Wasn't Myron going to call him?"

"She was your patient."

"Right. Now, she's my patient…" She stopped herself. She wanted to add, Since you and Myron signed her death warrant, but she couldn't. It wouldn't be fair, even though she felt less than fair at the moment. She also felt guilty even though there appeared to be other factors contributing to Theresa's death besides the chocolates. No matter how many times she ran the past twenty-four hours through her head, she still came up with the same verdict—guilty.

Theresa and Eugene had relied on her. She'd told them that she'd help them work out their problems. Instead, Theresa was now under a white sheet in the hospital morgue.

She reluctantly dialled Eugene from the phone in the residents' room, which was empty. The others were seeing their patients; Joanna had only had one and now she was gone. She had never counted on having to make this kind of call in psychiatry. She took a deep breath as she waited for someone to answer the phone.

A woman answered. It was the dreaded mother-in-law. "Is Eugene there, please?" said Joanna, her trembling voice sounding like it was underwater. When Mrs. Boychuk called out for Eugene, she was glad that she hadn't been recognized. Waiting for Theresa's husband to come to the phone, Joanna held the receiver tightly as if it were a life support keeping her from drowning. She hoped she could talk to him without crying.

She could hear Mrs. Boychuk whispering in the background and wondered if she'd guessed who it was after all.

"Hello," Eugene said.

"It's Joanna calling."

"You sound different. Do you have a cold?"

"No, no. It's about Theresa. We couldn't…couldn't save her." Her voice trailed off. She struggled to go on, choking back the sobs that threatened to overwhelm her. Haltingly, she described how things had gone, how they had tried everything, and how they didn't know yet what had happened.

When she finished, Eugene made an ugly sound that showed he needed his wife more than anyone would've predicted.

◇◇◇

Eugene didn't waste any time getting to the ward. Already, his boyish face bore the grief lines of someone who'd been suffering for months. Roberta was waiting outside the nurses' station with Theresa's suitcase at her feet. Joanna stepped out from behind the counter to greet Eugene.

"I can't tell you how sorry I am," said Joanna, swallowing.

He looked past her, avoiding eye contact.

Roberta handed the suitcase to Eugene. "I have her things here for you."

"That was fast," he said, grabbing the suitcase from her.

Roberta drew back and let out a deep sigh when she saw Myron coming down the corridor. She motioned for him to hurry.

"If there's anything—" said Roberta.

Eugene, apparently not wanting to hear any more, darted for Theresa's room yelling, "Theresa!"

A young man, newly admitted after a toxic drug reaction and jumpy at the best of times, leaped out of Eugene's way as if he'd been walking on railway tracks and had only just noticed the approaching train.

Joanna ran after Eugene. The room had been scrubbed down with ammonia, leaving no trace that the young mother had ever been there. Eugene stood there dazed for a few minutes before sitting down on the stripped bed with his head in his hands as though cementing the fact his wife was no longer there. Joanna struggled with what to do. Ordinarily, she would've sat down beside him, but she couldn't bring herself to do it on Theresa's bed. It felt sacred somehow. As she was thinking about what she could possibly say to ease his pain, she heard footsteps at the doorway. Joanna turned to see Myron standing there.

"Eugene," said Myron. "I—"

"Even her smell is gone," said Eugene looking up at Myron. "You people don't waste any time, do you?" He then lowered his head and sobbed. Huge wracking sobs that shook his body; his grief spreading to each wall, enveloping those around him. When his cries subsided, Eugene raised his head and said through tears, "I don't understand. I just don't understand."

Joanna said softly, "We don't know yet what caused her death. It was very unexpected."

An elderly female patient was hyperventilating just outside the room. "Who died? Did somebody die? Are we all going to die?"

Eugene was full of reproach when he said, "You were supposed to help her, not kill her."

Joanna wanted to say sorry again, but what good would it do? It wouldn't bring his wife back.

"Bloody murder, is what it is," said Eugene. "Bloody murder."

"Oh, Eugene…" Joanna's voice clogged with sadness.

"I trusted you!"

"Please calm down," said Myron.

"Calm down?" He stood up, fists clenched. "Get out of my fucking way!"

Disquieted, Myron stepped aside.

Joanna felt Eugene brush by her as if she were nothing but a

THE RUBBER FENCE

piece of furniture. He then returned, picked up Theresa's suitcase from the floor, clutched it, and flew out the door.

She called after him, "Eugene, please wait!" She ran to catch up to him.

He stopped abruptly. With a contorted face, his words came out in choking sound bites. "How could this have happened? You told me—they told me it was safe."

She had never told him it was safe, but now wasn't the time to argue. "As I said, we're not sure what happened."

They were near the area for outpatient services that opened off the corridor. The doctors were out, so the area was empty. She took Eugene's arm, directed him to one of the visitor chairs, and then sat down beside him.

He stared straight ahead. "I don't know what I'm going to do now."

She waited a moment then said, "Eugene, do you know if Theresa had any drug allergies?"

"No, why?"

"We have to check everything."

"Weren't you supposed to do that before she got the treatment?" His words hit her like a slap across the face.

"If there's anything I can do…" Joanna knew his emotions would be conflicted for some time. She took out a business card from her jacket pocket and handed it to him. "Please feel free to phone me. If we find out anything more, I'll call you as soon as I know."

Eugene nodded and slumped away, a beaten man. She stood there awhile, transfixed by his departing figure. She envisioned what appeared to be the spirit of Theresa propping him up as he went. As in life, she was the stronger one.

Joanna was still in a bit of a trance when Myron approached.

"How did it go? What did you say to him?"

"I encouraged him to call me."

"Good. You'll keep me informed."

"Of course. Teamwork, right?" she said. She hadn't meant to be sarcastic, but she was beyond caring. She didn't wait for an answer and headed for the stairs. She wanted to get off the ward and out of the hospital. She knew there was more at stake here than trying to find out who was right and who was wrong. Knowing Myron, he'd try to put this fatality behind him. But since Theresa had been her patient, Joanna had a part to play whether she liked it or not. She could prevent Theresa's death from becoming just another statistic—one more forgotten victim of sloppy medical practice. She could at least do that.

◇◇◇

"Hey, I just heard." It was Dennis coming up the stairwell looking about the same—tired and in need of a shower. "How are you doing?"

"Surviving."

"God," he said, hugging her.

"Thank you." His face appeared to be carrying a lifetime of sorrows. "What about you? The whole ward's been looking for you."

"I know."

"Did you get my message?"

"Yes. I would have come, but I wouldn't have been the best company."

"Not that it's any of my business, but you're looking a little rough."

"Life intrudes, you know?"

"Yeah." She nodded and teared up.

Dennis put his hand on her shoulder. "Look, if it's any consolation, I'm on your side. Myron's going to play hard ball even though he screwed up. Best defence is an offence, they always say."

She looked at him with surprise.

He put his hands up. "I know. I'm not good at confronting either." He shrugged. "I better find out what's going on with Marty." Without looking back, he walked away as if they hadn't encountered one another at all.

FORTY-NINE

MYRON'S ANXIETY WAS an unwelcome adversary during his squash game with Bernie that afternoon. It was as if he had to play against two instead of one. He didn't hold back as he used every opportunity he had to let off steam and get rid of the so-called monkey on his back.

The squash ball resounded against the wall as Myron whacked it back with a maddening force. He was playing well, but Bernie coolly outmanoeuvred him by tapping the ball lightly. Myron lunged, missed the ball, and fell.

"Son of a bitch!"

"Hey, this isn't the Masters."

Myron was in no mood to joke. He helped himself up.

"You're just off your game," said Bernie. "Theresa's death still bugging you?"

"I had no choice, you know that. You heard Roberta. Any more disruptions, and we would have had a mutiny on our hands."

"True, but I haven't seen you this upset since that analyst brother of yours beat you out of that university position."

"Bernie, now you're sounding just like him."

"Until I ask you to lie down and tell me about your rotten childhood, you have nothing to worry about."

Myron grimaced as he massaged his calf.

Bernie's face grew serious. "On the other hand, I wouldn't

be taking any holidays right now if I were you." He stretched his legs against the wall. "Does Bryce know yet?"

"No. He's visiting another hospital today." Myron grabbed his towel from his bag and wiped the sweat off his forehead. He wished he could wipe away the last twenty-four hours as well. "Look, these things happen. Bryce knows that as much as I do. No matter what animosity we show to one another, I know he'll be there to back me up."

"Are you sure?"

Myron nodded absent-mindedly, but later, as he changed, he wondered how the next few weeks would go. He had told Bernie that there wouldn't be a problem, but now... He wanted to get home and have a scotch. Maybe there, he could sort out his jumbled thoughts. If Bryce deserted him, then what? He'd have to defend himself with the board. He hoped it wouldn't come to that, but with the way things had been going on the ward, nothing surprised him anymore.

If only he could have a good roll in bed with Diane and get the relief a good orgasm could give him. Only then would he feel he had the fight within himself to see this bloody mess through. But the possibility of that happening was quickly dashed when he found a note from Diane on the fridge, reminding him that she and the kids would be home late. They were at some community concert organized by their synagogue's women's auxiliary.

When had his marriage gone stale? He knew he was partly to blame. He hadn't put the time and effort into making it work, but then again, neither had Diane. Wasn't that her job? He provided the income. If it weren't for him...Oh what was the use of going over and over it again?

At home, he had a few drinks and began to feel drowsy while watching a news special on the troops in Vietnam.

War was hell, but maybe it served a purpose. It was a way out for those whose home was a greater hell. He went to sleep thinking if he were younger, he might have enlisted just to find himself again and escape the bleakness ahead.

FIFTY

HER LEGS FELT like they'd been weighted with lead as she trudged up the walk to their apartment building. What had started out as an exciting adventure in a new profession had turned into a horror show. And with all that had transpired, she'd almost forgotten that Michael was due back that evening. Maybe he was already home. Would they meet like strangers? But what if he never came back? What if something had happened to him, and she never got to feel his arms around her again? She didn't know if she could take much more.

She opened their apartment door and was once again met with darkness. She took off her jacket, hung it up, and went into the kitchen. She hadn't eaten dinner or shopped for groceries in the past few days, so she had to scrounge the fridge for something to eat.

After settling for a plate of scrambled eggs and toast, she plopped herself on the sofa in front of the TV. It was now eight o'clock and the sky had turned a midnight blue. She was losing hope that Michael would come home. Not finding anything interesting to watch, she took her dirty plate to the kitchen and was scraping it when she heard the front door open. "Michael?"

He came into the kitchen carrying his overnight bag. He looked tired, and his face was unshaven.

In the early days of their marriage, she would've run to him. Now, she and Michael stood apart, looking at one another as if they were casual acquaintances. She wondered how his weekend had gone. Was there another woman? Was it Cindy?

He put his bag down on the floor, took off his jacket, and placed it over a chair. "How are you doing?"

She shrugged. "I've been better."

"I called the hospital this afternoon, and Annette told me what had happened. I thought you'd call me. I thought you would after I sent you the chocolates."

She opened her mouth in surprise. "You sent them?"

"Who else...?"

"Nobody, it's just..."

"What?"

"Nothing. That was nice of you." She watched him pour a glass of water from the tap. Why hadn't she thought of Michael? Maybe it was because he hadn't given her anything out of the blue in a long time. And with all that had been going on, Annette must've forgotten to tell her he had called. She wondered if he had given her the sweets to appease her—to make up for his fooling around with one of his students.

"I missed you." He turned to her, his blue eyes soft and caring. He was wearing a cologne she didn't recognize, a scent of wood and lime. When had he bought that and for whom?

She moved away from him and gripped the back of a chair for support. He studied her for a bit, as if waiting for her to reply in kind. When she didn't, he sat down on the chair across from her. "Funny," he said, "I went to this coffee shop in Gimli, and I saw this old couple teasing one another. They looked like they were in their seventies, and I wondered if we would ever end up like them, taking our dentures out together."

She smiled despite how she was feeling. Her smile then went as quickly as it had come. "I'm not big on triangles."

THE RUBBER FENCE

"It's over, Joanna. I never loved her."

"Never loved Cindy?"

There was a line on his forehead she hadn't seen before. "I was mad…stupid."

"And that makes it okay?"

He said nothing for a moment then, "No. Of course not." He sighed heavily. "Sometimes I get so wound up, I can't deal with you. You're so strong…" He paused. The line on his forehead deepened. "I've always loved you. Only you."

She wanted to say, Really? You can waltz on home and say it's only me, and I'm supposed to put all my feelings aside, all my thoughts of you and some other woman and that's it. We go on as before. She wanted to say all that, but didn't.

Instead, she said, "I don't know. I don't think I can do this anymore." She blurted it out despite the fact that only a short time ago there was nothing more she wanted than to work out their problems. It was like her voice now belonged to someone else—a more distant version of herself.

"I love you," he said again. He had hardly taken his eyes off of her since he'd walked in the door. The words were there, his face looked sincere, and yet…

She stood immobilized, as if she'd been touched in frozen tag. She wished she could repeat the same words back without reservation. But now it seemed as if her love was wearing a coat of grey.

"There isn't anyone else, is there?" he asked.

"Not really," she said. Was that true? Did she care for Sam now more than she thought?

"What do you mean, Not really?"

"I don't know what I mean. It was nothing. Nothing happened. I was just getting back at you, but you…I don't know what yours is…"

He studied her, as if he were trying to figure out what secrets she held. "I told you. I was mad."

"You think you're the only one who has a right to be angry? You think that every time you're upset, you can just fuck some other woman, and I'm going to wait around like you went out to buy a loaf of bread? Jesus, Michael!"

He curled his body, as if she'd hit him hard in the gut. Maybe he did love her. Maybe he did care.

She sat down on a chair opposite him and closed her eyes. "I know I haven't been easy to live with. I know I get obsessed with work and I think I have all the answers…and I don't listen to yours. But when you left, I thought I'd lost my best friend."

"Me, too."

She opened her eyes and saw that there were tears in his. Looking out the kitchen window into the black void of night, she said, "I think we should see a therapist."

FIFTY-ONE

UNLIKE MYRON'S ORDERED office, Bryce's overflowed with papers, plants, and haphazard stacks of books and journals. Framed degrees and honours figured prominently on one wall, and bookshelves filled the other. One of the frames was askew, and Joanna was tempted to get up to fix it.

Myron was beside her in a matching leather chair; any movement on her part was bound to draw attention, which was the last thing she wanted. She hadn't wanted this meeting. It was too soon after Theresa's death, and there were still too many unanswered questions. Bryce watered a fern while Myron gave his account of the unexpected fatality on 2B. Distracted by a spider plant that hung too close to her head, Joanna pushed its leaves from time to time and debated whether to move her chair backward or forward.

When Myron finished, Bryce put down his watering can and said, "There's going to be an autopsy and an audit. We have to ensure that we all tell the same story."

"Which is?" Joanna asked.

Myron said, "That somehow the patient stole some chocolates from the unit, and that the staff weren't aware."

"I can't say that. You expect me to cover up what I've done?"

"No one's suggesting you lie, Joanna," Myron said in a parental tone. "But if there are any pointed questions, we'll plead ignorance. We're doing this for your own good."

She wanted to spit at his smug face. She felt like she was becoming embroiled in something that, if not handled properly, could easily spin out of control, and she would be the casualty. She glanced at Bryce, hoping for some support, but he wasn't taking any sides.

As if he could read her thoughts, Bryce said, "No one is going to let you hang out to dry." His raspy tone suggested otherwise.

"I was the therapist assigned to the case," she said in an even tone that belied how she felt. "There are going to be a lot of questions. We are still trying to determine whether Theresa had a predisposed condition. What happened could've been an allergic reaction."

Bryce regarded her for a moment as if considering this possibility for the first time. He sat down at his desk and put on his reading glasses. Glancing at the report in front of him, he said, "We need to work together on this." Then, looking at her over the rim of his glasses, he added, "Even the mighty oak has to bend."

Myron seemed relieved, but Joanna felt discouraged. Sure, like Bryce said, the mighty oak had to bend, but it seemed to her that she was the only one being asked to do the bending.

FIFTY-TWO

THE ROMAN CATHOLIC service was brief but moving in the modern church with a wooden vaulted ceiling. In front of the altar lay a closed oak coffin with a spray of light pink roses on top, and beside that, Theresa's photo stood on a pedestal. The mostly empty pews on one side of the church, reserved for the young mother's kin and friends, underlined the rejection she must've felt in life.

Joanna sat alone on the left in the third row on Theresa's side, while near the front, on the right, sat the Boychuks. She prayed that Eugene's fury had dissipated enough for him to at least give her another chance to explain and express her regrets. Because of his outburst at the hospital, she had debated about coming to the funeral, but now that she was here, she knew she had made the right decision. It was the least she could do to deal with the guilt that continued to stalk her.

The Roman Catholic priest conducted the mass, which included a prayer for Theresa's final journey to heaven and some words of consolation for her family. At the end of the service, Eugene, in a charcoal grey suit and white shirt, walked up to the podium that had been set up on one side of the altar.

He cleared his throat and said, "Thank you all for coming." He took a few moments to review a piece of paper he had placed on the pulpit. Then he said, "Theresa and I met through friends in our teen years. It seemed we were destined to be together. We married young, too young it seems, now I realize, but that's what we did." He half-smiled before going on. "We couldn't make it on our own, which many of you know, so we ended up at my parents' place. It wasn't easy, as you can imagine." Eugene faltered, putting the paper back in his pocket and nodding his head.

Joanna looked over at Mrs. Boychuk, who was holding Marlene, but could only see a bit of her profile. Her erect posture gave the impression that she had little sympathy for her son's loss.

Eugene went on, looking at something in the distance. "Theresa, it's not going to be fun without you. I'm going to miss you. And so will Marlene. I hope that wherever you are, you're not worrying anymore. I'll be along to join you when I'm finished here. We'll still talk, right?" Fighting back tears, and with his head down, he walked back to his seat.

Joanna was surprised by what he'd said. Some couples, mainly elderly ones, were so close that when one went, the other followed soon after. But Eugene wasn't elderly. With his wife gone, how would he manage? In some ways, Theresa had been a buffer for Eugene.

Since all the mourners were invited to the reception at the Boychuk home, Joanna went as well, hoping to talk to Eugene. Family and friends milled about, sharing stories and eating lunch from the buffet of cold cuts, salads, vegetable crudities, pickles, and baking of all kinds. Instead of wine, fruit punch, tea, and coffee were served.

Marlene was passed around the crowd and ended up in Joanna's arms in the dining room. She resembled a life-sized doll, dressed in a yellow nylon polka-dotted dress with a Peter Pan collar trimmed with white lace. Her fine brown hair was

THE RUBBER FENCE

still thin, but had grown some. Joanna stared at the bundle in her arms and marvelled at the baby's clear, pink skin. Holding Marlene reawakened Joanna's own desire to have a child. There were countless women like her, who, for whatever reason, were unable to carry to term. They didn't give up on having a family. If only Michael had been more amenable to the idea of adopting, maybe this chasm between them wouldn't have developed. But he was too proud…or maybe he had come to the conclusion that their relationship wasn't going to last anyway, so why add a child to the mix? And yet, when she had brought up counselling, he had agreed.

"Here, let me take her from you," said Eugene warmly as he came toward her. "Thanks for coming."

Transferring Marlene, Joanna said, "It was a lovely service."

"Yes." He had a faraway look in his eyes. He then seemed to snap back and said, "Mom was just asking where her granddaughter was, so…" His voice trailed off. With Joanna following, he went through the archway to the living room where Mrs. Boychuk, dressed in a navy crepe dress, sat with a couple of women her age. When she saw Marlene, her face broke into a smile.

"There's the little darling, now," said Eugene's mother. He handed her the baby. Mrs. Boychuk kissed her granddaughter's head and cuddled her on her lap. She cooed at Marlene in an obvious display of affection—one that undoubtedly would have irritated Theresa no end.

As Eugene and Joanna turned to leave, Mrs. Boychuk said to the women beside her, "You know, I don't blame the doctors. She was a very, very sick girl. Who knows what would have happened to the baby if she had come home?"

"Mom!" said Eugene, facing his mother.

"What? I'm telling the truth."

"For God's sake, this is Theresa's funeral. Please. Couldn't you just let up for a few hours?"

"I was just saying the way it was, Eugene. You know it's true." Mrs. Boychuk looked at the other women and shrugged her shoulders.

"You're unbelievable!" Eugene was on a fast boil; his face reddened and the veins on his throat strained with anger.

"My Eugene. Such a good boy. He's so protective of her," she said in her sweet voice. "Why, I don't know. She did nothing around the house, that girl. What can I say?"

Eugene shot his mother another look. The exchange was brief but pointed. Sitting next to Mrs. Boychuk, the woman with brightly dyed red hair and a gold-capped front tooth clucked her tongue. Another woman bent down to adjust her heavy hose that had wrinkled around her ankles.

Mrs. Boychuk wasn't going to let the matter drop. "You want me to lie?" She turned to the woman with the dyed red hair. "He wants me to lie."

"Mom, just...shut up! Just shut the hell up already!" Eugene's body shook with fury. Joanna reached out and held his arm.

Gasping for air, his mother paled. Stroking her chest, she said, "Oh my God. I don't feel well. I have to lay down."

"Oh, Sophie," said the red-haired woman, stretching her arms out. "Here, give me the baby." Mrs. Boychuk reluctantly let go of Marlene and then allowed another woman to help her lie down on the sofa with a pillow under her head.

"I can't take it anymore," said Eugene, shaking his head. He walked out, passing his father, who was standing with two other men in the corner. Joanna noted that for once Mr. Boychuk

THE RUBBER FENCE

looked stricken, revealing that his skin wasn't as tough as she'd first thought.

As she left the house, Joanna heard Mrs. Boychuk say, "He's not himself, my poor Eugene. How could he be himself after having a crazy woman for a wife?"

◇◇◇

On a small concrete patio in the back garden, Joanna and Eugene sat on lawn chairs and said nothing for a while. Staring at the leaves of a birch tree, which were dancing in the wind, she found the crisp breeze refreshing after the drama indoors.

His head in his hands, Eugene said, "Why didn't I listen to Theresa? Why did I let her put up with all of this shit? What kind of man am I?"

Joanna pursed her lips. "There's no point in beating yourself up. It was a confusing time. You did what you could. Marlene's going to need you now, more than ever."

"If only I had breasts, huh?" He managed a weak smile.

"Hey, they're not all what they're cracked up to be. Some women can't breastfeed and their kids manage. Marlene will flourish as long as you give her your love."

He nodded. "Theresa knew you cared, even if she didn't tell you."

"That's big of you to say that. Thank you." She paused. "The audit report is going to take some time and there may be more questions."

She considered what she was about to say next. She didn't want anything to backfire at this point, but she felt compelled to let him know. "Eugene, there's a group for ex-patients. It's called MPS—The Mental Patients Society. They fight for the rights of the mentally ill, for them to have some say in their treatment. I'm sure they'd like to hear your story. Theresa's story. Maybe they could help you present what you know to the hospital board, present it in such a way that this kind of tragedy doesn't happen again."

Eugene's face showed nothing. He seemed to have gone somewhere else for the moment.

"But then again, maybe this is too early for you."

He looked out at the garden. A sparrow had stopped to rest on the fence. "I heard what you said. I was just thinking…If I do talk to them, can I give them your name?"

She hadn't expected this, so she stumbled, "Eugene, I work there. I don't think I'd be allowed to get involved."

She could see his eyes glaze over, his body tighten, and his lips quiver. She immediately regretted wavering, but she felt she had no choice. She had already done enough to put into question her whole career. Didn't he know that by suggesting she talk to the MPA, she was putting in jeopardy all that she had worked for? But why would he care? He had lost the most precious person in his life. She left feeling fluish, but she knew it wasn't the flu.

FIFTY-THREE

WHEN JOANNA MADE the appointment for herself and Michael to see a therapist, she wondered if she was up for the scrutiny. She knew that soon enough she would have to undergo analysis to become a shrink, but to do it now with Michael contradicting her perceptions, well, it was a scary thought.

Dr. Robert Leonard was known in medical circles as the doctors' psychiatrist. Joanna was lucky to get an appointment with him so quickly, as he was normally booked up for months in advance. Only through the pull of Professor Peterson, who was a close friend of Dr. Leonard's, was she able to get an early date.

Though Michael had agreed to go, he looked as if he were having second thoughts. His back stiffened when the receptionist, a trim matronly woman with salt and pepper hair, asked them to fill out a form. It was the usual request for medical information, a safeguard for both patient and doctor. If any psychotropic medication was prescribed, the doctor would have to know about any pre-existing conditions.

Dr. Leonard, a tall, handsome man of about forty with sandy coloured hair and a boyish grin, came into the waiting room, shook their hands warmly, and introduced himself as Robert. He didn't seem intimidating in the least in his khaki pants and navy crew neck sweater, not that Joanna had expected him to be, but after her dealings with the suited shrinks on 2B, she was expecting a similar demeanour. They were ushered into Dr.

Leonard's office, which had comfortable stuffed armchairs, a chintz sofa, and watercolour landscapes on the walls. Dr. Miriam Sahula, his co-therapist, stood up when they entered. She was pleasant, a little older than Robert, and fashionably dressed in tan leather pants and a matching cashmere sweater. Her soft speaking voice promised she'd be gentle.

After Joanna and Michael gave a stumbling but quick summation of their struggles, Robert and Miriam went to work. It wasn't long before they were able to extract several intimate details, including Michael's dalliances with students.

Joanna looked at her husband and said, "We weren't doing too badly were we, until…?"

A pained expression crossed Michael's face.

"I had two miscarriages. After that, I was scared to get pregnant again—didn't think I could go through losing another one. I wanted to adopt but Michael…"

Michael said, "You never know what you're going to get, do you? You could be trading one set of problems for another. I figured we were managing fine without kids, why add someone whose background we have no idea about?"

Robert nodded. "I agree it's a gamble, but for many couples it's proven to be the gift they needed."

Joanna said, "When Michael said no, I decided to get on with my career. I guess plunging into that realm blinded me to what was going on."

Joanna proceeded to cry over Michael's affair. She told the therapists about what she knew and what she suspected. She thought the therapists would help her deal with it, but instead they left it alone, at least for the present.

Robert said to Michael, "What was your mother like?"

Michael looked startled by the question. He said haltingly,

THE RUBBER FENCE

"She was good to me."

"And your Dad?"

"They didn't get along at all. My Dad worked long hours in his business and came home basically at all hours. He had a clothing store. It annoyed her no end; there were a lot of arguments. She yelled at him constantly."

"What did your Dad do when she did that?"

"He just laughed or tried to make a joke of it or disappeared into his shots of whiskey."

"Did that work?"

"No. She just got madder."

"And you? Did you have any trouble with your mother?"

Michael glanced at Joanna, "Like I said, she was good to me. But…she did have a temper. It helped that I stayed out of her way. She left me alone."

"She didn't leave *me* alone," said Joanna.

"That's true. My mom found it hard to accept my wife."

Joanna made a face. "I don't think anyone would've been good enough for her son. She picked on me whenever she had a chance. She could be pretty cruel with her jibes. She would say things to embarrass me, little zingers I called them."

Miriam said to Michael, "What did you do when you saw that happening?"

"Nothing. What could I do? I could never stand up to her. Like my Dad. My sister tried, and she went through hell because of it."

"What do you mean?" asked Robert.

"They don't get along, and my mother talks about Gloria to everyone. It's pretty nasty."

Robert said, "My mother had a way of reducing me to size, too. It's hard when you think you could lose your mother's love if you say the wrong thing."

Michael's brow tensed.

"Joanna," said Miriam, "an affair is not what it seems. It's often a way of fighting back."

"On top of everything else? Michael doesn't seem to have a problem fighting me."

"You never listened. I would—"

"Never?" Joanna interrupted. "That's not true, I—"

Miriam put her hand up for them to stop arguing.

"Sometimes," said Miriam, "couples think they listen, but they don't really hear what the other is saying. They're too busy trying to get their own point across. The other part of the problem is that we tend to be less than clear when we're upset. And also, we hear only what we want to hear. We hear that which reinforces our beliefs in ourselves and others. Anything counter to that, we discard. Having a successful marital relationship is a challenge. When you're both carrying your own family's script, you're basically talking different languages." She smiled. "It's easy to tune out."

Joanna absorbed the words. She couldn't help but think that Miriam was right. Joanna applied that logic in her work with patients, but she found it hard to do it in her own relationship. When she and Michael quarrelled, it got so heated that logic flew out the door. It was like that old story of the shoemaker's children having no shoes. Same held true for people in her profession. Much easier to treat someone else's maladies than your own or your family's.

Robert said, "Michael, I think it would be a good idea if I saw you alone, and Miriam can arrange an appointment with Joanna. It'll give you both a chance to talk about what you want. In confidence."

THE RUBBER FENCE

It was the 'in confidence' part that made Joanna twist her crumpled tissue into tiny pieces. She hoped that whatever it was that came up for the two of them, it would be something that brought them together, not something that tore them apart.

FIFTY-FOUR

HEADING TOWARD THE hospital gift shop, Joanna reflected on the last twenty-four hours. The counselling session had opened up areas that needed exploring, but it had done nothing to change the mood at home. She and Michael acted like they were afraid to say anything that might tip their relationship even further into negative territory. It appeared that they had agreed to stay the course until something more substantial from their sessions pointed them in a new direction. At least Cindy was out of the picture. Or maybe on hold. Either way, Joanna accepted that for now Michael was trying.

She picked up the city newspaper from the gift shop news rack and read the front page headlines: *Foul, Cries MPS on Young Mother's Death. She Was Electrocuted For Her Own Good.* The first paragraph outlined the interview with the head of the Mental Patients Society, who questioned the circumstances surrounding Theresa Boychuk's death. After paying for the paper, Joanna skimmed the article but couldn't find any mention of herself. She was sure the time would come when her involvement in the patient's life would become news fodder.

While she waited for the elevator to take her to 2B, she scanned the article again. It didn't look good for the board or the staff. Could she have done anything differently? Was she now doing the right thing?

The first thing she did when she got to the nurses' station

THE RUBBER FENCE

was check to see whether the autopsy had come back. It hadn't; there was nothing new. She closed Theresa's chart and was about to leave when she heard a familiar voice, "I'm sure he said nine o'clock."

Standing at the counter was a stupefied Rose in a flower printed blouse, beige cardigan sweater, and matching polyester pants.

"Rose, this is the fourth time you've asked me," said Annette, wide-eyed. "I've told you, Dr. Eisenstadt is very busy. As soon as I see that he's free, I'll tell him you're here. Now just go and wait in the lounge." Annette's tone was firm but motherly. She had been cautioned about talking down to the patients, but every so often, she slipped into it without thinking. Joanna couldn't blame her. Since many of the patients behaved like children, it became routine to talk to them like they were.

Resigned, Rose shuffled away meekly and sat down on a chair in the lounge. Annette said to Joanna, "I think I liked the old Rose better."

"You and me both," said Joanna as she watched Rose pull at the loose threads on the arm of her chair. "Does she have an appointment?"

"She says she does, but I've got nothing down here."

Joanna went over to the lounge and sat down beside her former patient. "Hello, Rose. How are you doing?"

Rose looked at Joanna as if she had no idea of who she was. "I don't know how I'm doing." She glanced at the ceiling as if Joanna were somehow sitting up there.

"I'm Dr. Bereza. I worked with you for awhile."

"So you say." Rose examined her fingernails. Finding some dirt under a couple, she began to pick away, trying to get them clean. "Dr. Eisenstadt took out some of my brain in his office. He took it out and then put it back."

Joanna found Rose's further deterioration unsettling. Was it complications from ECT, or was something else going on? This was more than depression. Joanna hadn't seen a diagnosis of schizophrenia but that didn't mean Rose didn't have it. Sometimes there were competing diagnoses in the file, but in the elderly woman's case, all Joanna had seen was depression. One thing for sure, Rose had lost her feistiness and with it, her spirit. It was as if she'd been lobotomized. More manageable now, but all that was left was a shell. She patted Rose's shoulder and went back to the nurses' station and encountered Carmen, who was coming on shift.

"I see Rose is back for more treatments," said Carmen, looking at the former inpatient.

Joanna sighed. "Yeah. I was hoping that once she was discharged, she'd get some support from her family, but I was probably being too naïve. Myron's going to try another bout of ECT. It's been a month since the last round." Joanna couldn't keep the sarcasm out of her comments. "I guess that bad old depression just won't stay away. Now she's got a layer of something else. Oh well, what's a good doctor going to do? If you can't fix one, then you have to keep trying. There are plenty of victims needing a cure."

"A little cynical, are we?" asked Carmen, sitting down beside Annette.

"Right about now, voodoo in Trinidad looks more promising than psychiatry."

Carmen was sympathetic. "Honey, you just got to hang in and believe that what you're doing is going to win out."

Joanna considered that and took another look at Rose in the lounge. "I hope you're right. Have you seen Sam around?"

"He's playing basketball with Jerome at the University gym."

"Maybe they got something there. Next life, I'm taking up ball."

"Yeah," laughed Carmen. She checked one of the charts and went into the medications room. Joanna grabbed her bag and told Annette that if anyone asked, she'd be back in an hour.

It was only a ten minute drive to the University of Winnipeg where Sam and Jerome were playing, but by the time Joanna got to her car in the hospital parking lot and made the commute, it ended up taking half an hour.

While she drove, she thought about how much 2B had changed since she'd arrived there. Since Theresa's death, it had become a colder place. It was as if everyone were watching their backs. Instead of pulling together, there were hushed groups discussing ward politics and expressing hope that none of them would be implicated. Sam had been there at her side right after the ECT catastrophe, but since then, Joanna hadn't seen him around. She wondered if Myron had had something to do with that.

She parked her car on Portage Avenue and then checked her face in the visor mirror. The strain of the past week had taken its toll. The dark creases under her eyes suggested she'd missed too many good sleeps in a row. It was hard to put her worries about her marriage and the hospital on the shelf when she lay her head on the pillow. She clucked her tongue, thinking that her appearance was the last thing she should be worrying about.

As she walked to the gym, her heart rate went up. She still

didn't know what she was going to say to Sam and how she was going to say it, but she needed to find out where he stood in all of this. Would he see her point? Was she wasting her time? She didn't think so, as she had always lived her life according to the motto: Nothing ventured, nothing gained.

She pushed through the double swinging doors of the gym and saw the two residents running across the basketball court. Sweat ran down their lean bodies like a slow drizzle from a rain spout. In their sleeveless shirts, their exposed arms showed a nice contrast; Sam's skin was fair whereas Jerome's was a highly polished bronze. Both unattached, their lifestyle suddenly seemed more appealing than hers. Marrying the love of her life had brought her joy but it had also brought heartache. She stayed by the entrance watching them play for a few minutes. Each shot was more masterful than the previous one. It was hard to tell which was the better player.

Sam noticed her first. "Hey, why don't you strip and join us?" With that gleam in his eye and his sexy tone, he sounded like the old Sam. Maybe she'd been imagining the distance between them.

"Now, there's an idea," chuckled Jerome. He shot a long ball, which rimmed the hoop, wobbled there for a bit, and then bounced out. He caught it and tried again, this time sinking it. Joanna clapped enthusiastically. Jerome winked at her and without missing a beat dribbled the ball down to the other hoop and sunk another beauty, which Sam picked up.

She took a few steps toward Sam. "I need to talk to you."

He threw the ball to Jerome and came over to her while Jerome continued to shoot in the background.

"What's up?" asked Sam, as if nothing out of the ordinary had occurred in the last few days.

"Have you seen the headlines?"

"Yeah," he said, his expression turning sombre.

"I'm thinking of talking to the MPS lawyer. I think it would help if he knew Myron pushed for ECT every chance he got to keep the statistics down."

"Whoa." He wiped the sweat from his brow with the bottom of his shirt. "That's one thing you don't do. You don't go against another doctor."

"Even if that doctor is in a conflict of interest?" Her voice rose as she said, "Not to mention his convenient ties with the drug reps and the extra money the hospital earns by doing ECT?"

He glanced at Jerome, who continued to shoot hoops. "It's not that simple."

Was he back-pedalling now? "Isn't it? I need you to back me on this. It would be so great if you—"

"Joanna, I really would but—"

"But what? You were the one who gave me this great spiel on us being nothing more than oily medicine men, remember? This is an opportunity for us to change the system. Or at least bring a magnifying glass to the process. We owe that much to our patients."

Sam's face twisted. He wasn't getting it, or if he was he didn't want any part of it. He kept looking over at Jerome, as if the other resident knew of an escape route that Sam had overlooked.

She was disappointed. She had hoped for more from him. "Sam, are you with me, or not?"

He hesitated. "What about your residency? Have you thought about that? It's in jeopardy as it is."

"Then I don't have much to lose, do I?" It was the opposite of how she felt, but she couldn't turn back now.

Sam's forehead pleated. "It's more than that. Even if you pursue this and you win, you could get blackballed from working anywhere else. Do you really think you can take on the system and come out with only a few bruises? It's too big."

She shook her head. She knew what Sam had said was true, yet there had to be a way.

He said gravely, "You know, manufacturers of ECT devices and drug companies are in deep; everything is intertwined. It's going to take a whole lot more than one death to change anything." He seemed so earnest. Was he on her side, or was he just playing it safe?

She decided it was the latter. "It's okay, Sam." She backed up, brushing him off with her hand in the air. "Go and play ball."

She looked back to see Jerome bounce the ball over to Sam. As he passed the ball, he said, "What's up, man?"

"One of life's finer moments," said Sam, smashing the ball down hard.

She walked away, feeling like she'd gone underwater for the third time while Sam stood on the shore doing nothing.

FIFTY-FIVE

IT SEEMED LIKE yesterday that Myron had first met her, an enthusiastic and bright intern. Now here she was, only a few months later, the pebble that had started the avalanche. She sat across from him in his office, more defiant than ever. Initially, he had avoided her penetrating gaze and had delivered the first part of what he had to say while standing at the window. It was grey outside; the sidewalks and streets were wet from a heavy rainfall. It suited his frame of mind. He had a pencil in his hand that he kept moving between his fingers. Nerves.

Now he turned to her. She was leaning back, her long legs crossed at the knee. Today, she had on a slim pantsuit that covered her legs, but that didn't hide her good figure. He let out a sharp breath and said, "Joanna, I've witnessed some unimaginable situations. If it wasn't for ECT, many more tragedies would've occurred. We've talked about this."

"We have."

"Look, I know how stressful it is to lose a patient. I've known many physicians who've acted erratically after a crisis. Maybe you should take a few days off to think this through."

"Can I go now?" She stood, looking anxious to leave.

Myron didn't know what he'd expected, but it wasn't this. He had never run across anyone as stubborn as she was. She reminded him of his younger self, when he'd been a brash, gung-ho student. Where had that spirit gone? Had he compromised too much to get to where he was now? Back then, he had also challenged one of his superiors—a professor—about the efficacy of some anti-psychotic medication. Hard to believe that he'd been so naïve back then. Much like she was now. She stared at him waiting for his answer.

"You could go far in this profession, Joanna. You have spunk. You could be a brilliant shrink."

She raised her eyebrows.

"If you go ahead and talk to the MPS, you'll be committing professional suicide. You know that."

"Who said I was going to—?"

"Have I made myself clear?"

Joanna nodded. "Absolutely clear." She headed for the door but suddenly turned and said, "Sam told you, didn't he?"

Myron unintentionally showed a whisper of a smile. In return, her face tightened in resolve and gave him the feeling that she could do anything.

After she left, Myron reviewed in his mind what they'd discussed. Fearing the worst, he said, "Fuck," and broke his pencil in half.

Joanna felt the wind lash her body as she strode through the parking lot to her car. She wished it would blow away the last few months and give her a fresh start. It was a good thing she was going for a run; maybe that would calm her bruised spirit.

She took her jogging shoes out of the trunk and slammed the lid down. Putting her foot on the bumper, she tied the lace.

Sam's voice called out, "I was hoping to catch you." She turned to see him walking toward her.

Shaking her head, she said, "I can't believe you told Myron I was thinking of going to the MPS. You blind-sided me."

He looked sheepish. "I was afraid you were going to blow it. I wanted to give him heads-up so he could caution you—warn you what this would mean. You're forgetting that Myron makes the decisions on who is ready to be boarded."

"So," she said and began to walk away.

He took her arm. "Joanna, don't be foolish."

She met his eyes. "I know. I'm supposed to bow deeply from the waist and say, Yes Myron, no Myron, you're right Myron."

"You could win the battle, but—"

"Lose the war." She frowned. "Maybe I misunderstood Myron right from the beginning. Maybe he said we should follow the hypocrite's oath, not the Hippocratic one."

"Is there nothing I can say…?"

"Yeah. You can go back and tell Myron that the second platoon failed its mission." She ran off before he had a chance to reply.

Joanna ran past pedestrians heading to the hospital and mothers out for some fresh air with their babies in strollers. It wasn't the best place to run, but she didn't have time to get to a park. Each time she stepped on the concrete, it was as if she were trying to crush an invisible bug.

FIFTY-SIX

WHEN MICHAEL AND Joanna got home, there was a message on their answering machine from Sam. He asked her to call the hospital. She had left her pager off during another marital counselling session and had forgotten to put it back on. She hoped Sam had phoned to apologize and had changed his mind about helping her out. Instead, it was news about Dennis.

"He what?" she said, nearly dropping the receiver.

Sam repeated, "Dennis committed suicide. His body was found this morning."

"Oh no!"

"What is it?" Michael looked alarmed and stopped unpacking the groceries they had bought on the way home.

Sam said, "Can you come in?"

"Yes," said Joanna, gripping the phone. "Of course. I'll be right down. Thanks for letting me know."

After hanging up, she leaned against the kitchen counter, thinking back on the last time she'd seen Dennis. He had looked awful, but she never thought he was at risk. How could she have missed that? How could all of them have? She had told Dennis to call if he wanted to talk, hadn't she? Looking for some answer, her mind circled like a Ferris wheel.

"What happened?" said Michael.

"One of the interns committed suicide." She thought for a moment. "I was going to introduce Dennis to you at the party, but he left early."

"Was that the guy with the Mercedes?"

"Yes." She tried not to think about how he had died, but she couldn't stop herself. What had he done? Pills? A gun? What struck her was how little she knew about him. In fact, what did she know about any of the staff she worked with? She'd done enough crying lately; she bit her lip to keep the floodgates closed.

When she entered 2B, the nurses' station was in chaos. Two deaths within a week were more than the staff could handle. Although everyone carried on with the basics—giving patients their meals and medication—a considerable amount of time and energy was spent discussing who knew what and how they could've missed the signs.

Dennis's patients were assigned to the other residents. Joanna thought she might get one, but given the fact that Myron considered her to be uncooperative, she wasn't surprised when she was passed over. If not for the ongoing investigation regarding Theresa's unexpected death, Joanna would've protested. But as it was, she had enough to deal with.

Dennis's suicide made the ward even gloomier. It wasn't so much the physical aspects of the work that seemed insurmountable, it was the emotional baggage that sapped everyone's energy. Blame was now being thrown around like the dirt a gardener spreads trying to cover bare spots in a yard.

Joanna found out from Sam that Dennis had gone out to his family's cottage at West Hawk Lake. He had taken a rubber hose, clamped it to the exhaust of his Mercedes, and then ran it through his car window. A neighbour found him a few hours later clutching an old photograph of himself with his sister and his mother. There was also a note on the dashboard, but the details of that had not been released.

Joanna stewed that she hadn't reached out more. She had noticed his unhappiness, but never in her wildest imaginings would she have suspected that he was capable of killing himself. He had confided in her a little—actually, very little—and because of that, she had taken for granted that he would've sought her out for more support if he really needed it. Now that she looked back, she could see that he had, in his own way, been crying out for help, but his cries had gone unanswered. They were all too busy tuning in to strangers or getting wrapped up in their own personal problems.

What was it about their work or personalities that blinded them to picking up on the obvious? To have one of their own fall down a hole, deep and dark as it must have been, and have no one there to extend a hand, that was the shame of it all.

Myron thought things couldn't get worse until he ran into Bryce in the men's staff washroom. He had just finished when his superior walked in the door.

"It's a mess, Myron," said Bryce, undoing his zipper at the urinal. "We not only have Dennis's tragedy on our hands, but we also have Eugene Boychuk demanding an inquiry into his wife's death. He's obtained a lawyer, and he has the support of a number of ex-mental patients. There's also been a reporter hanging around, ready to chew us up and spit out this place."

Myron went to the sink and turned on the water. "Don't go melodramatic on me. My reputation is—"

THE RUBBER FENCE

"Your reputation?" interrupted Bryce, his eyes bulging in his flushed face. "Do you know how quickly that can be erased? This hospital is on the line. Don't ever underestimate the power of those we treat. Or work with."

Livid, Myron said, "I don't think any resident—"

"You're not hearing me. This is no longer just a resident issue." Bryce joined Myron at the sink. "Do you understand what's happening out there? Dennis's death can remain an internal matter but—"

"A few mentally disturbed patients—"

"There's a talk show on the radio willing to listen to those crackpots. The public is demanding answers! You'd think we were doing something barbaric here."

Myron fumed with each interruption. He washed and rewashed his hands, as if the stain of current accusations could disappear with extra scrubbing.

"Damn the radio!" said Myron, turning off the tap. "Who are they going to believe? Eugene's just as crazy as Theresa was. And Joanna? C'mon, she's a neophyte."

"She may be inexperienced, but she's determined. She's passionate about patient rights."

Myron pulled at the cloth towel in the dispenser, yanking more clean cloth than he needed. "Jesus, Bryce, it was an accident."

"I know. But this was one accident too many." Bryce glanced at the bathroom stalls, as if at any moment an eavesdropper would open the door and reveal himself. He lowered his voice. "When there were other deaths, yes, we could say the old bastard's heart gave out. But in this case, it's decidedly different. If there's a choice between you and the hospital, you know what I have to do."

Myron was taken aback. "You can't be serious."

"I'm afraid I am. I know my limits. It's too bad you don't."

"Bryce—"

"What the hell happened with Dennis? He was your resident."

"If I could tell you, I'd be a genius."

"Well, we both know you're not."

Stung, Myron said, "Mincing words was never one of your qualities, was it?"

Ignoring him, Bryce wetted down a stray white hair in his eyebrow. Satisfied with his look in the mirror, he took some steps toward the door.

Myron bristled and couldn't help jabbing back. "How's that heart of yours? You should be careful. You don't want to drop dead from a heart attack." And then, with thinly veiled sarcasm, he said, "You know how impossible you would be to replace."

Bryce smirked. He looked down at Myron's fly, and said, "You better zip up Myron, unless you want to scare people with that limp dick."

Bryce was gone before Myron could reply. He pulled up his zipper but it stuck. "Fuck!" he said and banged the wall with his fist.

FIFTY-SEVEN

THE STAFF FLOATED around for days in a semi-fog until someone had the presence of mind to call in a counsellor to help them deal with the grief that threatened to go underground. The group session was scheduled at the end of the afternoon shift in the hospital meeting room on 2B. Someone remarked it was too bad the place couldn't be shut down until the staff could regroup. Since that was impossible, a bare bones staff of Carmen, Annette and a few others volunteered to man the unit so that others could go.

Charlie Giesbrecht, a suave man in his fifties, had arranged the chairs in a circle and placed boxes of tissue in places that would be easy for all to access. Most of the staff were there and the mood was dismal, which said a lot about the need. Unsure of Sam and Jerome, Joanna elected to sit opposite them. The other shrinks sat across from her as well.

Charlie started by saying, "Whatever you're feeling is completely appropriate. We all grieve in different ways. I understand that Dr. Dennis Williams wasn't here long, but long enough to make an impression. I've heard that a few of you shared some personal conversations with him, which you've probably reviewed in your minds a number of times. In cases like this, where a fellow worker has taken his own life, others in the workplace may be blaming themselves for not reaching out in time. This is especially true in the helping professions."

It was Charlie's words—in cases like this—that struck Joanna so sharply. Dennis was not a case. A week ago, he was a doctor helping others. Now, he was seen as this tragic individual who hadn't been able to cope. What was even more heartbreaking was that Dennis had been surrounded by psychiatrists, social workers, and nurses yet no one had seen it coming. *No one.* What kind of madness was that?

Charlie broke through her train of thought. "It would be helpful if we could begin by talking about how you first found out about Dennis's death. Who would like to start?"

Charlie's gaze went around the room, but no one volunteered. They all looked at one another hoping someone else would go first. The counsellor said again, "Anyone want to start? I know it's hard." He was trying, but all he got was silence. At least half the faces were averted from his penetrating gaze.

"Bryce," said Charlie, "I heard you were one of the first ones to know."

"Yes." Bryce cleared his throat. "Jerome called me at home and told me the news."

"He called me, too," said Myron. "Then I called Bernie."

Charlie had struck a match, but the fire was slow in building. The chief shrinks had said little, skirting their emotions. There were more nods around the room, and a few more staff members recalled how they'd been informed. Joanna's head stayed down as she fought for control.

Then Jerome spoke up. "Marty, that was one of Dennis's patients, was acting up on the ward when…" He stopped to take a deep breath. "That night, Marty kept yelling, 'no needles, no needles'. He repeated, 'Dr. Dennis said no needles'. So I went and checked the records, and when I didn't see a notation, I called Dennis on his pager. He was supposed to be on call. I left a

THE RUBBER FENCE

message. I waited and waited. When I didn't hear back, I thought maybe he had turned it off. I never expected…It was a few hours later when the police called. I assume when they found him, they checked his pager and traced it to the hospital. They phoned to let us know that they'd found him in his car. They said it looked like he'd committed suicide."

"Did they tell you how it happened?" asked Charlie, leaning forward.

"In the garage," said Jerome. "He asphyxiated in his Mercedes."

"He loved that car," said Sam.

"We had supervision the day before," said Myron. "He didn't complain about anything."

Joanna doubted whether Myron would have heard Dennis even if he had complained. She suspected that Myron's pressuring, both professional and personal, was a major contributing factor in Dennis's downward spiral.

"You knew him quite well, didn't you Joanna?" asked Roberta.

"Not really. I don't know if anyone did. I noticed that he had let his grooming go, but I thought he was preoccupied with his mother and didn't think more of it. Now I wish I had."

Charlie said, "There's little any one of us can do when somebody decides to end their own life. They're usually so determined, they find a way despite our best efforts to turn their spirits around."

"He left a note," said Bryce. "The police said he mentioned he had a lot of stress. There's more, but I'm not at liberty to say right now."

Myron said, "I was his supervisor, if there's anything I—"

Interrupting, Bryce said, "I cannot say anything more at the moment. I can't make it any plainer than that." There was a bite to his words, and Myron scowled in frustration.

"I'll have to remind everyone here," said Charles, "that emotions are running high. A lot of you are naturally angry about what happened. Whatever you're feeling, it's good to let it out, but please do so without any finger pointing."

Charles's advice hit a brick wall. The meeting served to open up the topic of Dennis's suicide, but it only skimmed the surface of what everyone was going through. At the end of it, there was talk of what a good idea the group session had been, and how nice it'd be to have a follow-up meeting, but with patients requiring attention, time was at a premium. The best Bryce could promise was that he would consider the idea.

A day later, Bryce called a meeting in his office for all the shrinks on 2B, including the remaining residents. No one knew for sure what was on the agenda, but they were sure it was something big. Bigger than setting a time for a second go-round with Charlie.

When Joanna walked into the office, she had never seen Myron so agitated. His face was pale, and he kept pulling his white shirt sleeves down under his suit jacket as if the shirt was one size too small.

Bryce started by saying, "I called you in today because Dennis's death and what led to it may get out in the press. There may be a lot of awkward questions."

"Such as...?" said Myron.

"The police have given me permission to divulge the contents of Dennis's suicide note. I mentioned at the group

THE RUBBER FENCE

meeting with Charlie that Dennis had complained of stresses here and at home. There's more. He divulged in his note that he was homosexual."

Joanna had noticed his effeminate mannerisms but had left the question of his sexuality open.

Bryce cleared his throat and continued. "Dennis wrote that he couldn't let go of the fact that homosexuality was listed as a psychiatric disorder. He felt doomed to fail."

Myron tented his fingers and leaned forward. "I had some idea, but I wasn't sure."

"You suspected, and yet you badgered him?" Joanna's anger coloured her words. "When we discussed Marty, you underlined that being gay wasn't normal."

Myron said, "It's in the DSM."

"The DSM has been revised before," said Joanna, "and we all know they're working on further revisions. I know none of this can help Dennis now. I wish it could. The point I'm trying to make is that Dennis may have been getting this message his whole life, that there was something the matter with him. That he wasn't *normal*. It would be hard to live with that. Especially as a psychiatrist."

She choked on the last words. She felt that if she didn't leave right away, she'd lose it and be called hysterical by half the men in the room. "He was normal," she said and quit the room.

She didn't know how long she'd been standing at Dennis's old desk when Jerome entered the psychiatric residents' room. "How you doing, girl?"

"Funny. He was here, and now he's gone. What are we all fighting for anyway?"

"A little taste of glory before we're snuffed out, enough bread to put food on our table and a roof over our heads. But more than that, we're fighting to do good—to help ease the suffering of what troubled minds can do to people. You know that, girl. I don't have to tell you that."

"I guess that's where I get stuck. I wish to hell we could have seen it coming."

"We all do."

She looked out the window. The grass continued to grow, the clouds continued to form. Life was strange how it went on after those you cared about were no longer with you. When her grandmother had died, Joanna had been struck by similar thoughts. It wasn't fair.

Jerome frowned, and she noticed how those lines showed up as different shades of black on his handsome face. "You're naïve if you think there's anything you can do to change the status quo."

"Is that what you really think?"

"I do. You've got to remember, hospital boards are entities unto themselves. They're lobbied by drug manufacturers and those who supply the medical apparatus that keeps this place humming. They're not about to change just because a patient died and a young resident killed himself. All you're going to end up doing is creating more misery for yourself."

"All I wanted was to learn how to be a good shrink."

"You already are," he said, pointing to her, "and you will continue to be, but you got to think about the big picture."

"That's exactly what I've been thinking."

He arched his eyebrows. "We're looking at different screens, aren't we?"

"What do you mean?"

"It's like taking medicine that doesn't taste good. The taste doesn't always reflect how it's going to work. Think about it."

THE RUBBER FENCE

He let out a deep sigh. "Now, I have to go check on Marty. He thinks the bogeyman got Dennis."

"Oh, forgot to mention it," she said. "I heard about Mrs. Kowalski. She's going to a new home."

"Yeah. And Natasha is leaving that asshole."

"Congratulations."

After he left, she thought about what he had said. Could she look the other way and still feel that she had served her patients?

FIFTY-EIGHT

LIFE CONTINUED ON 2B, but it's heart had been punctured, and the wound was slow to heal. It was as if a veil had been thrown over the ward, muting the colours and dulling the sounds. The staff discovered there'd be no replacement for Dennis as the term was well underway. The psychiatric staff would just have to double up on the work as needed. Jerome took Marty and Bernie assumed responsibility for the other two cases that Dennis had carried. The latter two were short-term—a couple of depressed females who were both discharged shortly after admission with a diagnosis of situational depression. One had shown up in emergency after the death of a child, and the other, after a motorcycle accident that had left her paralyzed. They would be followed up on an outpatient basis.

But for any new patients coming onto the ward, Joanna was the only one free at the moment, and for this reason, she'd have to accept whatever came her way. She had struck out on her first two. One more that went awry could mean the death of her professional dreams. Worried about her future, she decided not to speak to the MPS lawyer. She wasn't proud of her stance, but she knew that there were some things, like Jerome had said, that were too hard to fight.

Was it only a few weeks ago that morning rounds were an exciting part of her day? At rounds, she could learn how to discriminate between the neurotic patients that showed up, the hysterical ones, and the ones who were truly insane. But after what had happened, Joanna faced each day's rounds with trepidation.

She no longer trusted Myron. Not that she had in the beginning, but back then, she hadn't known how far he would go to get his way. And also, back then she'd had the support of Dennis and Sam. With her marriage in disarray and psychiatry looking bleak, she hoped the slump she was in wouldn't spread and become a full-blown depression—one with no doors leading out.

Myron and the residents walked into Theresa's old room, where a new patient, Mr. Ted Zorn, a burnt-out alcoholic in his sixties, was sitting on the bed the young mother used to occupy. Still grieving for what could've been, Joanna found the change disrespectful. It felt strange to have another patient fill that spot so quickly.

Myron asked the old man to stand up and take a few steps. Mr. Zorn complied and then remained standing, looking fragile and diminished in their presence. With his wizened face and terrible posture, he could easily have passed for a man a decade older.

"Notice his splayed feet?" Myron said. "With his demented condition, his gait is severely affected."

Although Joanna had heard Myron talk bluntly before in front of other patients, she couldn't get used to it. He obviously hadn't taken a course in bedside manners, or if he had, he must have slept through the basics. Either way, she found him rude.

"How much rubbing alcohol did you say you drank?" asked

Myron.

Mr. Zorn stumbled and braced himself by his bed. "I…I…What d'ya say again?"

Myron repeated the question.

"Uh, two quarts, maybe. Thereabouts. I don't measure when I'm drinkin'." He laughed at his own joke.

Myron sniggered. "If you drank that much, sir, you'd be dead."

"Maybe a cup, then. I…I can't remember."

Myron nodded as if he hadn't expected a precise answer anyway. "We're going to keep you here for a few days, all right? Maybe a week. Let you dry out, okay old-timer?" He patted the man's arm.

Mr. Zorn sat down on the bed, looking content. Joanna wondered if the look had to do with the fact that he was going to get help, or the fact that the mob in his room was leaving.

In the corridor outside Mr. Zorn's room, Myron elaborated on the patient. "What we have here is a classic case of Korsakoff's syndrome. Years of abuse have resulted in serious brain damage. It's unlikely he'll ever recover."

"Pickled brains," said Sam.

"What's the course of treatment?" asked Jerome.

Myron warmed to the question. "Vitamin B and Valium to prevent seizures. So now you know what all that imbibing can do for your intellect."

"Yes sir, that's why we smoke pot," said Sam.

The residents shared a laugh, and for a moment it felt to Joanna as if everything was as it should be. But the feeling was quickly dashed by Myron saying, "Joanna, this would be an interesting case for you to take on."

"The man is hardly coherent."

THE RUBBER FENCE

"Exactly. It'll give you a chance to experiment with some pharmacology. Of course, if you'd rather, you could always do family therapy with his family...that is, if you can find them." He had delivered the last with a smile. If he'd intended to humiliate her, he'd succeeded.

"Seems a little rough, Myron," said Sam.

Ignoring his senior resident, Myron checked his watch. "Well my illustrious students, I have an appointment. Carry on." He walked off, leaving Joanna deflated.

Jerome said, "Just ride it out. Of course he's ticked off with you. You, Dr. Bereza, are a mighty thorn in his side. Anyhow, you can't do much with this one. There'll be others."

Joanna exhaled sharply and made a mental note to get the social worker on the case right away. There was no way she could do any psychotherapy with this one. The only way to deal with this kind of patient was to refer him to an alcohol and drug counsellor. If indeed his brain was fried, there'd be no hope of helping him get back to a more lucid time. At least she could guide him to assistance that might prolong his life.

In the end, her decision to refer the patient to social services satisfied both Myron and Bryce, who were anxious to free beds and get patients moving. It would be a matter of days before some external solution could be found, but at least all felt there was forward movement with Mr. Zorn.

If only other problems in her life were as easy to work out. With the audit and the autopsy report on Theresa's death still to come, the ongoing work was like a prelude to a storm—one with an intensity no one could predict.

FIFTY-NINE

SINCE IT WAS a suicide, the Williams family decided to dispense with anything formal and have prayers instead at the funeral home for anyone who wanted to come and pay their last respects to Dennis. Joanna was frankly surprised that he had any family that could take charge, but an aunt flew in from Toronto to make arrangements and also to find another caregiver for Dennis's sister. His mother was still in Germany in grave condition and unaware of her son's passing. She hadn't been told for fear the information would send her over the edge.

Dennis rested in a closed coffin flanked by two urns of white lilies on white marble columns. The air was ripe with the pungent scent of the pale blossoms, underlining the finality of another life. Beside the casket, the undertaker had placed an easel with an eight by ten colour photo of Dennis. It was an undergraduate photo, and there were circles under his eyes even then.

There were ten mourners, scattered here and there. Joanna, Bernie, Sam, Annette, Roberta, and Jerome sat in the middle pews. Myron and Bryce had stayed behind to secure the ward, as they put it. Joanna suspected they'd rather be there than face the family. In the right front pew, Dennis's sister, an emaciated woman with scraggly brown hair, sat flanked on one side by her aunt from Toronto, and on the other by an elderly man, whose shoulder she rested her head on. Near the back, a young man with long curly blonde hair sat crying into some tissue. He was all alone, and Joanna could only guess that he was someone who had loved Dennis very much.

Annette was close to tears herself; she had lost a sister to cancer recently, and seeing others suffer refreshed her sorrow. She grabbed Joanna's arm as they came away from the coffin. A very short man with thick, shiny black hair and slanting eyes passed them. He nodded to Annette and then stood by the coffin in prayer.

"Will you look at that?" said Annette, through tears.

"Who is it?"

"Axel Ng, the maintenance man. You have to die for him to show up."

Joanna suppressed a chuckle. For a fraction of a second, there was nothing sweeter than Axel showing up to bug Annette one more time. For that fraction, she felt that nothing had changed. But it had.

SIXTY

THE ONLY GOOD thing that arrived along with the mess at the hospital was a rekindling of her marital relationship. Michael and Joanna had each met with a therapist alone; she with Miriam, he with Robert. She felt affirmed when Miriam told her, "Of course, you'd be upset. Any woman would under those circumstances."

And Michael later told her that Robert had understood how impotent he felt at times being married to a strong woman. He said he had acted out because he felt he could not win with her. "You're strong, Joanna. I could never stand up to my mother. When you get on your high horse, it triggers all kinds of things for me."

It was true. She always had an answer. She was more like her mother than she wanted to admit. One of these days, she'd have to have a conversation with her about that. How had her parents managed to stay married all these years?

Through more marital therapy sessions, Joanna came to understand that forgiveness was key. Still, at times, resentment raised its ugly head. Why wasn't she good enough? But then she'd answer, *It isn't always about me.* She tried to leave the disturbing thoughts alone, knowing they would only massage old wounds if she brought them up with Michael. She'd done enough of that in their sessions together.

Michael wasn't happy with himself. He knew he'd been an ass. He knew he had to find another way to deal with his feelings of inadequacy. He vowed to let her know when he felt she was coming on too strong—when he felt put down.

It had taken awhile, but they came together as if they had never been apart, falling asleep in each other's arms after an hour of lovemaking that seemed as fresh as the crisp air in spring.

◇◇◇

D-day for Mr. Zorn arrived, and Joanna was only too happy to sign his discharge papers. Although still quite shaky, the old man was now presentable—shaved and dressed in a clean plaid shirt and brown tweed pants. The clothing was courtesy of the social services department.

His social worker held his tattered grey suitcase and a brown paper bag containing medications. She said to Mr. Zorn, "You're going to a new home—an intermediate care home. They'll take good care of you there."

Joanna shook his hand. "I wish you well. You're looking so much better."

Mr. Zorn stared at her curiously.

"I'm Dr. Bereza. I've been working with you all week." She had seen him a number of times to get his history, but also to ensure that he knew what plans were being made on his behalf.

"You're a doctor?" asked Mr. Zorn, shaking his head. "You're too young to be a doctor."

Joanna smiled. "And you're too young to be in this much trouble. Take care of yourself."

With Mr. Zorn out of the way, Joanna steeled herself for the next event on her schedule. She made her way down to the meeting room where available staff, medical students, and visiting psychiatric personnel from other mental health facilities, were gathering to hear Myron's latest report on the benefits of ECT. She assumed he had to do this every so often just to keep the troops on side.

The chairs had been arranged lecture style, and Joanna sat down by Carmen on the left side. She looked around the room and estimated there were about sixty personnel. By the far wall sat Sam and Jerome. Bryce was seated in the first row with a couple of older men, each immaculately dressed in well-tailored suits. She wondered if they were board members or doctors from the community.

She stole another glance at Sam. Her relationship with him had cooled significantly; it seemed he did his best to avoid her. She was sure that Myron had gotten to him, but then again, maybe she'd misread Sam right from the start. The hippy resident had been a lovely distraction. He had raised her spirits, but her involvement with him had also muddied the waters at home.

Myron was in top form as he expounded from the podium. He didn't look at all like a doctor under siege. At times, he directed his points directly at Joanna. Was he trying to provoke her? She didn't shy away from his gaze. Carmen noticed too and poked her at times in the side. Joanna felt her rage bubbling to the surface.

After about fifteen minutes of mostly dry statistics coming out of some research in America, Myron summed up the findings. "In cases of chronic depression, electroshock therapy has proven ninety per cent effective, with relatively few cases of tardive dyskinesia. The benefits far outweigh any side effects, and that is why it's become the treatment of choice when all else fails. Are there any questions?"

Joanna struggled with all that she'd heard. Myron was still championing ECT, even after her patient had died. He had not

THE RUBBER FENCE

mentioned Theresa at all.

A young male medical student wearing glasses raised his hand. "Is there any research being planned for this hospital?"

Myron said. "I'd love to get some going again. I'm in discussion with some pharmaceutical companies who have expressed interest. The efficacy of the drugs used to sedate patients needs further study."

Joanna could not bear it any longer and put up her hand, but Myron ignored her and took a few other questions instead. After he'd answered those, she waved her hand again. This time, he was forced to acknowledge her.

"Yes, Joanna."

"What about the headaches that patients report after having ECT?" She saw the audience turn toward her. She felt unsteady and hoped her nervousness wasn't obvious.

"You can get headaches from anaesthesia. Doesn't mean anything."

"What about loss of memory?"

"This isn't the place for—"

"What is this place for? Is this the place where, if you haven't got time to talk to the patients, you zap them?"

"You're out of order here."

"Am I?" Joanna took in the room. She wondered how many supporters she had. Sam was an enigma. His face showed nothing. She quickly scanned the audience for Jerome, but she couldn't see him. The only comfort she had was from Carmen, but she wasn't a doctor. Joanna had never felt so alone in a crowd before. She trembled as she said, "I wish this was a court where you'd be compelled to tell the truth—the truth that ECT doesn't help everyone."

Myron sighed. "Nothing does. But it's the only—"

"What you did was unconscionable." Her blatant retort raised the tension in the room. "Theresa would still be alive if—"

"I was wrong, Dr. Bereza," Myron almost shouted. "An analyst friend of mine said you were suffering from penis envy. At the time, I disagreed. I said you were naïve at best. Now I can see that he was right on the mark, but he didn't go far enough." Turning his attention to his audience, he said, "What we have here is a classic case of the messiah complex."

The room went quiet.

Joanna was not to be deterred. She shouted back, "Resorting to your straightjacket labels isn't going to work."

"You're hysterical. This kind of exchange serves no one. I'm sorry this session has been disrupted. This lecture is over."

"I'm not finished."

"Oh yes you are. In more ways than one." Myron stomped off, leaving Joanna rattled from the exchange. The audience buzzed as it dispersed. Sam glanced at Joanna but left without coming to her aid—not that she wanted help from him. But some words of support would've been appreciated. It was then that she saw Jerome. He gave her a half-hearted smile and a small shake of his head letting her know clearly that she had gone too far.

Carmen put her arm around her. "I got to give it to you, girl, but I don't know where this is going. I don't want to lose you."

"Yeah. I don't want to lose me, either."

SIXTY-ONE

THE CJMR RADIO station was situated in a low, small concrete building on a busy one-way street in the heart of Winnipeg. In its recording booth, the talk show host, Stone Flanagan, was working up a steam. He was in his fifties, gruff, and bearded, and not one to back down no matter what the topic. That was probably the main reason he drew the largest share of talk show listeners in the city. He was on one mike and Joanna was on the other. When she had agreed to be on his show, she'd known she was kissing her residency good-bye.

"Let me get this straight," said Stone. "You say you gave Theresa Boychuk chocolates just before her first shock treatment."

"Yes, I did." Joanna quickly gave an overview of that fateful morning. "If I'd had any say, there would've been a different outcome."

◇◇◇

With the heavy traffic on Portage Avenue, Myron was having a hard time concentrating on the radio program. Diane had phoned him at work and told him that CJMR had advertised that Joanna was going to be on the show. He had tried to get in touch with her to persuade her to abort her plans, but he couldn't reach her in time.

Stone said, "And the psychiatrist in charge of the ward suggested you lie?"

"Yes. He told me to say she stole them, as if that were the reason for her death. She shouldn't be branded a thief when she's no longer here to defend herself," said Joanna with some emotion in her voice.

Myron couldn't believe what he was hearing. He knew she was altruistic, but this was ridiculous. He knew that tonight, when he got home, there would be calls from Bryce and incensed board members demanding he do something to stem the bleeding.

Joanna continued, "She was making progress. She didn't need ECT."

"So what you're saying is pretty damning. Now that you've spoken up, aren't you afraid that you've ruined your chances of becoming a psychiatrist?"

Infuriated, Myron turned off the radio, and then he had to swerve into the right lane to miss a van that was turning into the left one. Unfortunately, he didn't notice the truck sneaking up on the inside.

The sound of metal scraping upon metal jarred his ears. His head went forward, banging on the dashboard. It took a few moments for him to realize that the accident was more than a fender bender. He felt his forehead; a bump was already forming. He looked in his rear-view mirror and saw an ugly red spot. Other than that, he seemed to be okay. He'd find out later if he had whiplash.

The truck driver, a burly man in a red plaid shirt, was walking toward him. When Myron got out of his car, he saw that the truck was barely scratched, but his Porsche's passenger side was seriously dented. Paint chips lay on the ground, and he couldn't open the car door. Shaken by the impact, Myron tried to remember how it had happened.

SIXTY-TWO

OCTOBER ARRIVED WITH a blast of arctic wind. Donning her hooded winter coat, Joanna wished it were the only protection she needed. A week had passed since her radio debut, and the reverberations kept coming. Michael had praised her performance and told her a number of times how impressive she sounded, but she had her doubts. He was her number one fan, and fans don't always see the whole picture.

As she walked down the corridor to the nurses' station on 2B, she tried to put the radio show and all the events that followed Theresa's death behind her. Annette was at the typewriter filling out a requisition form. Jerome and Carmen looked very chummy as they bent over a chart together. Behind them, Sam and Roberta were occupied with a new patient at the counter.

The patient, a young woman in her twenties, tall with Nordic features and dressed in bright floral pyjama bottoms and a knitted cable sweater, said to Sam, "Have you talked to Zach, yet?"

"Zach?"

"He's a computer in Seattle."

Sam tried to keep a straight face. "We've been trying. He must be unplugged."

Joanna walked up to Carmen, just as she was saying to

THE RUBBER FENCE

Jerome, "If you think it's bad now, when I first graduated, you had to stand up every time a doctor came into the room."

"At attention, no doubt," said Joanna.

Jerome sniggered. "Hey, that wouldn't be too bad. We could all use a little more respect."

Carmen gave her a hug. "You did it, girl!"

Joanna smiled broadly. Roberta did an about face and walked into her report room muttering to herself.

Jerome said, "With the autopsy report showing a likely drug reaction along with a grand mal seizure, the board is checking ECT patients for the past five years. The way things look, Myron may as well start packing."

Joanna frowned. "I wouldn't put it past Myron to sail through this unscathed."

"At least, girl" said Jerome, "they're leaving you alone."

"From what I've been told, the board wouldn't dare tag this on me. They can't afford any more bad publicity." Even though she now had some breathing room, she knew that Jerome had been right about what he'd said awhile back. It was near impossible to change the status quo. It had taken a few unexpected deaths, a lot of unwanted publicity, and an aggressive move by the MPA to move things only a little.

Sam approached Joanna with an unfathomable expression on his face. "You did the right thing."

"That's a shock, coming from you."

"You know hindsight is—"

"Twenty-twenty."

"I just hope it works out for you. Maybe a residency somewhere else will pay off. I just don't want you to think—"

She put her hand on his arm, stopping him in mid-sentence. "Sam, I learned a lot. I'll be okay." She regarded his face and was hard pressed to recall what the big attraction had been. She didn't know what else to say and left him standing there.

Annette winked at her as she passed by. "Hey, Joanna. If you see Axel in your travels, tell him I work on 2B, okay?"

Joanna smiled. "You bet." She knew she'd left Sam in an awkward fashion, but it was what it was. Too much had happened. She had gone to him for the support that was missing at home and didn't realize she had to find it in herself first.

Coming out of the hospital, Joanna saw Eugene and about a dozen MPS protesters parading on the front lawn with posters: *FREE WILL and DEMOCRACY for PATIENTS; WE MAY BE CRAZY BUT WE HAVE RIGHTS; BAN ECT—Treat us, not Shock us.*

She stopped to listen to a reporter speaking to a camera beside the protesters. "The recent death of a young mother has placed the progressive Manitou General Hospital under the microscope. In the wake of the furor, the Board announced Dr. Myron Eisenstadt's full cooperation in the review. The ward psychiatrist, stung by the recent criticism, is considering returning to New York to pursue further psychoanalytic studies…"

There'd been a rumour that Myron and Diane had separated. Maybe the idea of New York was not only an escape from the trials at the hospital, but also a retreat where he could go and lick his marital wounds.

"Joanna!"

Hearing her name, she turned to see Theresa's husband waving at her with Marlene in a stroller beside him.

THE RUBBER FENCE

She smiled and gave him the thumbs up, which he returned. As she continued down the sidewalk to William Avenue, she thought again of Theresa and Rose—two women who had touched her life more than they would ever know. That was the beauty of her profession. You gave, but you also got back. The sad part was that, no matter where she worked or how hard she tried, she'd lose a few.

Just ahead, Michael stood waiting by Joanna's car. They had an appointment to see a social worker at the Children's Aid Society. They hadn't decided yet to adopt, but at least they were both bent on exploring what adoption would mean.

With every step she took, the voices of the protesters grew dimmer, and the reporter's voice faded. "To reassure the MPS, Dr. Bryce Morley reiterated that…"

As if to underline the moment, the wind wrestled with Joanna's hair. She tucked the loose strands behind her right ear and caressed her grandmother's gold hoop earring.

ACKNOWLEDGEMENTS

In 1972, when I worked as a social worker on a psychiatric ward, I was shocked to discover that ECT was still being used. I arrived at my new job enthusiastic about family therapy and naive about the benefits of other treatments. Some of my feelings and experiences from that time have been woven into this novel, but none of the patients or staff portrayed existed.

Today, according to some statistics, 100,000 people receive shock treatment annually in America. As a result, the controversy regarding this treatment continues.

I am indebted to the many caring people—both staff and patients—I worked with during my time in the mental health field, which also included work in the community in the late 1970s and 1980s. The struggle to help those who suffer is ongoing.

The Rubber Fence was originally a screenplay titled "Shrinkproof." From those bones came the novel. I appreciate all the constructive comments I got back then from *Upwords*, my Vancouver screenwriters' critique group: Monty Burt, Brian Casillio, Glynis Davies, Gayl DeCoursey, Hal Gray, David Jones, Michaelin McDermott, Marilyn Norry, Jennifer Ryan, and Rudy Thauberger.

The novel was later submitted chapter by chapter to my writers' critique group in Campbell River. Kristin Butcher, Sheena Gnos, Shari Green, Jocelyn Reekie, Janet Smith, and

THE RUBBER FENCE

Liezl Sullivan gave me wonderful notes. Judy Johns, Nancy Mann, and Janet Ogg, my beta readers, found a few spots that needed tending.

I was also lucky to have the keen eyes and talent of my copy editor, Ellie Sipila, who combed through my manuscript to ensure that all was as it should be.

My family, bless them all, have read various incarnations of my screenplay and now my novel. Thanks to my daughters Karen and Robyn, my son-in-laws John and Diego, and my grandchildren Michael, Chloe and Mimi for their encouragement. They've endured my growing pains with this story.

And a special gratitude to the love of my life, Robert, who's been so patient with my writing obsession. Without his invaluable support, I couldn't have told this story.

ABOUT THE AUTHOR

Diana Stevan is the author of the well-received debut novel, *A Cry From The Deep,* a time-slip romantic adventure, and the novelette *The Blue Nightgown*, a coming of age story.

Her varied background includes work as a clinical social worker, teacher, professional actor, and freelance writer-broadcaster for Sports Journal, CBC Television. She's had poetry published in *DreamCatcher*, a United Kingdom publication, a short story in the anthology, *Escape,* as well as articles for newspapers and an online magazine.

Diana lives with her husband, Robert, on Vancouver Island in beautiful British Columbia.

Made in the USA
Charleston, SC
14 March 2016